Lee Christine is the author of six romantic suspense novels. Her first crime novel, *Charlotte Pass*, was published in 2020 and was a finalist for Favourite Romantic Suspense Novel in the 2020 Australian Romance Readers Awards. Her second crime novel, *Crackenback*, was published in 2021 and her third, *Dead Horse Gap*, in 2022.

Lee lives in Newcastle, NSW, with her husband and her Irish Wheaten Terrier, Honey. To read more about Lee Christine, visit http://leechristine.com.au.

Praise for *Charlotte Pass*

'This intriguing, page-turning mystery will have you gripping the handle of your hot beverage of choice, if not spilling it entirely.' *TasWriters*

'Ice, snow, fog and darkness set the scene in Lee Christine's chilling delve into the niche genre of romantic alpine crime.' *Newcastle Weekly*

'This is a murder mystery in the classic tradition, revealing a cast of characters from the past and slowly revealing secrets and connections. And this comes interwoven with a side serving of romance for the present day characters.' *NZ Booklovers*

'Not afraid to tug at your heart strings in one paragraph and have you gasping in shock at the next, this is a confident and assured book that will keep you guessing until you reach its nail-biting conclusion.' *The Manning Community News*

Praise for *Crackenback*

'A nail-biting cat and mouse game in play.' Living Arts Canberra

'I did enjoy this one; empathetic characters, wonderful settings and a gripping narrative.' Reading, Writing and Riesling

'Lee Christine is certainly making her mark in crime fiction with memorable characters involved in cracking good plots set in the stark beauty of the Snowy Mountains in the heart of winter—the perfect time to commit a seriously good crime.' Blue Wolf Reviews

'Lee Christine has produced a novel of great merit. *Crackenback* builds on the success of *Charlotte Pass* and in its place we have another absolutely thrilling read.' Mrs B's Book Reviews

'*Crackenback* is a strong, multi-layered work of crime fiction with good lashings of Australiana, wit and enough tension to cause an emotional avalanche.' *The Manning Community News*

LEE CHRISTINE

Dead Horse Gap

ALLEN&UNWIN
SYDNEY·MELBOURNE·AUCKLAND·LONDON

First published in 2022

Allen & Unwin
83 Alexander Street
Crows Nest NSW 2065
Australia
Phone: (61 2) 8425 0100
Email: info@allenandunwin.com
Web: www.allenandunwin.com

A catalogue record for this book is available from the National Library of Australia

ISBN 978 1 76106 607 8

Set in 11/15 pt Sabon LT by Midland Typesetters, Australia
Printed and bound in Australia by Griffin Press, part of Ovato

10 9 8 7 6 5 4 3 2 1

The paper in this book is FSC® certified. FSC® promotes environmentally responsible, socially beneficial and economically viable management of the world's forests.

For Honey, who never tires of hearing my story read aloud many times over, and who demands only treats and daily walks in return.

Prologue

They didn't call him cowboy for nothing.

Most pilots would have aborted the landing on the tiny airstrip, unwilling to descend over the mountainous terrain in the dark, but he knew the runway was there, and he was confident he could make it. He should have landed hours ago, but a blizzard had forced him to fly around the weather. Now, long after darkness and aviation last light, the pilot made a bumpy approach into Khancoban Airport in the Snowy Mountains. He was accustomed to night flying thanks to years of crop-dusting after dark, and he had confidence in his Cessna. He had checked it prior to departure, checked he had enough go-juice, checked that he himself was fit to fly.

Fierce gusts buffeted the light plane as he worked the throttle, controlling his descent. Focused on his instruments, his mind totally in the cockpit, he checked the plane was straight and level, checked his airspeed was good, checked his altitude and GPS track. He looked up, scanning the darkness for the visual cues he needed to put the light plane safely on the ground. The clouds parted, and in the momentary wash of moonlight he glimpsed the three-kilometre stretch of water he'd been searching for. He closed the throttle, raised the nose and extended the undercarriage, slowing the Cessna before it dropped into the bank of fog hovering over the Khancoban pondage. He switched on his landing lights. Two bright beams appeared on each wingtip.

Tension gathered at the top of his spine. In the reflection of his landing lights, he could see the strands of fog becoming thinner.

Now. Any moment now.

The pilot let out a triumphant whoop. He was over the water, flying at a slow 70 knots and one minute away from landing. He chose full flap before opening the throttle to maintain his approach as the flaps ran to position. The airstrip was short and devoid of runway lights, but it was there, waiting in the darkness, just on the other side of the concrete spillway.

Five seconds to landing, and the pilot glimpsed the turbulent water below, gushing from the spillway and flowing into the Swampy Plain River. Then he was touching down, applying the brakes as soon as the wheels struck solid ground.

Euphoria raced through his body but it was immediately replaced by horror at a looming shape blocking the runway. Unable to stop in time, he wrenched the plane to the left, hoping to ground loop whatever it was. Time slowed. The plane careered to the left, a tyre exploding like a bomb. Above the blood pounding in his ears, he heard the grating, tearing sound of metal as the right wing clipped the tractor and was torn from the plane. The engine hit the ground, flinging fuel across the airstrip and sending the control column slamming into the pilot's chest. With the breath punched out of him, he groped for the Cessna's door handle, sparks spraying like fireworks all around him.

One

Detective Constable Mitchell Flowers had never been a fan of light planes. As a passenger, he worried about the single engine failing, or the lone pilot suffering a medical emergency. But as he walked across the part-asphalt part-grass runway of Khancoban Airport, it was clear that neither of those things were responsible for this accident. The burnt-out tractor with a slasher on the back in the middle of the airstrip was quite obviously the culprit.

It was 6.45am and first light in the Snowy Mountains in New South Wales, two degrees above zero, minus six with the wind chill. Flowers had woken with a dull headache brought on by too many hours in front of a computer screen and too few hours' sleep. Negotiating the snowy hairpin bends along the Alpine Way had intensified the headache into a painful throb on the left side of his skull. He reached into his coat pocket for a tab of anti-inflammatory tablets, popped out two and swallowed them dry.

As he neared the wreckage, a uniformed officer straightened up from where he'd been taking photographs of a landing wheel that had rolled some distance away. Bald and heavy-set, he had the kind of bushy moustache blokes his age had grown in the seventies and never shaved off.

'Sergeant Walt Collins, Khancoban Police,' the officer said, hitching up his pants by the belt.

Flowers held up his ID. 'Detective Constable Mitchell Flowers, Sydney Homicide.'

'Sydney?'

Here we go, thought Flowers, not missing the officer's unimpressed expression at a wet-behind-the-ears detective with a full head of hair homing in on his turf.

'That's right.'

'I asked for the Queanbeyan boys.'

'I was in Queanbeyan for a court case,' Flowers replied, careful not to sound defensive.

It had just gone midnight last night when Inspector Gray had called his mobile and told him to get himself to Khancoban. *A plane has crashed on the Snowy Hydro airstrip. Possible sabotage according to early reports. The pilot's dead.*

Sergeant Collins looked past Flowers to the gravel road where a small group of onlookers had gathered outside the locked gate. 'So, you're it?' he asked.

Deal with it, Flowers wanted to say. Instead, he answered calmly, 'My partner will be here soon.' How soon that would be Flowers had no idea, so he took out his notepad and pen and asked, 'So, what happened here?'

Sergeant Collins gave a heavy sigh and gazed at the two blackened vehicles roped off with police tape. 'The plane came in late last night. The airport manager heard it and raced down here. He did his best but there was nothing he could do. Fire and Rescue put out the blaze.'

Flowers followed the sergeant's gaze. A fire truck was parked on the other side of the airfield, its two crew members on watch.

'What state is the body in?'

Sergeant Collins shook his head slowly, his eyes grave. 'Burned to a crisp.'

Flowers jotted down shorthand in his notebook. Just his luck he was on his own at his first plane crash, and one where foul play was suspected. He shivered inside his heavy-duty police jacket and wondered what Detective Sergeant Ryder would do if he were here.

No doubt his more experienced partner had attended multiple plane crashes in the past. He'd done everything else.

Flowers glanced back towards the burnt-out vehicles. 'Why was the tractor on the runway?'

Collins spread his hands. 'Nobody seems to know.'

'Who had access to it?'

'Only the bloke who does the mowing, apparently.'

Flowers nodded. 'I'll figure out what other resources we'll need to bring in, and I'll get in touch with the Coroner's office.' Beyond the wreckage, several large pieces of jagged metal and other general debris were scattered across the grass, torn from the aircraft before it had been engulfed in flames. 'Do we know who the pilot is—*was*?'

'We're pretty sure it's Art Lorrimer. The wreckage is consistent with a Cessna 210, which he flies. He was due to land here yesterday, but the weather turned bad.'

'Is he local?'

'Not to Khancoban,' Collins said. 'The family have a grazing property down Tooma way, White Winter Station.'

'Have they been notified?'

'Not as yet.'

Flowers looked at the growing number of people gathering at the gate. A sign bearing the Snowy Hydro logo warned: Khancoban Airport, No Entry, Authorised Personnel Only.

'Was anyone waiting here for him to land last night?'

'Not to my knowledge.'

'How long does it take to walk into the town? Five minutes?'

'If that.'

'So, maybe he wasn't getting picked up, maybe he intended on walking into town. I'll make some enquiries, see if he booked a room anywhere.' Flowers pocketed his notepad and pen, the acrid smell of burnt rubber and aviation fuel surrounding the wreckage turning his stomach. 'I'd better take a look at the body,' he said, glad he'd decided to skip breakfast.

With Sergeant Collins close behind, Flowers ducked under the police tape, the stench poisoning the otherwise pristine breeze blowing off the pondage on the other side of the spillway. As they moved carefully towards the burnt-out vehicles, it became clear from the angle of the plane that the pilot had attempted to turn away from the tractor. The right wing had detached from the fuselage while the undercarriage looked to have been ripped out, possibly from colliding with the tractor's slasher. But that would be for the Australian Transport Safety Bureau to work out.

'You have photographs of all this?' Flowers asked, burnt grass crackling under his boots.

'Yep.'

As they drew closer to the plane, Flowers held up a hand for Collins to stop. He could already make out the charred skull and torso from where they stood and, to his mind, there was no doubt how the pilot had died. 'We need to leave this to forensics,' he said, turning away from the grisly scene. 'We touch any part of that and it could crumble to black ash.'

As they walked back towards a large, corrugated-iron shed, the lone building gracing the airport, Flowers phoned Harriet Ono in Canberra. She was Ryder's most trusted forensic pathologist.

'Boy Wonder!' Harriet's voice reverberated in his ear. 'Why are you calling me?'

Flowers winced at the nickname she'd bestowed on him when he'd first been partnered with Ryder. 'Shouldn't you be in an autopsy or something? I was getting ready to leave a message.'

'I couldn't resist answering when I saw it was you. What's up?'

Flowers gave her a rundown of the situation. 'I need a team up here real fast. Can you do it?' He watched as Sergeant Collins headed into the shed. Both roller doors were open and two men were sitting at a table inside, deep in conversation. 'I think a rep from the Transport Safety Bureau could be here already.'

'Probably, they're based in Canberra as well. What's the weather like?'

Flowers surveyed the sky. 'Fine, partly cloudy with a light breeze coming from the south—'

'Righto, smart-arse. Listen up, the local police or emergency services can cover the crash site if there's strong wind or rain threatening. That's it, until the body is removed. I don't want anyone contaminating my crime scene.'

'So I'll take that as a yes?'

'Of course it's a yes,' she said irritably. 'Where's Ryder? Is he okay?'

'Fine. Busy juggling court appearances and a whole bunch of other stuff. I'll tell him you were worried though. Thanks, Harriet, see you when you get here.' He hung up before she could give an outraged reply. Hiding an amused smile, Flowers went to join the others, relieved that the crime scene would soon be in the hands of one of the best police pathologists in the business.

The shed was part office, part rec room and part hangar. A yellow plane, hardly bigger than a toy, was parked at the far end. Flowers sat down at the table and Sergeant Collins made the introductions. Zane Alam from the Transport Safety Bureau was slightly built with shiny black hair. By contrast, Benjamin Hoff, the airport manager, was blond and lanky and dressed in pilot's white.

No chance of mixing these two up, thought Flowers, despite their identical aviator sunglasses. Taking out his notepad again, he spoke to Ben Hoff first.

'Why was the tractor parked in the middle of the runway?'

'I have no idea. When I left, it was parked beside the shed, like it always is.' Hoff's reddened eyes shifted to the blackened scar on the airstrip. 'It's *never* left on the runway—for obvious reasons.'

Flowers turned to Zane Alam. 'Do you think the pilot made an emergency landing?' Despite the tractor and slasher, it seemed an obvious question to ask.

'That will all come out in our investigation,' Alam said. 'From initial reports, and these are purely anecdotal, Detective, the pilot may well have landed safely if it weren't for the tractor. Several members of the community heard the plane come in, as did Ben. No one reported hearing engine failure.'

Flowers noted this down, nodding for him to continue.

'The pilot wouldn't have seen the tractor until after he'd touched down,' Alam went on. 'This airstrip doesn't have runway lights that can be switched on remotely from the plane. If it had, they might have given him a slightly better chance of seeing the tractor sooner and taking evasive action.'

Flowers frowned. 'Pilots can turn on runway lights?'

Alam nodded. 'Not all airports are big enough to have control towers, but some do have runway lights. The pilot tunes in to a particular radio frequency that allows him to switch them on. This pilot would have approached slowly because of the short runway and lack of lighting. When he touched down, he'd have lost too much speed to get the plane back in the air, but he'd still be travelling too fast to avoid a collision. Everything would have happened in seconds.'

Silence fell over the group. Flowers stared at the grey tabletop and tried to imagine the pilot's panic when he realised the runway was blocked. 'Where are the keys to the tractor kept?' he asked after a while.

Hoff turned and pointed to a desk barely visible under multiple stacks of paper. 'In the desk drawer, over there. It's still locked, and the shed wasn't broken into.' The skin on Hoff's left cheek was raw, as though he'd been singed by the fire.

'Who else has access to this place, and to the tractor key?' Flowers asked.

'Besides me, there are two other pilots,' said Hoff, before reciting their names and phone numbers.

Flowers nodded and wrote down the details. 'Who was the last person to use the tractor?'

'Our regular maintenance man, Orville Parish. He's been cutting the grass here for over ten years. You wouldn't find a more responsible person.'

Flowers made a note of the name. 'Is the key in the drawer the only one you have?' he asked.

'Yes,' Hoff confirmed. 'As I said, the tractor was parked in its usual spot when I left the airport around five.'

Flowers wrote down *hot-wired*? 'Has anything unusual happened lately, anyone hanging around?'

'Nope. It's been pretty quiet.'

'What about kids?' To Flowers' way of thinking, joy-riding on a tractor at night might be something kids would do.

'Haven't seen any. The local kids know better, but we have a lot of tourists in town now with the ski season under way.'

'Any CCTV cameras?' Flowers hadn't sighted any, but it was always good to check. Plus he'd be reporting all this to Ryder, so he needed to be thorough.

Hoff shook his head again. 'No, we don't have cameras here.'

'What's this airport mainly used for?' Flowers asked with a frown, gazing out at the short runway.

'A bit of everything,' Hoff said. 'Private planes are able to land here, and the National Parks and Wildlife fly out when they do weed control. Of course, the Snowy Hydro use it, and sometimes a resident needs to be flown to hospital.'

'That's probably my team,' Alam said suddenly.

Flowers looked up. Sure enough, the recognisable sound of a helicopter rotor cutting through the air could be heard in the distance.

'That chopper isn't going to land here, is it?' he asked, surprised that he sounded a lot like Ryder. 'I won't risk the crime scene being compromised.'

Alam shook his head. 'There's plenty of space for it to land on the other side of the road.'

'Good.' Flowers stood up. 'Nothing happens until the police forensics team gets here. Our investigation takes priority.'

Two

Detective Sergeant Pierce Ryder kept his eyes on Nerida Sterling's olive-green jacket and black helmet. Detective Sterling was two places ahead of him in the chairlift queue at Thredbo Ski Village in the Snowy Mountains, standing alone with her snowboard. The Chili Peppers' 'Higher Ground' blared from a speaker overhead, enhancing the holiday atmosphere. Ryder slid forward on his skis, using his poles to stop him from running into two young snowboarders in the line in front of him. They were brimming with excitement about how much air they'd caught on their last run down.

'Excuse me fellas, I'm a single,' said Ryder, his neck warmer pulled up to the bottom of his goggles. The pair cordially parted, giving Ryder the space he needed to move ahead of them. He glided past, nodding his thanks, but they took no notice, already discussing which run they were going to take next.

Ryder drew level with Sterling. Careful not to let his left ski drift anywhere near her snowboard, he stared straight ahead. Her right foot was free of its binding in readiness for the ride up, and the last thing he wanted to do was trip her.

An empty chair rounded the corner, scooping up the couple ahead of them. 'Have a good one guys,' the liftie called before beckoning Sterling and Ryder forward.

With his poles tucked under one arm, Ryder glided towards the designated red line stating 'wait here' then watched over his shoulder as another empty chair approached from the rear. To anyone watching, they were strangers about to share a ride up the mountain, not two members of the Sydney Homicide Squad. When the chair nudged them in the back of the knees, they sat simultaneously.

Ryder brought down the safety bar, watching Sterling from the corner of his eye. 'How was your counter surveillance?' He spoke quickly, conscious of their limited time.

'Safe. I made sure I wasn't followed.'

'I'm glad we were due to meet today,' he said, pulling his neck warmer down so his voice wasn't muffled. The day was mostly clear but a chilly four below zero. Ryder's lips were already stinging. 'Flowers is in Khancoban.'

Sterling stilled for an instant then wrangled her snowboard onto the footrest. 'Right now?'

Ryder nodded. 'As we speak.'

'For the plane?'

'Yes. Did you hear it come in?'

'No, the sirens woke me up though. I thought it was a road accident until I saw a post on the Khancoban Community page saying it was a plane. Why are Homicide involved?'

They were high on the chairlift now, with no chance of being overheard. Even so, Ryder looked straight ahead, disguising their conversation to anyone who might be watching.

'A tractor was left on the runway and the pilot was killed. If it was intentional there'll be an investigation. So don't worry if you see us around town.'

'Okay.'

'How're things otherwise?'

'The same. I have nothing new to report.' Sterling curled her mitten-covered hands around the safety bar. 'If someone's dealing drugs in the pub, it's not happening on my shift. Maybe it's time I put the word out that I'm looking to score a hit.'

Ryder took a deep breath. He could sympathise with her frustration; he'd been undercover himself several times and it was tough and lonely work.

'Listen to me, Sterling, it's your first assignment and it's normal to be frustrated, but it can be dangerous to try and *make* things happen. Buying drugs and having them in your possession creates a whole new set of problems. If you buy marijuana, what are you going to do if they insist you smoke it with them, or if they want you to take some other drug?'

When Sterling didn't answer, he went on.

'Disposing of the drugs becomes a problem too.'

Sterling nodded. 'I hadn't thought that far ahead.'

'That's why we have these meetings. You've been undercover for eight weeks. I know that feels like a long time when nothing's happening, but don't lose sight of the fact that it's been six *months* since Scruffy Freidman's body went floating down the Thredbo River. That day, the drug squad lost whatever information they thought they'd get from him and the trail went cold on my investigation here. So don't feel pressured to make things happen.'

Just then, the chairlift came to a sudden stop.

'Someone's probably fallen over on the unloading ramp,' Sterling said.

'That's good,' said Ryder, as the chair swung gently, 'maybe we'll get an extra minute.'

'Someone found out Freidman turned, Sarge.'

'No doubt.'

Freidman had approached the drug squad and offered to turn informant in exchange for protection. In a show of good faith, he'd tipped them off that a murder was imminent in the Snowy Mountains. But it was Freidman who'd turned up dead.

'The way I see it, Sterling,' Ryder went on, 'you're in Khancoban to make connections and build relationships with the locals and regular visitors. You're a woman spending a season in the snow, improving your snowboarding on your days off, like thousands of others.'

'I understand. I'm just worried that half the ski season is over and I haven't learned anything useful.'

'I'm not saying there won't come a time when asking to buy drugs is a reasonable course of action, but now is not the time. In my experience, it's usually the little things that crack the case open, not something big like you see in a TV drama. A guy talking himself up in the pub, and you overhear him and think *ah ha*! Or the same thing could happen when one of us is listening to an intercepted phone call. When you hear it, you'll recognise it for what it is.'

'Thanks, Sarge. What you're saying makes sense.'

The chairlift began to move again.

'How are you, otherwise?' Ryder asked the same question every time, concerned for the young detective's mental health. It took nerve to pretend you were someone else while remaining strong and focused. For reasons unknown to Ryder, Sterling had been hungry to take this assignment, fully aware she would be separated from her family, friends and co-workers for months. It was up to her to prove she had the mettle for it.

'My head's fine, Sarge.'

'If you need to be pulled out—'

'No worries there.'

They were drawing closer to the station. Whoops of laughter rang out from the slope below as the chair in front moved over the safety net.

'Stay safe,' he said, dragging up his neck warmer.

When Ryder's skis hit the snow, he stood up, Sterling half a second ahead of him. Once clear of the unloading area, he watched her head to a safe place where she could sit down and buckle in her loose boot. He skied past, cruising along the top of the track while looking for an easy entry into the run. Ryder's girlfriend, Vanessa, was a ski-patrol officer at Thredbo, but despite her intensive tuition, he was an average skier at best. He looked for a groomed run to take him all the way down the mountain, recounting Vanessa's instructions in his head. Somewhere behind him, Sterling would be taking

13

her time adjusting the bindings on her snowboard before heading in a different direction.

Ryder pushed off down the slope, his weight on his downhill ski despite how unnatural it felt. He made a wide turn, picking up too much speed before he remembered his edges. Pointing his skis a little uphill, he transferred his weight and made another wide radius turn. Someone shot past in a blur and Ryder's nerves tingled as he tightened his grip on his poles. Colliding with someone at speed would put him in a hospital bed quick smart.

Aside from the physical risk, it had made sense for him to meet Sterling in Thredbo. He was staying at the Golden Wattle, the ski lodge in Thredbo that Vanessa's sister Eva managed, while he was attending court in Queanbeyan. Eva's ski lodge was a convenient midpoint between the court and Sterling's Khancoban operation.

After a few more turns the run levelled out to a gentler slope. Confident on the easier gradient, Ryder glanced around but the area was deserted save for a ski instructor surrounded by a group of primary-school-aged kids. Reaching up, he slid open the vent on his helmet. The ski apparel was another reason for them to meet on the mountain—the helmets, goggles and face coverings made it almost impossible for anyone watching to recognise them.

Ryder relaxed, his body no longer needing his full concentration to stay upright. He exited the trees halfway down a wide run and traversed to the other side, careful not to miss the narrow trail that would take him through the trees again, and down the slope to the Golden Wattle Lodge.

Vanessa was outside the lodge near the bottom-floor exit, her back to Ryder as he skied across the clearing. Dressed in her red ski-patroller's uniform, her hair pulled up in its usual high ponytail, she was moving between a couple of trestle tables she'd set up in the snow. As he came to a stop beside her, she looked around and took out her earbuds.

'Hi. How did you go?'

To anyone within earshot, the question was a simple enquiry about how he'd handled the conditions, but Vanessa was fully aware he had a member of his squad undercover, and the movements and responsibilities that went with it.

Ryder clicked out of his bindings and leaned over to pick up his skis. 'I didn't stack it, so on the whole pretty good,' he said, his thighs burning from the continuous snowplough he'd used to get him safely down the last section of track in one piece.

'I told you we'd get those old footballer knees loosened up,' she said with a smile.

'Careful, not so much with the old. What are you up to?'

'Waxing my skis. I don't start until eleven and they needed it. Want me to do yours?'

Ryder looked at the skis clamped to the trestle tables. Vanessa was dripping hot wax from a block onto the undersides of the skis. The process looked a lot more complicated than waxing a surfboard.

'Will it help my skiing?'

'It'll make you go faster.'

'No thanks.'

She laughed, and Ryder learned over and kissed her gently on the temple, happy she was enjoying working in the snow again. After meeting while Ryder was investigating a case in Charlotte Pass, Vanessa had given up her ski patrolling to move to Sydney with him, but she'd hated being stuck in a sales job demonstrating skis rather than using them. Eventually, she'd made the decision to return to Thredbo for what would be her final season, while Ryder stayed working in Sydney.

He watched as Vanessa continued waxing her skis. As it turned out, with him in Queanbeyan for court, they were seeing a lot more of each other than they'd anticipated. But their permanent move to the country once the season wrapped up was looming large in Ryder's mind. With Vanessa's parents retiring, the time had come for her to take over the running of the family property, as she'd promised them she would. And Ryder had promised Vanessa he'd be right there beside her.

He sighed and touched her lightly on the back. 'As much as I'd love to stay and watch this fascinating process, I need to shower and change.'

She turned to look at him enquiringly, as though she were trying to read his thoughts.

'Drive safely,' she said quietly, 'and say hello to Mitch for me.'

Three

Half an hour after leaving the airport, Flowers crossed the second bridge at Tooma then turned right into Possum Point Road. Two single-storey buildings sat side by side on the banks of Tumbarumba Creek. One was the local pub, the other a perfectly maintained heritage building with white columns and dormer windows. A sign out the front advertised boutique accommodation. After the horrific scene at the Khancoban airstrip, the setting was peaceful and inviting.

Ryder was waiting in his unmarked four-wheel drive outside the pub. Flowers pulled in beside him and lowered his window.

'Morning, Sarge. The Lorrimers' property's a bit further on. Sergeant Collins said if we reach the Southern Cloud Lookout, we've gone too far.'

'Righto.' Ryder slid on his sunglasses. 'I'll follow you.'

Flowers shifted the car into reverse, pebbles from the unsealed surface crunching beneath his tyres. With a longing look at the counter-lunch sign on the wall of the pub, he pulled out onto Tooma Road.

Welcome rain had turned the rolling pastures green, the grass several shades lighter than the tree-covered hills in the distance. On both sides of the road, grazing sheep and cattle were up to their bellies in feed. Flowers smiled. The scenery was enough to warm the heart of any diehard city boy.

Minutes later, he turned into the driveway of White Winter Station, the car vibrating as he crossed the cattle grid. Closely planted poplars lined the driveway for several hundred metres before the road wound downhill. A two-storey Georgian-style homestead with tall chimneys lay nestled in the valley below. Several large sheds and water tanks to the rear of the house were a handy distance away, while the circular driveway gave easy access to a smaller building on the other side.

They parked in tandem near the left corner of the house and climbed out into the weak winter sunshine. A curved pathway led to a huge garden to the left of the home and was shaded by old jacaranda trees not yet in bloom.

'Nice place,' said Ryder as they walked towards the front steps. The smaller building across the driveway turned out to be a garage, a later addition built in the same style. Through the high lattice fence at the back of the garage, Flowers glimpsed the steel rails of cattle yards.

'Sorry I was busy when you came through Khancoban, Sarge,' Flowers said. 'We could have driven down here together.'

'It was important you met with the pathology team. As it turned out I was only about ten minutes ahead of you.'

Flowers nodded, his empty stomach churning with dread. Breaking news of a loved one's death was the worst part of police work, and the one thing that never got easier. He glanced at Ryder. The detective's shoulders were set square, the frown line between his eyebrows deeper than normal.

'From time to time you might need to take the unofficial lead in this investigation,' Ryder said in a barely audible voice as they climbed the front steps. 'I still have evidence to give in court, and with Sterling undercover . . .'

'Yes, Sarge,' said Flowers, surprised, excited and a little daunted all at once.

Ryder had made it clear to the squad that, ideally, he wanted the drug-related murder of Scruffy Freidman solved before he transferred out of Homicide to the regions in eight weeks' time. Now they also had the mysterious plane crash to investigate. As exciting as it was that Ryder was entrusting him with the lead, it couldn't have come at a worse time for Flowers. But now wasn't the time for him to dwell on his personal problems.

'Thank you, Sarge, for the opportunity,' he said, as they stepped onto a wide verandah cluttered with cane chairs and lounges. 'I'm aware the other guys are more senior than me.'

'Your instincts are better,' Ryder said simply.

Flowers pressed the doorbell buzzer then listened for it ringing inside. When all remained silent, he opened the screen door and rapped loudly on the glass panel. If Ryder wanted him to take the lead, there was no better time to start than now.

Footsteps echoed on a hardwood floor, and a woman who looked to be in her late thirties opened the door. She was dressed in workout gear, her platinum blonde hair swept up in a bun. She peered at them through the screen door, her expression wary.

Flowers flashed his badge and introduced them both. 'We understand Art Lorrimer's siblings reside here?' he asked.

'That's right,' the woman said a little breathlessly. She dragged a sweat towel off her shoulder and wiped it over her face. A workout video could be heard playing from somewhere inside the house.

'We'd like to speak to them if possible. It's concerning their brother, Arthur,' Flowers said.

'Oh, okay, I'll get my husband. He's the only one home at the moment.' The woman stepped back and closed the door.

It was an unusual reaction, and from Ryder's raised eyebrows he was thinking the same thing. Most people expressed concern, even panic, to find two detectives on their doorstep, but this woman was calm and measured, if a little wary.

'I wonder how old the other siblings are,' Flowers mused. 'Art's thirty-five, but she looks about forty.'

'I assumed they'd be younger than Art too, seeing they're all living together,' said Ryder. 'Maybe not.'

It wasn't long before the woman was back. 'Dan's in the shower cleaning up,' she said, holding the door open. 'One of our heifers threw a calf this morning. You'd better come in.'

Flowers followed the woman down a shadowy hallway. 'In here,' she said, showing them into a room on the left. 'Dan won't be long.'

She left them alone, and Flowers wondered if she had returned to her workout. The prospect of impending bad news concerning her brother-in-law didn't seem to have impacted her, but just as that thought came to mind the music was switched off.

The room was enormous, with flowery wallpaper and velvet drapes pulled back from the windows. Flowers moved across the carpet square to the impressive cast-iron fireplace at the far end, where the air temperature was even colder, the grate depressingly empty.

'I can see why she's working out,' he muttered, eyeing a water-colour in a heavy gold frame as he went to stand beside Ryder at the window. 'This place is cold as a grave.'

Ryder didn't answer, and Flowers winced inwardly at his poor choice of words. He might be starving, freezing his butt off and have a headache banging like a bass drum, but he wasn't going to screw up the opportunity to take the lead whenever he was asked to. He'd worked hard to dispel Ryder's initial misgivings when they'd first been partnered together, and over time he'd gained his respect. Now, their partnership was solid, bordering on friendship even, and Flowers valued that.

The door flew open, and a man who looked to be in his early forties came in. Dressed in a Wallabies jersey, jeans and runners, his blond-turning-silver-grey hair was damp and brushed back off his face. 'Detectives.' Dan Lorrimer looked from Ryder to Flowers. 'Kristin said you wanted to see me—something about Art.'

'Yes. You might want to sit down,' Flowers said.

'Oh God,' Lorrimer said quietly, but he did as Flowers suggested and sat in a stiff, upright chair while waving them towards a comfortable-looking sofa. 'Please, take a seat.'

Flowers sank into a lounge covered in oversized cushions so plush he doubted he'd be able to get up again. Ryder remained standing.

Flowers cleared his throat. 'I regret having to inform you that a plane, piloted by your brother, Arthur, crashed on Khancoban

Airport just after ten o'clock last night. I'm sorry, but your brother didn't survive the accident.'

'Oh my God, are you certain it's Art?' Lorrimer asked. 'Has someone identified him already?'

Flowers heard Harriet's voice in his head. *We'll need more time with this one. We're going to be scraping him off here.*

'The plane caught fire,' Flowers said quietly. 'He'll need to be identified by DNA.'

'So, you can't be certain it's him? I'm sorry, it's just that Art rarely comes home.'

'The plane was a Cessna 210. Your brother did communicate with the airport yesterday afternoon.'

'Jesus.' Lorrimer rubbed a hand over his forehead then looked up as Kristin came into the room. 'Art's dead,' he told her, his face drained of colour.

Kristin moved towards her husband. She'd changed into black leggings and an oversized jumper, but her feet were bare. She sat on the floor beside his chair, crossing her legs in a yoga pose and looking to him for an explanation rather than to Flowers or Ryder.

'He's been killed in a plane crash,' Lorrimer said, his voice shaky.

'You didn't know he was flying in?' Ryder spoke for the first time.

Lorrimer shook his head. 'I had no idea.'

'Maybe he was going to surprise you,' Flowers suggested. When Lorrimer didn't comment, he asked, 'Is there anyone from the old days he's still friendly with? A good mate he might have called?'

'I wouldn't know who Art associates with anymore,' Lorrimer said quickly. 'He's been gone a long time.'

'Well, if anyone comes to mind, please let us know. We're trying to work out where he was going to stay.'

'Yes, I'll do that.'

'We'll have to let Heidi know,' Kristin said suddenly.

'And Ethan,' Lorrimer added.

'Heidi's your sister?' Flowers asked.

'Yes, she and Art are twins. Oh God.' Lorrimer shook his head. 'This is going to be hard on Heidi.'

'Heidi still lives here at the property?' asked Flowers.

Kristin raised an eyebrow. 'When it suits her.'

'Kristin.' Dan gave his wife a reproving look.

'Well, it's true. She doesn't even bother to let me know if she'll be here for dinner.'

Dan frowned. 'That's your fault because you keep asking her. Let her fix something for herself. Most of the time she eats at the hotel anyway.' He looked at Flowers, and then at Ryder. 'I'm sorry. We shouldn't be bickering in front of you, especially at a time like this. Heidi often stays at her boyfriend's place, but she's never moved in full-time with him, or officially changed her address. Kristin and I find all the comings and goings fairly disruptive.'

'I'm sorry, honey.' Kristin reached up and put a hand on Lorrimer's thigh, rubbing it a little. 'Are you all right?' she asked.

He nodded. 'Yes, I'm just trying to think.'

Flowers cleared his throat. 'And Ethan, he lives here too?'

Dan nodded. 'It must seem strange that we're all under the same roof right now, but it hasn't always been the case. Ethan moved back about three years ago after being medically discharged from the army. He needed work and somewhere to live, and I needed help here. He knows better than anyone how things work around this place.'

Flowers nodded. 'Mr Lorrimer, I was wondering if you could give us Art's contact details?'

'I'm sorry, I don't have any.'

'Does Art have any children?'

'Not that I'm aware of.' Lorrimer leaned forward and linked his fingers. 'We're not close, Detective. Art was the black sheep of the family, as they say.'

'That's okay. Sergeant Collins up at Khancoban Police is contacting Cessnock Airport, where your brother departed from. If that's his regular airfield, they'll have details of his next of kin.'

'You said he communicated with the airport. Did he have engine trouble?'

'They spoke about the weather. Ben Hoff, the airport manager—'

'Yes, I know Ben. He's a mate of mine.'

Flowers nodded. 'Mr Hoff suggested he land elsewhere because the conditions were so dicey. Apparently your brother agreed, but then flew in after dark anyway.'

'That sounds like Art. He never did like anyone telling him what to do.'

There was an uneasy silence. Flowers decided to wait for Dan Lorrimer to carry on the conversation.

'You mentioned Walt Collins. I would have expected him to be the one to break the news to us, or maybe a police officer from Tumbarumba.' Lorrimer looked at both of them. 'How come you guys are involved?'

Ryder cleared his throat. 'We need to establish whether negligence or foul play were factors in the crash.' He looked at Flowers. 'Detective Flowers has been at the site this morning.'

Flowers nodded and gave them a brief rundown of how the accident had occurred. 'The Transport Safety Bureau will do their own investigation, but we need to find out how a tractor came to be on the runway.'

'Of course.' Lorrimer looked at Kristin then. 'I assume if Art did have a significant other, she'll want to take care of the funeral arrangements. Otherwise, we'll do it.'

Kristin nodded silently.

Flowers had the impression something unspoken had passed between them. He took his notepad and pen from his pocket. 'If I could get Ethan and Heidi's phone numbers, that would be great.' Dan Lorrimer might be estranged from his youngest brother, but that didn't mean the other siblings hadn't kept in touch.

Lorrimer fished his mobile from his jeans' pocket and scrolled through until he found the numbers. After jotting them down, Flowers asked if Ethan and Heidi also worked on the property.

'No, I'm the only one who works here full-time now, and Kristin takes care of the house. Our two children are at school.'

'And Ethan and Heidi, where do they work?' Ryder asked.

Lorrimer pocketed his phone. 'Ethan's contracted to work on the bushfire salvage operation. I think they're cleaning up around Batlow at the moment. Heidi does bar work, in Khancoban.'

Flowers scribbled down the information, his mind racing. 'Which hotel?'

'The Ramshead Tavern.'

Flowers wrote it down, though the name was already familiar to him.

'Thank you. You should call your brother and sister after we leave,' he said, hoisting himself up from the pile of cushions. 'People have started posting about the crash online. There's a chance they already know.'

Four

'I can book you a room at the Golden Wattle,' Ryder said, watching as Flowers mopped up the gravy on his plate with the last of their damper.

When they'd arrived back at the Tooma Hotel the place had been full of lycra-clad cyclists, but the group had left en masse ten minutes ago and the bar was empty again save for himself and Flowers and an elderly woman sitting by the window.

'Would you like me to?' Ryder asked again. 'The lodge isn't full.'

'What's the internet speed like?'

'It's not great.'

'No thanks, Sarge, I'll find something else.'

'Okay.' He wondered if the internet speed was really the issue, or if Flowers preferred to have the evenings to himself, which Ryder could understand. 'I wouldn't recommend you staying in Khancoban though, it's too close to Sterling. Thredbo's a better option.'

Flowers frowned. 'Thredbo it is then,' he said quietly.

Ryder picked up his coffee cup. 'It's just that it's safer to maintain some distance from a squad member who's undercover.'

'Yeah, I get that. How was she today?'

Ryder held the cup in his hand. 'Frustrated by the lack of progress. She was considering putting out feelers about where she might score drugs.'

Flowers eyes widened. 'What did you say?'

'That it was a bad idea.' Ryder recounted his conversation with Sterling. 'It's a town of three hundred people. It's only a matter of time until she learns something.' The thought of Sterling's body floating down the Thredbo River like Scruffy Freidman's often kept him awake at night. 'So, what's your take on this plane coming in?'

Flowers picked up his lemon squash, the ice clinking in the glass. 'Even though Art Lorrimer was an experienced pilot, it was a massive risk. Ben Hoff said he would have been looking for visual cues to get his bearings as he came in, like the town lights, the pondage and spillway, because the airstrip is short, and it doesn't have runway lights.'

'Was he making an emergency landing?'

Flowers shook his head. 'Alam doesn't seem to think so. Not according to the preliminary reports anyway. Several people heard the plane, but no one reported sounds of engine failure. Judging by the heat of the blaze, he wasn't short on fuel either.'

Ryder glanced at the eldery woman by the window. She was standing up now, preparing to leave. 'It was a dangerous landing, and that was *before* he saw the tractor.'

'That's it.' Flowers raised his eyebrows. 'He must have had a good reason to risk it.'

'Maybe he had cargo on board.'

Ryder reclined in his chair as the woman passed their table. She was tall, with shoulder-length silver-grey hair and expensive-looking jewellery, which seemed at odds with the armful of branded Vinnies bags she was carrying. She smiled pleasantly as she passed by. Ryder and Flowers nodded to her.

When the woman was out of earshot, Ryder leaned forward and spoke in a low voice. 'Tell Harriet Ono to test the wreckage for trace levels of illicit drugs. If he had weed there won't be anything left, but a half brick of coke would show up.'

'You think he could have been the transporter?' Flowers asked, his voice equally hushed.

'It's a long shot, and it's probably just Freidman's murder playing on my mind. Still, I can't help thinking that a small plane landing late at night on a closed airstrip is suspect and warrants more investigation, and that's leaving the tractor aside.'

Ryder paused as the bar worker spoke to the elderly woman. Flowers turned to watch.

'Hello, Wendy. Where are you off to?'

'Tumbarumba,' the woman said.

'Found a few treasures, have you?' the barman asked, conscientiously polishing glasses.

'I have managed to find a few things, yes.'

'Well, you drive safely now.'

After the woman had left, Flowers turned around to face Ryder again. 'Let's go with your hunch for a minute. Say Lorrimer *was* bringing in drugs, someone must have had a reason to kill him, to put the tractor there.'

Ryder nodded. 'He could have been skimming money off the top, or he could have had a mountain of cash or drugs on board, and someone got greedy, not realising the plane would go up like that.'

'But they would have known a plane crash would bring people running from everywhere,' Flowers argued. 'Why not put a bullet in his head and toss him in the Swampy Plain River, it's right there? Why a *tractor*?'

Ryder resisted the self-satisfied smile tugging at the corner of his lips. He'd made the right decision giving Flowers the lead in this investigation; his partner's mind was already in overdrive. Ryder wanted the Freidman case solved before he transferred out of Homicide, and if the Lorrimer case was related, it would be ideal to wrap up both and exit on a high. His most urgent task was bringing Sterling out from undercover before he left, even if Vanessa had to go to the farm ahead of him, though he wasn't going to voice those concerns to her yet. In the meantime, giving Flowers as much experience as possible would leave him well-positioned in the squad for whenever Ryder's replacement was brought in.

He shifted his thoughts back to what Flowers had asked. 'Why a tractor? I have no idea. Look, it could be anything, but remember to check with Ben Hoff how often Art flew in. It could differ from what Dan told us.'

'Yes, Sarge.'

Ryder sighed. 'I really hope it wasn't bored kids trying to give Ben Hoff heart failure when he turned up for work the next day. Stupid pranks can ruin people's lives.'

'Or something just as tragic, like the lawn-mowing guy forgetting to put on the handbrake, though I think that's unlikely.'

'Hmm. You'd better tee up an interview with him too.'

'I will. Sergeant Collins is guarding the accident scene this afternoon but I'm hoping he'll fill me in on Art Lorrimer's background tomorrow. I get the feeling Collins has been in town a long time. You know him, don't you?'

Ryder nodded. 'I got to know him quite well when Benson and I were here investigating Freidman's murder.'

'I thought it was the same guy.'

'Speak to Collins, and Ben Hoff.' Ryder looked at his watch. 'I'd say Dan has broken the news to his siblings by now.'

'How about Heidi Lorrimer working at the Ramshead Tavern with Sterling? That could prove useful.'

'Very useful. I'll talk to Sterling and find out how well she knows her. What did you think of Dan and his wife?' Ryder asked.

'Dan seems like a pretty regular guy. He didn't pretend his relationship with Art was close when it wasn't. Kristin . . . she struck me as a bit odd, but each to their own.'

'She was wary when she opened the door, but once she knew we were police asking about Art, her wariness disappeared,' said Ryder.

Flowers nodded. 'I noticed that. It was like she was expecting trouble.'

They were quiet for a while, each preoccupied with their thoughts. When Ryder looked at Flowers, his partner was washing down two painkillers with a mouthful of lemon squash.

'Feeling better?' he asked, looking at Flowers' empty plate.

'Yeah, it's the first thing I've eaten all day.'

'That's not like you. I see you're still getting those headaches. What's going on?'

'It's all those reports you've got me writing.'

Ryder didn't buy his partner's flippant response. 'You had a bad concussion a while back, Daisy,' he said, an image of Flowers' head wrapped up in bandages flashing into his mind. 'They're learning more and more about the long-term effects—'

Flowers smirked at the use of his nickname and shook his head. 'Sarge, don't worry, it's not that. It's lack of sleep and too much screen time.'

'You're sure?'

'I'm sure.'

'Okay, let's hit the road.' Ryder grabbed his keys and sunglasses off the table and stood up. It wasn't his place to tell Flowers to go to bed earlier. 'Make sure you get your accommodation organised this afternoon. And call me if you get stuck.'

Five

The big guy with a straggly grey beard that tapered to a point in the middle of his chest had been in a celebratory mood all night. On arrival, he'd told Sterling at the bar that a difficult job he and his co-workers had been grappling with had come together just before the end of their shift, after which they'd adjourned to the hotel.

'Back in the sixties,' he said loudly, using his size and position as foreman to hold court over his co-workers. 'Back in the sixties, Buzz Aldrin came to Australia, and there was a litter of kittens at the property where he stayed around these parts. He named one of those cats Apollo. That cat lived for nearly twenty years.'

'Ah, bullshit,' whined a weedy kid who looked about seventeen.

A guy wearing black glasses and a cap looked away, trying to hide his mirth.

From his seat at the head of the table, the big guy slowly lowered his near-empty schooner glass. 'Hey, sweetheart?'

Oh geez, here we go. Sterling straightened up from the table she'd been wiping down. 'Yes, mate. Can I get you something?'

'What's your name, love?'

'Ida.'

'I'm Gus.' He pointed to himself and then to the teenager. 'That's Spider. Who would you believe, love? Me or him?'

Sterling gave the group a friendly smile. 'I can't help you there, Gus, I'm not a local.' The group were the only customers left in the bar, and she and Elijah had been hoping they'd push off for the last half hour.

'I can tell you're not a local,' Gus said with a good-natured wink.

'I've been here ten years and I'm still not a local,' Elijah said to no one in particular as he approached the group. 'Come on, guys, five minutes to closing.' The young publican held out his hand. 'Pass me those glasses will you, Gus?'

Gus began stacking the glasses then looked at the young man who'd doubted his story about the cat named Apollo. 'Well come on, Spider, look alive.'

Elijah joined Sterling behind the bar after he'd locked the door a few minutes later. 'Finally. Boy, do I feel for Spider.'

Sterling straightened up from where she'd been stacking the dishwasher. 'I think he'll be paying for doubting Gus's story for a while.'

Elijah chuckled. 'Are you up for a drink, or would you rather head home?'

Sterling hit the button for wash. 'I think I might just head home.'

'Yeah, whatever works. Thanks again for coming in at short notice and covering Heidi's shift.'

'I was happy to help out. It's incredibly sad her losing her brother like that.'

'I know, it's awful. Look, I don't know when she'll be back, but would you mind working her shifts in the meantime? If it doesn't suit, I can ask around, see if I can find someone else at short notice.'

'No, I'm happy to take the extra shifts,' she said, slipping on her coat. 'I need the money.' *And the time listening in on the locals' conversations.*

Elijah gave her a grateful smile. 'You're a lifesaver, Ida. If today is any indication, we're going to be busy with all these extra people in town.'

'That's good for business,' she said.

'Yeah, my mortgage is finally going in the right direction.'

31

Sterling smiled and went to get her coat and backpack from her cubicle in the small staff room. When she returned Elijah was unlocking the door for her.

'See you tomorrow,' he said, letting in an eye-watering blast of freezing air.

'Yep, goodnight.'

With her backpack slung over her shoulder, Sterling stepped out into the sub-zero temperature, the deadbolt engaging with a clunk behind her. The group of co-workers had taken their friendly argument outside and were standing around one of the picnic tables. Hoping they'd organised a ride home, Sterling turned up her collar, crossed the grassy area covered in frost and began her counter surveillance. She'd already committed their physical appearances to memory as well as the names she'd managed to pick up.

Two cars sat alongside hers in the carpark. One she knew to be Elijah's, the other was a white twin-cab utility. Figuring the twin-cab belonged to Spider as he was the only one underage and drinking Coke, she pulled on her beanie and gloves and unlocked her fifteen-year-old Forrester. The cabin was like a fridge, but Sterling hardly noticed as a sweep of headlights lit up the car's interior. She turned the engine over, leaving it to idle a little before reversing out. As she pulled out of the carpark two men from the group broke away from the others and began walking towards the ute.

Nestled below the western face of the Snowy Mountains, Khancoban was deserted at night: its few shops, the Snowy Hydro Information Centre and even the service station lay in darkness. But as Sterling rounded a wide curve in the road, a wash of light in the near distance lit up the murky sky. *Portable lights at the airport*, she thought, *so the various teams can work through the night*.

Minutes later, and without passing another car, Sterling pulled into the driveway of a split-level house and parked in the double carport. With the owners away, the house was in darkness, the nearest neighbours fifty metres down the road. The home was built on a gentle slope with a set of stairs leading to a wooden deck and the main entrance above. Below the stairs, at ground level, a plain wooden door led directly into a rumpus room. Using her phone torch to see the lock, Sterling let herself in. The room was long and narrow with exposed-brick walls, the only splash of colour the handmade quilt with a mountain design covering the queen-sized bed. When she was certain everything was exactly as she'd left it, she hung up her coat and dumped her things on the bed. After turning on the split-cycle air con, she headed for the brown-and-beige oil heater recessed into the far wall.

That old heater doesn't work, the owner had said when she'd shown Sterling through the place. *But if we removed it, we'd need to brick up the wall.*

Crouching in front of the heater, Sterling removed the fascia and laid it on the carpet, then turned back to where her mobile phone and Glock were hidden inside. The mobile in her backpack had been set up for Ida Stevenson and given to her by Ryder. Leaving the pistol where it was, she took out her personal phone then carefully replaced the fascia.

While her personal mobile was booting up, she stripped off her white shirt, skinny black pants and boots and felt the tension leave her body for the first time that day. With only a single, wind-out window and with no internal access to the floor above, the rumpus room was the only place in Khancoban where Sterling felt safe.

As expected, Flowers had left her a message, so she called him back when she was tucked up in bed with a hot cup of tea.

'Nerida,' he said quietly. 'How's everything going?'

'I didn't expect to be so late. I'm in for the night now.'

'That's good.'

'I left Thredbo early to help Elijah out. Heidi Lorrimer was rostered on to work tonight. The pilot was her brother.'

'I know. We found out you worked with her when we visited the Lorrimers' property today. How well do you know her?'

'I don't really. She's standoffish with me—though not with Elijah, but she's relying on him for work. I'm covering her shifts until she's ready to come back, so it'll mean more night work for me.'

Ryder might have been her handler, and her first contact in an emergency or anything requiring an immediate response, but it was Flowers who checked in with her every night. It had started at Ryder's suggestion, as a way of keeping them all in the loop. Of course, Ryder hadn't known that her decision to accept this under-cover gig was in part an attempt to put some distance between her and Flowers after their hook-up a while back. Flowers had been understanding when she'd given him her reasons for not wanting to take things further. But the 'cooling down' break wasn't quite working out as planned. They were talking nightly even when they didn't have anything to report on the case.

'It doesn't matter how late it is when you get in,' Flowers was saying now. 'I'm often up until two or three in the morning anyway.'

Sterling grimaced and turned down the electric blanket. 'What on earth are you doing, and how do you function the next day?'

There was a short pause, then: 'I don't need a lot of sleep.'

'Clearly.'

'Has Heidi Lorrimer ever mentioned her twin brother, Art?'

'No, I've never had a conversation with her about her family. How are they holding up?'

'Dan Lorrimer was shocked. He didn't know Art was flying in. It sounds like they're estranged.'

'Well, they wouldn't be on their own there. Do you know what went wrong with the plane yet? The lights are still on at the airport.'

'Only that it slammed into a tractor someone left on the runway.'

'Do you have any idea how it got there?'

'Nope. Hopefully I'll find out tomorrow when I start talking to more people.'

'Ryder warned me I'd see you around.'

'Maybe not that much. He wants me to stay in Thredbo.'

'Oh, are you at the Golden Wattle?'

'No way, too many loved-up couples there. I found a self-catering unit. There's half a dozen of them further down the hill.'

'That sounds nice.'

There was a pause that made Sterling think the wistfulness in her voice might have come through.

But if Flowers noticed, he didn't let on, and merely said, 'Ryder told me what you were thinking of doing.'

'Asking around for a dealer? He didn't completely rule out the idea.'

'I'm glad you listened to him, Nerida. Ryder's three or four steps ahead of us.'

'I know, Mitch. He's the undercover Jedi.'

Flowers' shout of laughter had her holding the phone away from her ear. 'Oh man, don't tell him that,' he begged. 'We'll never hear the end of it.'

Sterling yawned and snuggled further into the blankets. The wind velocity had increased in the last half hour, making the iron roof on the old bird aviary down the side of the house bang with every strong gust. Maybe she'd need earplugs tonight.

'Are the owners still away?' Flowers asked.

'Yes,' she said, slurring the word as she struggled to keep her eyes open. 'They're still holidaying in their caravan. They couldn't give me a definite date for when they'd be back.'

'You're falling asleep, Nerida,' she heard Flowers say, 'go to bed.'

She opened her eyes wide, forcing herself awake. 'I'm in bed already.'

There was a pause, then, 'Oh, okay, I'll let you go. Thanks for calling me back.'

'Don't worry. I always will.'

Six

'How long have you been in Khancoban?' Flowers asked as he sat opposite Sergeant Collins at the local police station. Now that the initial rush of sorting out the crime scene and organising forensics had passed, it was worth investing some time in building a relationship with Collins. Flowers knew from experience that his life would be a lot easier if the local boys were on board.

'How long?' Collins leaned back in his chair. 'Forty-six years and counting. Only eighteen months to go.'

'Where was that taken?' Flowers pointed to a framed photograph hanging on the wall. The sergeant was standing in front of a substantial hut built entirely of river stones save for its iron roof. Younger, and wearing an ear-to-ear grin, he was holding up the biggest trout Flowers had ever seen.

Collins swivelled around to look at the photograph. 'That's at Geehi. You would have passed through it yesterday if you came along the Alpine Way from Jindabyne.'

'I did. It looks like a beautiful spot right by the river.'

'A group of old fishermen built that hut. There used to be more huts like it, but we keep losing them in the bushfires.'

'Are they all fishing huts?'

'No, the really old ones were built by stockmen.' Sergeant Collins turned back to face Flowers. 'Others were built by skiers. Even the Snowy Hydro Scheme built some for their workers during the original build. They're all heritage listed now.'

'Wow, I didn't know that.'

'Oh yeah, there are over a hundred scattered across the Alps.'

'Do people still use them?'

'Absolutely they do, all the time.'

Flowers frowned. 'It's a shame so many have burned down.'

'Some have been rebuilt.'

'That's good. Dan Lorrimer said his brother Ethan is working on the bushfire salvage operation.'

'Doesn't surprise me. A lot of people are.'

There was a brief silence, so Flowers nodded at the photograph again. 'How much did that big whopper weigh?'

Collins smirked. 'Over nineteen pounds.'

'So, there's more fishing on the horizon in retirement?'

'Sure is, though not at Geehi, too many tourists down there now. I have a secret fishing spot up the river.'

Mention of the river brought a different image to Flowers' mind: Scruffy Freidman's bloated body snagged between two large river rocks. He blinked away the memory before smiling at Collins and taking out his notepad and pen, determined to prove to Ryder that his faith in him hadn't been misplaced.

'So, my partner, Detective Ryder, has looked at Art Lorrimer's record. You must have known him fairly well; he spent a bit of time in the station here.'

'Yeah, I got to know Ryder when he was up here investigating Freidman's death,' Collins said. 'He didn't crack the case, though, not that it matters. Freidman was no loss to anyone.'

'I was actually referring to Art Lorrimer,' Flowers pointed out. 'You must have known *him* well.'

'Oh.' Collins huffed out a breath, moving from side to side in his swivel chair. 'Well, you know kids, some go through wilder stages than others. But Art wasn't a real bad egg, if that's what you're getting at. Now, I can only speak from back in the day, but he was different to his brothers and sisters.'

'Different how?' Flowers asked.

'Well, for starters, Dan and Ethan went to boarding school in Sydney for their final two years, and so did Heidi if I remember rightly. Art had a different calling. He had a ton of energy, was outdoorsy, good at whatever sport he tried. I think his parents realised that school wasn't for him. He was teaching skiing and snowboarding at sixteen.' The sergeant chuckled. 'I remember him getting into a few fights that ended with me reading him the riot act.'

Flowers nodded and scribbled in his notepad. 'His record shows he was charged with two counts of possession, and one with intent to supply.'

Sergeant Collins studied him for a long moment. 'Look, when he was working up at Perisher full-time he started mixing with a different crowd. It was around then that he was charged with possession. Personally, I don't think he was intending to sell the weed found on him when he was charged. It's just that he had more of it on him. He paid his fines, did his community service, and you can see from his record he's stayed out of trouble ever since.'

Flowers looked up. 'Or he hasn't got caught.'

Collins didn't answer, just fixed him with a dead-eyed stare. It was obvious Collins had taken his comment the wrong way, as if Flowers were insinuating a member of the force had turned a blind eye or been part of a drug racket. Flowers didn't flinch. It happened all too often.

'Well, you're the detective,' Collins said eventually. 'I'm sure you'll get to the bottom of it.'

'I'm sure we will.' Flowers turned to a fresh page in his notepad. 'So, did you see much of Art Lorrimer after he'd completed his community service?'

'No, and I was happy about that,' Collins stressed. 'I heard on the grapevine he was learning to fly. Once he got his licence, he was off.'

'Did he come back from time to time?'

'I assume he did. I know he came back for his father's funeral, and then later for his mother's.'

'What about his old friendship group? Any of them still living in Khancoban?'

He glanced up to see Collins running a hand over his head as though smoothing down imaginary hair.

'I couldn't be sure about that. You need to understand what kind of a town this is. Originally, the place was built to house the Snowy Hydro workers. A lot of kids whose parents worked on the Murray 1 and Murray 2 power stations left town to find work. Khancoban is mostly a tourist town now. People come here to ski, hike and fish, or to visit the snowfields in winter, or maybe take a tour of the Snowy Hydro and learn—'

'But Lorrimer came from a property in Tooma,' Flowers interrupted, attempting to shift Collins' focus back to the deceased pilot. 'Why was he spending so much time in Khancoban?'

'All the young people in these small towns know each other. They play footy together, go to school together, ride horses together. They make friends from all over, Tumbarumba, Thredbo, Jindabyne, even Corryong. The border's only across the river.'

'Yes, I know where the border is,' Flowers said, ignoring Collins' tone, which had turned slightly condescending. 'So, do you remember whether any of Lorrimer's friends were charged at the same time?'

The sergeant thought for a few moments. 'I recall charging a couple of the others. I'd have to search my records and get back to you with the names.'

'That would be helpful, Sergeant.' Flowers closed his notepad, signalling the discussion was coming to an end, and tucked it safely away in his pocket. He'd tried taping his interviews the way Ryder did, but he found it annoying replaying the recording over and over. His notepad was old school, but he could flip to the appropriate page in seconds when he needed something.

'How were things down at the airstrip this morning?' Flowers asked.

'Forensics finished late yesterday afternoon.'

'Yes, I had a message from Harriet Ono.'

'The safety bureau was going to work through the night. I'll shoot down there again once we're finished here.'

'I think we're all done for now,' Flowers said, standing up. 'I'll come with you if you're heading down. I need to get the maintenance man's address from Ben Hoff.'

'I can give you that.' Sergeant Collins jotted down the details on a notepad. 'Orville's place is only two minutes up the road,' he said, tearing off the page and handing it to Flowers. 'Everything is close by in Khancoban.'

After thanking Sergeant Collins, Flowers left the station. He had just enough time to speak to Orville before he met up with Ryder.

'Orville meant "gold town",' Orville Parish told Flowers as he led the way down a central hallway to the back of his single-storey house. The older man wore a grey tracksuit, a battered cap with a petrol-company logo on it, and slippers. He was small and wiry with bowed legs, making Flowers wonder if he'd spent a lot of time riding horses.

'One of my ancestors discovered gold up in Kiandra in the late 1800s,' Parish said. 'Not enough to make him wealthy, but enough to give the family a start. Our clan have lived in this area ever since.'

Parish stopped at the kitchen door. 'Can I get you something to drink?'

'No thanks, I'm good.'

'Right, well let's go and sit down in the sunroom.' Parish led him into a bright room overlooking a well-maintained yard.

'You've got a nice spot here.'

'Can't complain.' Parish sat in a recliner rocker and pressed a button on the control to bring up the footrest. 'Kiandra's a ghost town since the old courthouse museum burned down years ago. Nothing left up there except a few old pieces of mining equipment and a handful of graves.' He waved his hand at a chair, indicating Flowers should sit. 'I've been expecting you, Detective.'

'We'll get started then.' Flowers left his notepad and pen in his pocket, feeling a more relaxed conversation with Orville was the way to go. 'Ben Hoff said you've been mowing the airstrip for about ten years now?'

'That's right. I mow a few other lawns, but the airstrip is the only job where I use a tractor.'

'Was the tractor that was left on the airstrip new?' It had just occurred to Flowers that Parish might not have been familiar with it.

'It was there when I got the job.'

Flowers raised his eyebrows. 'So, it was old?'

'Maybe twenty years. Some of the older models are better than the ones they make these days.'

'Like a lot of things,' Flowers said with a smile. 'Mr Parish, could you run me through what happens on a typical day when you're working at the airstrip?'

'Well, Ben rings me when the lawn needs to be cut and gives me a suitable time to turn up. In the shed, Ben unlocks the drawer and hands me the key. When I'm finished, I park the tractor beside the shed and take the key back inside.'

'And you give it back to Ben?'

'Exactly right. And if Ben's not there I hand it to one of the other pilots, but he's there most of the time.'

Unable to help himself, Flowers pulled out his notepad. 'Who was working when you finished the mowing two days ago?'

'Ben.'

'And you remember handing him the key?'

'I do, but I don't hang around and watch him lock it in the drawer. I give him the key and head off.'

Flowers leaned forward in the chair. 'Mr Parish—'

'Orville.'

'Sorry, Orville. How do you think the tractor came to be in the middle of the runway?'

'Buggered if I know,' the old man said, taking off his glasses and putting them on a small table next to his chair. 'Someone must've deliberately driven it onto the runway. You couldn't push it out there.'

'And it was done after dark,' Flowers said. 'It's school holidays and the town is full of families with teenage kids. Could a few of them have mustered up enough bravado to take the tractor for a joyride?' It was on Flowers' list to talk to the tourists staying in Khancoban.

'I don't think it was kids,' Parish said. 'It's too coincidental that a plane comes in after dark when the airport is closed, on the same night someone puts the tractor on the sealed bit.'

'That's where the Cessna would have landed?'

Parish nodded. 'On the sealed section, not on the grassy areas on either side. That's where the tiger moths and other little planes take off and land. This was a bigger plane and would have landed on the sealed runway.'

'Hmm. The key was still in the drawer and the shed hadn't been broken into,' said Flowers. 'The tractor must have been hot-wired.'

Parish pressed his lips together. 'It's possible. Anyone could do it, it's all on the internet. You just take off the fascia and the wires are right there. But if it was someone who uses the same model tractor, they wouldn't need to hot-wire it.'

'Why not?'

'Because those tractors have a common key.'

Seven

Ryder paced back and forth in front of the window at the Golden Wattle Lodge, waiting for Benson to pick up from the station in Parramatta. Outside, snow was turning the trees white. It was a perfect day in Thredbo, with little wind and a fresh cover of snow blanketing the ground, but Ryder had no time for the view.

He looked up as Vanessa came into the room carrying a bowl of muesli and fruit. 'Eva put this aside for you,' she said, putting it down on the bedside table. 'It's ten-thirty and you haven't eaten.'

'I've been waiting for Benson. I was trying to prepare the report for the Coroner but then Flowers rang with a lead.' He switched his phone to speaker and put it on the table beside the muesli. 'You grew up on a property. How much do you know about tractors?'

Vanessa frowned. 'A bit. What do you want to know?'

Ryder killed the call when it went through to voicemail. 'Is it true that one key can operate different tractors manufactured by the same company?'

'Yes.' Vanessa shrugged on her ski-patrol jacket and began fiddling with the zipper. 'Oh, wait, some of the newer models could have individual keys. How old is it?'

'About twenty years.'

'I'd say that one would likely work off a common key.'

'That's what Flowers said when he called.'

'You tossed and turned all night,' she said, fixing watchful eyes on him as she zipped up her jacket. 'You're not getting cold feet about moving to the farm, are you?'

'No, of course not,' he said, though he couldn't deny the hollow feeling in the pit of his stomach every time he thought about it. 'What makes you think I'm having second thoughts?'

'I'm just asking.'

Ryder turned away from her to pick up the cereal she'd brought him, then turned back to face her again. 'I've got a lot on, that's all. I'm just trying to stay across everything. I want to wrap up as much as I can before we go.'

Vanessa nodded and moved towards him. 'Sorry, but I have to get going. I have another eleven o'clock start.'

Ryder put his free hand in the centre of her back as she kissed his cheek. 'Thank you for bringing me breakfast,' he said. 'Take care on the mountain today.'

'I will. You too, Detective.'

Ryder watched Vanessa leave, and when Benson still hadn't returned his call by the time he'd finished his muesli, he pocketed his phone, car keys and wallet and left the suite.

Eva was in the kitchen rolling pastry. Despite being several years older, several centimetres shorter, and with blonde hair where Vanessa's was dark, the family resemblance was unmistakable.

'You make the best Bircher muesli, Eva, thank you,' he said, rinsing his bowl in the sink. 'Have you heard from Jack?'

Ryder had grown to like Eva's partner, despite his initial misgivings about the guy. As a hostage negotiator and back-country survival expert, Jack Walker's skills were in high demand. Eva was often left to manage the lodge on her own.

'I was speaking to him last night,' Eva said. 'They're starting to wrap things up, so he should be home soon. He's happy you're coming and going, and that Vanessa is here for the season.'

'I am too. Vanessa is good company for you, and I'd rather her be happy in her job, even though I miss her when I'm in Sydney.'

'She never took to that sales job, did she?'

'No. She told me she'd rather be skiing than talking all day.'

'That's Vanessa.' Eva put down the rolling pin. 'I meant to ask you if Mitch had found somewhere to stay.'

'Yeah, he's in a place down by the river.'

Eva frowned. 'I thought he may not want to stay here because of what happened . . .'

Ryder shook his head. 'I don't think he remembers anything about the situation here, he had a pretty bad knock on the head.' He smiled a little. 'He's probably dreading the thought of spending all day and night with *me*. We'd never get a break from the case.'

'Well, I hope he knows he's always welcome here,' Eva said.

'I'll invite him over for dinner. That'll be an offer he can't refuse.' Ryder shrugged on his heavy-duty police jacket. 'Thanks, Eva.'

Just then his phone's screen lit up with Benson's name. With a quick wave, he hurried out of the kitchen. 'Hello, Benson.'

'Sorry, Sarge, I was on another call.'

'Anything I need to worry about?' Ryder asked, picturing Benson, Brown and O'Day working at their desks in Parramatta.

'Nothing we can't handle.'

'Good.' Ryder passed through the lobby where a young man was vacuuming. 'Have you had a chance to look at the updated case notes on the plane crash?' he asked.

'I saw that Flowers had updated the file,' said Benson, 'but I haven't read it yet. I'll look at it now.'

The rush of freezing air caught Ryder's breath as he pushed open the double wooden doors and stepped outside. In the clearing out the front, two young boys were having a snowball fight, their parents watching on from one of the picnic tables.

Ryder rounded the corner of the lodge where his four-wheel drive was parked at the top of the driveway. Shivering, he listened as Benson tapped away at the keys.

'Okay, I've read it.' Benson's voice crackled in his ear. 'So, the tractor that was on the airstrip could have been started with a key from any tractor of the same make?'

'Right. Can you see where Flowers has put in the make and model?' Ryder asked, unlocking the car and grabbing the plastic scraper from the door pocket.

'Yep, I can see that.'

Ryder began scraping away the ice stuck to the windscreen. 'I want you to call every dealership that carries that make of tractor. We're after a list of previous owners from the last twenty years.'

Benson's soft whistle came down the phone.

'I want details of sales and trade-ins, starting with towns in the Snowy council areas,' Ryder said. 'A desktop analysis will do for now.'

'Yes, Sarge.' There was a pause, then, 'What's that noise?'

'I'm getting the ice off my windscreen,' Ryder said irritably.

Benson chuckled. 'You're not regretting staying in Thredbo?'

'Not on your life. I get to see Vanessa, and Eva's cooking is first class.' Ignoring the ten centimetres of snow that had built up on the roof and bonnet, Ryder slid into the driver's seat and dumped the scraper back in the door pocket.

'Eva's just as entitled to your expense account money as anyone else,' Benson said.

'My thoughts exactly.'

'I must admit, I'm jealous, Sarge.'

Ryder felt a pang of sympathy. Benson's wife had decided to stay in Queanbeyan with their children when he'd accepted a promotion that involved a move to Sydney. 'Listen, Benson, this might be a desktop analysis for now, but if we need another pair of hands down here, you're first in line.'

'I appreciate that, Sarge.'

'Hold on a minute, I'm backing out.' Checking all mirrors twice before shifting his attention to the rear camera, Ryder reversed slowly. Only when he reached the end of Eva's driveway and turned onto Crackenback Drive did he speak again. 'It's a long shot but someone on that tractor list might have a history with Art Lorrimer.'

'And they could have a record,' said Benson.

'Right, as well as the same tractor key.'

Satisfied the task was in good hands, Ryder brought the call to an end. He drove past the duck pond then wound his way up the steep, narrow road lined with ski lodges. When he made the sharp turn onto the Alpine Way, snow slid from the roof and tumbled in a shower onto the road.

At the top of a long, steep rise, he glanced at the vast views of the valley on his left. A car had pulled off the road, and a woman was posing for a photograph on a long wooden seat made from an old tree trunk. The words carved into the log marked the spot. Dead Horse Gap.

Ryder flexed his fingers inside his gloves, pushed the button to activate his seat warmer, and settled in for the drive to Tooma.

The first sound to greet Ryder when he climbed out of the car at White Winter Station was the whine of an automatic hedge trimmer. A man wearing overalls and gardening gloves was standing on a ladder trimming a two-metre-high hedge that grew beneath one of the old jacarandas. A wheelbarrow nearby was overflowing with leaves and branches.

Ryder watched the man silently as he waited for Flowers to park beside him.

'Is that a maze over there?' Flowers asked, slamming the door and pointing to a square of high hedges. 'Those things used to freak me out when I was kid.'

Ryder smiled as they walked towards the house. 'Did you think you'd never get out?'

'Yeah.'

This time it was Dan Lorrimer who answered their rap on the door.

'Detectives,' he said, peering past them to look at the gardener. 'Come in.'

He showed them into the same cavernous room at the front of the house, though the temperature was slightly warmer this time.

A woman who looked to be in her early thirties stood close to the fire. She was shivering, possibly due to the ripped jeans and loose knitted jumper that hung off one shoulder, leaving it bare.

'Heidi,' Dan Lorrimer said gently, 'these are the detectives who were here yesterday, Detective Ryder and Detective Flowers.'

The woman folded her arms tightly across her chest, as if by hugging herself she could trap her emotions inside.

'Hello, Heidi,' Ryder said, ignoring her shivering. 'Please accept our condolences for the loss of your brother.'

'Thank you,' she murmured, watching as Kristin Lorrimer came into the room.

Heidi was not at all what Ryder had expected. Her blonde hair was cut in a pixie style, the pink tips matching the pink-and-gold Japanese fans dangling from her ears. Her eyebrows didn't arch but instead slanted upwards in a straight line towards her temples.

'Kristin, would you go and ask Ethan to come in?' Dan said to his wife, his voice laced with frustration. 'I'm surprised he didn't see the detectives arrive.'

Kristin disappeared without a word and Dan herded them towards a large dining table. 'Why don't we all sit down here?' he said. 'You can start, detectives; Ethan can catch up when he gets here.'

Ryder sat next to Flowers, Dan and Heidi opposite them. 'We are in the process of preparing a report for the Coroner—not that there is any dispute as to how your brother died,' began Ryder, 'but his body can't be released until he's been formally identified by DNA.'

Heidi drew a tissue from the sleeve of her jumper and wiped her seeping eyes. Dan put an arm around her shoulders and gave her a comforting squeeze. 'You're okay,' he said in a reassuring tone.

The man who'd been working in the garden came in. Ethan Lorrimer was Ryder's height, his wide shoulders and muscular frame testament to years of physical work. More mountain man than grazier, he wordlessly pulled out a chair and sat at the head of the table, eyeing them warily.

Once again, Ryder introduced himself and Flowers, then left it to Flowers to go over what they'd just told Dan and Heidi.

'We've also been in touch with the relevant people at Cessnock Airport,' Flowers said. 'They've confirmed that Art did log a flight plan to Khancoban two days ago. They know of a former girlfriend of Art's but no one current. Daniel is listed as his next of kin on the paperwork they have, but all of you are equally his next of kin.'

Heidi and Ethan exchanged glances while their brother stared down at the table.

'Well,' Dan said eventually, struggling to control his voice, 'it doesn't seem like Art had a significant other in his life, so I suppose we'd better start making funeral arrangements.'

'You can go ahead and make preliminary arrangements,' Flowers said, 'but you'll need to wait until the body is released before you can set a date.'

Dan nodded while Ethan and Heidi said nothing. To Ryder, it was obvious the firstborn reigned supreme in the Lorrimer household.

'We've opened an investigation into the suspected murder of your brother,' Flowers said. 'The likelihood of a tractor blocking the runway when he flew in after dark is too coincidental to be an accident.'

Heidi began to weep again, wiping the tears away with her tissue. Ethan rested his elbows on the table, his hands clasped together.

'We know Art has a record,' Ryder said. 'Detective Flowers has already spoken to Sergeant Collins about the historical drug charges.' He looked at each Lorrimer sibling in turn. Ethan was glowering. Heidi was shredding the tissue between her fingers and didn't meet his eyes. Dan was still, his gaze fixed on Ryder as though he were delivering a sermon. 'Do any of you know if Art had trouble with anyone in the past, someone who may have still held a grudge against him?'

Ethan unclasped his hands and leaned back in his chair. 'Art had problems with a lot of people,' he said, his voice half an octave lower than his brother's. 'He got mixed up with the wrong crowd years ago and got into drugs . . . it caused a lot of problems.'

'Who with exactly?' Flowers asked.

'Art owed certain people a lot of money—the kind of people with long memories,' Ethan said. 'They used to turn up here looking for him.'

That explained Kristin's wariness when she opened the door yesterday, Ryder thought. 'Are you talking about an organised crime ring?'

Ethan nodded.

Ryder caught Flowers' eye. 'Do you remember their names?'

'No,' Dan said. 'We never knew who they were.'

'Do you remember anything distinctive about them?' asked Flowers.

'Yes,' said Ethan. 'They didn't look like the kind of people who pay their taxes.'

There was silence from everyone at the table. Ryder looked at each of the Lorrimers again. 'When did this start?'

As Dan and Ethan thought back, it was Heidi who answered. 'When I was away at school, fifteen years ago. Dan and Ethan were back home by then.'

'That's right,' Dan said. 'Mum and Dad were worried every time someone knocked on the door. Dad, Ethan and I would band together and get rid of them.'

'Did you pay them off?' asked Flowers.

Dan nodded. 'In the beginning, but they kept coming back.'

'Art was learning to fly at the time,' Heidi said. 'The day he got his licence, Mum gave him money to buy a plane.'

'He took off not long after that, and we didn't see him again,' Ethan said, shaking his head. 'He was rewarded with money for doing the wrong thing all his life, and he didn't even have the decency to come home and see his family.'

'He needed a way out,' Dan argued. 'The pilot's licence was the only qualification he had. It enabled him to find work and shift around if they found him. Have you ever thought that he might not have come home because the people we've been talking about might have been lying in wait for him?'

'He couldn't pick up a telephone?' asked Ethan.

A tense silence brewed between the brothers before Dan said softly, 'Maybe he was thinking of us, and he deliberately stayed away so he didn't bring us more trouble.'

Ethan stared at his brother. 'Listen to yourself. Art was born selfish. He never thought about anyone other than himself.'

'Ethan—' Dan began.

'No. Art never lifted a finger to help us with this place. He didn't care that you were running the station singlehandedly, or that Heidi and I were working other jobs so the bills could get paid. No way. Art's priority was Art.'

Heidi sniffed loudly, her shoulders shaking. 'He did come home for Dad's funeral, and for Mum's,' she said.

'I'm sorry, detectives,' Dan said, looking at his sister. 'I think Heidi needs a rest.'

'We're just about done,' Ryder said, raising his eyebrows at Flowers in a silent question.

'There is one more thing,' Flowers said, taking out his phone. 'You might recall a man's body was dragged from the Thredbo River about six months ago?' Flowers held out his phone. 'Could this be one of the men who used to come by here?'

Impressed at how quickly Flowers was linking the information and seeking to verify his suspicions, Ryder watched the Lorrimer siblings study what he guessed was the Crime Stoppers image of Scruffy Freidman.

'Do you remember seeing this man's photograph on the TV and in the newspapers?' asked Flowers, showing each of them the photo.

Heidi gave a vague shake of her head and avoided everyone's eyes, while Dan shifted in his chair. Ethan ran a hand across his jaw, his dark brows drawn together as he stared at the phone.

'Have you seen this man before?' asked Ryder.

'I remember seeing that photo,' Dan said eventually. 'Ethan and I talked about it. We thought he looked like one of the men who used to come here, but we weren't certain.' He pointed to Flowers' phone. 'He has a buzz cut and a bushman's beard in this photo. From memory the guy looking for Art had long hair. It's hard to tell if it's the same person.'

'We thought about calling the police but decided it wasn't worth it,' Ethan said.

'Why was that?' asked Ryder.

'Crime Stoppers said he was known to police, and they were looking for information relevant to his murder. We genuinely couldn't tell them anything about it.'

Dan nodded. 'And we didn't want to bring Art's history to the attention of the police again. All that trouble was a long time ago.'

Flowers put his phone away. 'Samuel Freidman, commonly known as Scruffy, had close ties to a drug operation in the mountains.'

'Really?' said Ethan. 'Then he probably got what was coming to him.'

Dan gave his brother a sharp look then spoke to Flowers. 'Detective, you said earlier that it was too much of a coincidence for the tractor to be on the runway the same night Art flew in.'

'Yes.'

'If someone intentionally sabotaged the plane to kill Art, and this Scruffy Freidman is the same man who used to come here, are we in danger from these people as well? Kristin and I have the children to think of.'

'It's hard to say,' said Flowers. 'Their beef could have been purely with your brother.'

Dan gave a heavy sigh. 'We may not have been close to Art, but we're anxious to know who did this to him.' He looked at Ethan and then Heidi. Both nodded in silent agreement.

'Rest assured, we're chasing every lead,' said Ryder. 'We want this case solved as quickly as possible.'

Having wrapped up the interview, the detectives stepped onto the front verandah to find Kristin reclining in a wicker chair. She stood up when she saw them, a coffee mug cradled between her hands. 'I'm trying to catch some sun while it's out. My vitamin D levels are low.'

'You're doing the right thing then,' said Ryder, after searching his mind for the appropriate response.

Kristin joined them at the top of the stairs. 'It's difficult in winter when the days are short.'

'You can take vitamin D supplements,' put in Flowers.

Ryder had to forcibly stop himself from rolling his eyes.

'I do, but my levels still aren't high enough, and this house is so cold in winter.'

'Ah, fair enough,' Flowers said with a smile. He pointed to the hedges where Ethan had been working. 'I was wondering, is that a maze over there, that tall, square hedge?'

'A maze?' Kristin gazed out across the circular driveway to where Flowers was pointing. 'Oh, no, Detective,' she said with a serene smile, 'that's the old cemetery.'

Eight

'I wonder how they all get along,' Flowers said when they reached the cars. 'It must be like living in a share house.'

'Heidi seems different to the others, doesn't she?' Ryder said.

'Hmm. There's definitely tension between her and her sister-in-law.' Flowers glanced back at the house where Kristin Lorrimer was watching them leave. 'And I don't know what to think about Ethan.'

'Kristin must feel a bit powerless,' Ryder said in a quiet voice, his back to the house, 'like she doesn't have a say in the decision-making regarding the property, including who lives in the homestead.'

'Yes, she wasn't part of the discussion about Art's drug history, though it's obvious she knows about it. She defers to her husband.'

'I'm sure they'd discuss things privately,' said Ryder, jangling his car keys.

'Did you notice how close she was to the window?' said Flowers.

'I did. Perhaps the vitamin D thing was an excuse to sit close by and eavesdrop.' Ryder nodded at the tall, shaded hedges. 'So, that's the family cemetery.'

'Yep, and it looks like Ethan's the gravedigger.'

Ryder snorted and unlocked his car. 'Your imagination's running wild, Daisy. I'll see you at the airport.'

When Flowers arrived in Khancoban thirty-five minutes later, he found Ryder stonewalling reporters who'd emerged from two regional news vans parked at the entrance to the airport.

'Detective, was the pilot making an emergency landing?'

Ryder spoke to the short, stocky male reporter who had shoved a microphone close to his mouth. 'It's only been two days since the crash occurred. The Australian Transport Safety Bureau have completed their work here, but we won't know the answer to your question until we receive their report.'

'Detective?' A blonde woman edged out the other reporter. 'It's obvious this is being treated as a murder, otherwise Homicide wouldn't be here. Do you have any idea how the tractor came to be in the middle of the runway?'

'No, but I can assure you that is the focus of our investigation. Thank you.'

'Detective?'

'Detective?'

Ryder gestured to Flowers and they began to walk towards the main shed. Flowers waited until the reporters had given up the chase before saying, 'Your drug hunch could be right on the money, Sarge. We know Art had prior drug charges, and I reckon Scruffy was one of the enforcers putting the screws on the Lorrimers.'

'There's no doubt in my mind they recognised him but decided between themselves not to go the police,' Ryder said as they approached the shed. 'Did you get on to the other pilots who use this airport?'

'Yep. Both can account for their whereabouts on the night of the crash. One is still holidaying with his family on the New South Wales south coast, the other was in Melbourne on business. Both stories checked out. Ben Hoff was the only one on duty the day the plane came in.'

They rounded the corner of the shed and the expanse of the airfield opened up before them. The remnants of the plane and tractor had been cleared away, leaving only an ugly section of scorched earth. Further out, the grass was speckled with numerous patches of red spray paint where forensics had marked and photographed items for evidence before the crime scene had been disassembled.

They found Ben Hoff alone in the shed. 'Not open yet?' Flowers asked from the doorway.

Hoff put down the armload of books he was carrying and looked up. 'Not until forensics and the safety bureau tell us they don't need access to the site anymore.'

'Ah, gotcha.'

Hoff wiped his forehead with his shirt sleeve, sweating despite the coolness of the day. 'At least it's given me the chance to clean up around here. I've taken a couple of loads to the tip already.'

'It's looking tidier,' said Flowers before glancing at Ryder. 'This is my partner, Detective Sergeant Ryder.'

Hoff nodded to Ryder. 'Is there something I can help you with?' he asked warily.

'We're checking everyone's whereabouts the night the plane came in,' said Ryder. 'Can you tell me where you were at 10 pm two nights ago when Art Lorrimer died?'

Hoff flushed a dull shade of red. 'I already told Detective Flowers I was at home. I rushed down here after I heard the crash.'

'Can anyone confirm you were home beforehand?' asked Flowers.

'My wife can.'

'Okay, we'll check in with her,' Flowers said easily. 'I also spoke to Orville Parish. He remembers handing you the key when he finished work, so that fits with what you told us. Apparently, the tractor you had here could be started by anyone who owned a similar make and model. Were you aware that many tractors have a common key?'

'No, I didn't know that. I'm a pilot, not a farmer.'

'It could explain why the shed wasn't broken into, and why the key was still locked away in the drawer. We're searching for people who own, or have owned, similar tractors in the area.'

Hoff's expression turned guarded, giving Flowers the impression he wasn't going to say any more. But then he picked up the stack of books and said, 'That sounds like a big job.'

'It'll take a while. But we'll get around to everyone eventually.

Oh, one more thing, how regularly did Art Lorrimer fly in?'

Hoff shook his head. 'I can't remember the last time I saw him.'

Deciding to leave things there, Flowers looked at Ryder then raised a hand in farewell. 'Thanks for your time, Ben.'

'I don't know what it is about that guy,' Flowers said as they walked back to the cars, 'but he strikes me as cagey.'

'He's defensive all right,' said Ryder, 'or maybe the word's "reactionary".'

When they drew level with the reporters, the same pair made a half-hearted effort to engage them, but a firm shake of Ryder's head had them retreating to their vans.

'Are there any other airstrips around here?' Ryder asked.

'Yeah, I thought of that too,' said Flowers. 'There's an abandoned one down at Geehi but it's riddled with rabbit warrens. There's no way *anything* could land there.'

'Hoff said he couldn't remember the last time he'd seen Art,' said Ryder. 'That could be true in a literal sense, but what if Art used to fly in during the dead of night and Hoff knew, but looked the other way?'

Nine

'Ida, table eight needs clearing.'

Sterling looked up from the schooner she was filling to see a family donning their jackets and beanies. 'Be there in a sec,' she told Elijah as he passed by the bar on his way to delivering two meals from the kitchen.

Setting the glass down in front of the customer, she held the machine for the bloke to tap his card then grabbed a tray and hurried out into the packed dining area. Taking the opportunity to scan the room full of diners, she noticed a few familiar faces in the crowd. Sergeant Collins was having dinner with a man she didn't recognise, and Gus, Spider and the crew had been forced inside by late afternoon rain. Apart from those few locals, the pub was packed with tourists, many of whom had stopped in for an early dinner on their way home from the ski resorts.

Sterling was grateful for the double shift despite her aching feet. Wiling away time in the rumpus room had grown so unappealing she'd taken to running twice a day when she couldn't get up to the ski fields.

She was making her way back to the bar when a voice raised in anger cut through the hum of conversation. A man jumped up from where he'd been having dinner with his two male companions and said heatedly, 'Deer, feral dogs and pigs do as much damage as the horses.' He had his back to her, so all Sterling could see was his bomber jacket and blue jeans with two white skulls on the backs of his thighs.

'Yes, and we cull them. The brumbies are destroying the alpine environment,' one of the other men argued, not caring that everyone around them had stopped talking to watch.

'They're an important part of our wartime history,' said the first man.

'I agree with you on that.'

'Oh, shit, here we go,' said Elijah as Sterling joined him. 'The brumby debate; when will it all end?'

'I don't know enough about it,' said Sterling, watching the three men argue. 'What do you think?'

'What do I think? I think I'm going to ask them to leave.'

Elijah approached the table; both men were standing now. The man facing Sterling had messy red hair and his pale complexion was blotched with crimson. The third man pulled his cap over his eyes and leaned back in his chair, making it clear he was not taking part.

'Come on, fellas,' she heard Elijah say, 'people are trying to enjoy their dinner. Dial it down or take it outside.'

Right then Sergeant Collins rose and walked towards the group. A hush fell over the room, prompting the men's seated companion to lift the brim of his cap and look around to see what was happening.

'You two are disrupting everyone's evening, including mine,' Sergeant Collins said. 'No one here cares for your opinions. Now sit down or leave.'

The room held a collective breath, and then the redhead snatched up his keys and left. The man with the skulls on his jeans sat down. A few patrons clapped as Sergeant Collins returned to his table.

'That was close,' Elijah said, keeping watch on the two who'd remained as Sterling began cleaning up behind the bar.

The door opened, and the patrons turned as one, fearing the redhead had come back to have another go. But it was Heidi Lorrimer who walked in, accompanied by a guy Sterling hadn't seen before.

Collins looked up and spoke to Heidi as she passed by. She nodded briefly, then followed her companion to the only unoccupied table, which was partly positioned in a foyer leading to the amenities—with little privacy, heavy foot traffic and a 1980s arcade game close by, it was the pub's least popular table.

Sterling hesitated, but when no one approached the couple, she tucked a menu under her arm and made her way over to them. She knew how to do this; knew what to say to people who had lost a loved one.

Heidi had taken off her jacket and was hanging it on the back of her chair. Her companion was slim, with a dark moustache and a patch of hair under his bottom lip. He was wearing blue jeans, a maroon hoodie and a plain black beanie.

'Hello, Heidi,' Sterling said, gazing squarely into the other woman's eyes. 'I didn't know your brother, but I just wanted to say how deeply sorry I am for you and your family.' The surprising thing was her condolences were heartfelt. Losing a sibling would be horrible. Losing a twin had to be worse.

'Thank you,' Heidi said simply.

Sterling glanced at Heidi's companion, but the man remained silent. 'Can I bring you something?' Sterling asked briskly, reluctant to linger.

The guy ordered two beers, a draft for him and a bottle of local craft beer for Heidi.

'No problem. Would you like to see a menu?' She glanced at Heidi. 'Although I'm sure you know it off the top of your head.'

Heidi started to answer but the guy interrupted. 'Just leave one here.'

Sterling headed back to the bar, a chorus of disparate voices creating a hum of conversation as she weaved her way between the tables.

'*I'm going to be sore tomorrow . . .*'
'*Mum, can I have your iPad?*'
'*Who's playing in the footy tonight?*'
'*I wonder if this will delay the Lorrimers' plans for . . .*'

Sterling almost broke stride, so unexpected was the snippet of conversation spoken in a quiet baritone. Fighting the urge to look around, she shifted her gaze left and right, searching the tables for empty plates. The man who'd spoken was sitting with Sergeant Collins.

She spotted a family who'd finished their mains. 'Can I clear these away?' she asked.

'Yes, thanks,' replied the mother.

Sterling took her time stacking the plates, glancing every so often at the sergeant's companion. Committing him to memory, she carried the dirty dishes back to the kitchen.

'How is she?' Elijah asked as she flipped the top off Heidi's craft beer.

'She's quiet, but that's to be expected.' Sterling straightened the glass, checking the head. 'Do you know the guy she's with?'

'Not sure. He could have been in here before.' He picked up the beers when they were ready. 'I'll take these over. I want to give her my condolences.'

For the first time since the dinner rush began there was a lull at the bar, so Sterling grabbed a cloth and began wiping down the taps. Excitement rippled through her body. Finally, she had information to pass on to Ryder, though she had no idea if the partial sentence she'd overheard was valuable or not.

When she looked up, Gus and his entourage were leaving. Gus winked, and she sent him a cheeky wink in return. Ryder wanted her to get to know the locals, so if she needed to flirt a little, so be it. When the diners at another table stood up, she hurried to the kitchen, impatient to be on her way. 'Any more mains to come?'

'Nope,' the kitchen hand answered. 'We're onto dessert.'

'Heidi and a friend came in five minutes ago. I'm not sure if they're going to order anything,' Sterling said.

'No problem.'

'Is it okay if I head off?' she asked Elijah when he joined her. 'Chef's finished the mains, and the place is starting to empty out.'

'Absolutely, you get going,' he said. 'Simon's here until closing time.'

After collecting her coat and bag, Sterling left the hotel and headed for the carpark. The rain had eased to a light shower. Soggy grass squelched under her Doc Martens.

I wonder if this will delay the Lorrimers' plans . . . the man had said. Minutes before, Sergeant Collins had been speaking to Heidi, so presumably the man was referring to Art Lorrimer's death. So, what *were* the Lorrimers planning?

Forcing everything from her mind, Sterling began her counter surveillance, peering left and right past the fur-lined edges of her hood. Of the dozen parked cars, Collins' police vehicle, Spider's dual-cab ute, plus hers and Elijah's made up four. Of the remaining eight, two SUVs sported skis, snowboards and bikes, while two more were packed to the roof with pillows and toys. That left four sedans.

'Hey.'

Sterling swung around, her heart hammering.

'Yeah, you.'

She turned in the direction of the voice. 'What's up?'

A scrawny figure with a mop of dirty blond hair straightened up from between the cars. 'Can you buy us a bottle of vodka?' She recognised him as one of the underage drinkers she'd seen hanging around the pub lately.

Sterling unlocked her car. 'Sorry, it's illegal to buy alcohol for minors.'

Two shadows emerged from behind a tree and joined the boy who'd asked the question. 'We'll pay. We've got money,' he said, clearly the ringleader.

'Sorry, I work here. I'll lose my job.' Sterling slid behind the wheel and started the engine. Clicking the phone into the bracket on the windscreen, she hit the record feature and recited the registration numbers she'd memorised. Should the underage trio be watching, hopefully they'd think she was calling the police, or someone in the hotel.

Leaving the phone recording, she slowly reversed out, reading aloud the registration numbers of the two remaining cars. She checked her rear-view mirror, pleased to see the trio had melted into the darkness. Hopefully they were off home, sober.

She pulled out of the carpark, impatient to call Ryder once she was on her own phone and tell him what she'd overheard. She'd been tempted to ask Elijah about the man having dinner with Sergeant Collins, but she couldn't risk raising the publican's suspicions. She had to remember she was a woman on a working holiday, not a detective, and Ida Stevenson would have no interest in a middle-aged man dining with the local police sergeant.

Headlights lit the cabin as the driver of a car parked by the kerb behind her switched their lights onto high beam.

'Turn it down,' Sterling muttered, her heart jumping as the car swung onto the road then accelerated to sit on her tail. With her own engine not fully warmed up, she maintained a steady speed, hoping the driver would overtake.

She decided to turn left when the way home was straight ahead, feeling increasingly unnerved when the car behind did the same. She made a second turn, looping back to the hotel. She'd taken Ryder's advice and left some items in her cubicle that she could go back for in case something like this happened. She turned left again, glimpsing the shining lights of the hotel not far ahead. Just then, the driver pulled out onto the wrong side of the road and floored it. Sterling maintained her speed, watching in her side mirror as the car began to draw level. And then the vehicle was beside her, the driver tooting and young men hollering from the open windows as they passed by.

The red glow of taillights disappeared into the darkness as the car turned right, screeching around the corner in the direction of the Alpine Way.

'Idiots,' she muttered, pulling into the carpark for the second time that day. Cutting the engine, she sat in the darkness until her heart rate had returned to somewhere close to normal. She walked quickly into the pub to retrieve a plastic bag from the cubicle in case there were other people watching.

'It's always tempting to head straight home once the danger has passed,' Ryder was saying, 'but you did the right thing going back in and getting the groceries you left there.'

'I have an assortment of things in the cubicle,' Sterling said wryly, sitting on the edge of the bed to unlace her boots, the phone on speaker beside her.

'Good work. And you've never seen the man with Sergeant Collins before?'

'No.'

'Flowers said he's big on fishing. Do you think he might've been a fishing mate?'

'I don't think so, Sarge. They weren't that upbeat, they were more serious. And it was after Collins spoke to Heidi that the other man said, "I wonder if this will delay the Lorrimers' plans for . . ." whatever.'

'Okay, it's likely they were talking about Art's death then. What did he look like?'

Sterling spent the next few minutes giving Ryder a description. Outside, rain fell steadily, the constant gurgle of water through the downpipe by the window oddly comforting.

'This is good work, Sterling,' Ryder said. 'The three of us need to keep our eyes and ears open. It's too dangerous for us to ask Collins outright who this man was. He'll wonder who tipped us off. It could blow your cover.'

There was a pause. Sterling began massaging the arch of her foot.

'See if you can make a personal connection with Collins. You'll work out the best way to do that. And bring Flowers up to date when you're talking to him tonight, otherwise I'll do it tomorrow morning. We're on the early-morning flight to Williamtown.'

'Yes, Sarge.'

'We should meet up when I get back too.'

'Same place?' Sterling asked.

'Perisher. I'll let you know the day and time.'

Ten

The red-brick house was set a few streets back from the water at Lemon Tree Passage, a small village at the tip of the Tilligerry peninsula. In summer, the population swelled with tourists drawn to the calm, safe waters of Port Stephens, but during school term the streets were empty. The trampoline in the front yard of the house next door stood quiet and there were no kids riding bikes or skateboards.

They'd touched down at Williamtown Airport at nine-thirty and only twenty minutes later they had arrived at the house, thanks to Detective Everett from Newcastle having a car ready for them.

Flowers drummed his fingers on the steering wheel, keeping watch in the rear-view mirror. Everett and two members of his forensics team were only minutes behind in their car.

'I keep thinking about what Sterling overheard,' said Flowers.

'Could be something, or nothing,' said Ryder. '*I wonder if this will delay the Lorrimers' plans . . . for Art's funeral?*' He shrugged. 'It would make sense. He has to be identified by DNA.'

'I hope we find the name of his dentist inside. Does he own this place?'

Ryder shook his head. 'It's a rental. Everett has the keys.'

'Here they are now,' Flowers said, reaching for his doorhandle.

As the police gathered on the footpath, Flowers nodded to the forensics guys they'd met briefly at the airport.

Detective Everett handed Ryder a set of keys. 'Cessnock Airport gave me his address. The woman next door knew the name of the managing agent, so I picked up the keys early this morning.'

'Thank you,' said Ryder. Turning to Flowers, he held out the keys. 'Lead the way, Detective.'

Flowers went ahead across the overgrown lawn, then jogged up five easy steps onto a porch, bare except for a pile of brittle liquid-ambar leaves gathering around the doormat.

'We'll wait out here until you're ready for forensics,' said Everett.

Flowers unlocked the door and stepped into a cold hallway with patchy grey carpet. The hallway ran from front to back, its white walls scarred with scratches and scuff marks. To the left was a sparsely furnished main bedroom with a hastily made bed and a lounge chair that looked as old as the house. Behind the wardrobe's mirrored doors were shelves containing jeans, sloppy joes and T-shirts. Three pairs of black pants and three white shirts hung from the rail.

Ryder flicked a spare wire hanger. 'Work uniforms I'd say, and he was probably wearing the clothes that usually hang here.'

Flowers crouched down and examined the four pairs of shoes in the bottom of the wardrobe.

'Anything?' Ryder asked.

'Nope.'

They crossed over to the lounge room where a brown modular couch faced a TV mounted on the wall. A ghetto blaster sat atop a low cabinet. 'I bet this is probably full of CDs,' Flowers said, walking over and sliding open the cabinet doors. 'Yes, CDs and . . . here we go, an old flight bag.'

He pulled it out and dumped it on the arm of the lounge. 'A birth certificate and some prescription repeats, the doctor's name will be on that,' he said, handing one to Ryder.

Next, he pulled out a small stack of business cards held together with an elastic band and flicked through them. 'Dentist,' he said, passing a card to Ryder who was already on his phone.

'We don't have time to go through everything now, Daisy. Bring it with us.'

Flowers moved on to the second bedroom. An unplugged iron stood on top of an ironing board, next to an empty clothes hoist by the window.

'O'Day,' he heard Ryder say in the hallway. 'I've sent you a photo of a business card. Contact the dentist and request Lorrimer's dental records, then send them through to Harriet Ono. Make it urgent.'

'Definitely a man cave,' Flowers said after they'd checked a couple of empty suitcases and three canvas duffle bags they'd found in the third bedroom.

'We'll get forensics to test those for trace elements,' said Ryder.

'There's not one family photo in this place, no paintings on the walls, no books or even a magazine.' Flowers looked around then walked into the kitchen and opened the fridge. The freezer was empty, the fridge stocked with beers and the basics. He scanned the bare kitchen benches and shook his head. 'Not even a fruit bowl.'

'His clothes would fit in the suitcases,' Ryder mused. 'He could disappear in a hurry.'

'It's creepy,' said Flowers, 'it could be any dude living here. Only what we found in that bag tells us it was Art Lorrimer.'

'Right. His phone and laptop probably went up in the plane.'

Flowers trailed behind Ryder as he went into the bathroom. 'He has no online presence either, I already checked,' he said. 'No social media.'

'That's odd for someone in their thirties.'

'There's not even a website advertising his joy flights.'

'How does he get business then?' Ryder asked, opening the vanity unit.

'Through those experience websites. Customers book online. All they have to do is turn up at the airport with their printed voucher.'

The bathroom was standard with only some razors and deodorant in the small vanity unit. 'Plenty of strands of hair in here,' said Ryder, poking a bar of soap on the side of the basin.

The final room was a small but functional laundry with a dryer stacked on top of a front-loader washing machine. A square wooden deck at the back of the house couldn't even boast the most basic of barbeques, while the yard was a tangle of overgrown shrubs.

'I don't get it,' said Flowers, gazing through the window at the broken rotary clothesline. One of the arms had been bent all the way to the ground as if kids had swung on it too many times. 'This guy was an adrenaline junkie; he had a plane and was into snow sports. There isn't even a pair of skis. A ghost could live here.'

'But there is a boat.'

Flowers swung around, a fishy aroma filling his nostrils. Ryder had thrown open the internal doorway leading into the garage. There, taking up the entire space, was a white fishing boat and trailer.

Flowers watched a little water taxi pull up to the marina while Ryder spoke to Brown at Homicide.

'Forensics are going through the house and garage now. Can you confirm the appointment I have with Cessnock Airport this afternoon? Remind them that a team from Newcastle will be with me, and they'll be impounding Lorrimer's car.'

Flowers sipped his takeaway coffee and watched a well-dressed couple disembark from the water taxi.

'Flowers is on the twelve-forty pm flight back to Canberra,' Ryder was saying, 'so call him if you need anything. And, Brown, when you've got the airport on the phone, ask them for Lorrimer's mobile number so we can apply for a warrant. We need a copy of his call log.'

A water police boat arrived and began cruising between the boats moored further out in the bay, as though they were looking for something. Flowers shifted his gaze to the couple. They were walking towards a schmick blue-and-white restaurant on the marina. When he turned back to the police boat, it was already motoring out of the bay. He mentioned it to Ryder as they walked to the car.

'They were patrolling around the boats that were anchored further out. Maybe we should give them a call, see if they suspect someone's bringing drugs into Port Stephens.'

'You think Lorrimer was meeting up with someone offshore?' asked Ryder.

'It's happened before.' Flowers unlocked the car and slid in behind the wheel. 'There were a few fishing boats in the marina, and yet Lorrimer kept his in the garage. He could take the boat out and slip it anywhere.'

'Maybe he doesn't want to pay the marina fees,' said Ryder.

'Maybe.'

'I'll look into it.' Ryder pulled the seatbelt across his chest and clicked it in. 'Let's say he is hauling in something besides fish. He goes home, puts it in one of those duffle bags, drives to the airport and from there he can transport it anywhere.'

'He's been done for possession before.'

Ryder was quiet for a bit. 'Once I get a copy of his flight log this afternoon, I'll look for patterns and recurring destinations. Let's go meet the ex.'

Ten minutes later, Dawn Fleming led them into the front room of her home. Stockily built, with short red hair and wearing rimless glasses, she held a swaddled baby in her arms and gave them a friendly smile. 'Would you like to have a look at Mabel before you sit down?'

Flowers glanced at Ryder then nodded. 'Sure.'

Dawn gently lifted back the edge of a soft white shawl to show them the baby. 'I'm a home carer.'

'Oh wow!' Flowers gazed in wonder at a tiny koala the size of his hand. Blissfully asleep, the young joey was clinging to the furry back of a toy koala three times its size. 'That's so cool.'

'How do you become a home carer?' Ryder asked, looking as smitten as Flowers felt.

'Through the Port Stephens Koala Sanctuary,' Dawn said, sitting down and inviting them to do the same. 'Her mother was killed on the road, so I took a few weeks' leave from work to look after her. The sanctuary can't take them all.'

'Will they take her when they have space?' asked Flowers.

'No, most of the ones in the sanctuary will be there for life because of blindness or a head injury from being hit on the road or falling out of a tree. Mabel will be released where she was found when she's big enough. The koala's digestive system grows accustomed to the gum leaves in their area, they won't eat if you return them to a different one.'

'That's something everyone should know,' said Flowers. People like Dawn restored Flowers' faith in humankind. If he hadn't been on a tight schedule to make his flight, he would have liked to learn more about the sanctuary, but Ryder wanted him back in Thredbo so someone was close to Sterling.

'You said on the phone you wanted to talk about Art,' she said. 'I can't believe you think he was murdered. It's so upsetting.'

'Yes, I'm sorry,' said Flowers. 'A pilot at Pokolbin gave us your name, though he did stress you were a former partner.'

'Oh yes, Art and I broke up years ago.' She looked at Ryder and then back to Flowers. 'I've bumped into him a couple of times at the shops, that's all. I don't know if he was in another relationship.'

'The airport had his older brother, Daniel, listed as his next of kin. Do you know Dan?' asked Flowers.

Dawn shook her head. 'I never met any of Art's family.'

'You've never been to their property in Tooma?'

She shook her head again. 'In all the time we were together, Art didn't go home once.'

'You must have thought that was strange?'

Dawn had a habit of wrinkling her nose when she was about to answer in the negative. 'He told me early on he was the black sheep of the family, that he didn't enjoy country life.'

'Did Art do drugs?' Ryder asked.

Dawn's eyes widened and she glanced over her shoulder towards the back of the house. 'I moved back in with Mum after Art and I broke up. She doesn't know about that.'

The hairs on the back of Flowers' neck stood up. 'So, he *was* involved in drugs? In the drug trade?'

'I wouldn't go that far. We used to smoke a bit of weed together. I haven't touched it since then.' She smiled at the furry bundle in her arms. 'I've got better things to do with my time.'

'What about hard drugs?' Ryder asked. 'Coke and meth?'

'God, no! We used to have a joint on the nights when Art didn't have to fly the next day. How would he have done his job if he was using that stuff?'

'Would you have known?' Flowers asked.

Dawn was silent for a few seconds, thinking about the question. 'I'm fairly sure I would have.'

'Where did he buy the weed?' Ryder asked.

'I don't know. He always had it on him though.'

'Did he own a boat when you lived together?' Flowers asked.

'Yes, he loved fishing.'

'Would he often bring home a catch?' asked Ryder.

'Most of the time.'

Flowers leaned forward. 'Can you tell us what he was like? We're trying to get an idea of his personality.'

'The other pilots used to call him "cowboy" because he was a bit of a thrillseeker.' Dawn smiled and visibly relaxed. 'But the Art I knew was laidback and calm, which I think are good traits if you're a pilot. He never worried about money and that used to annoy the hell out of me. I was always trying to save, and Art would spend every dollar he had.'

'So, he wasn't thinking about his future?'

'No, Art lived in the moment. He once said something about family money. I assumed he meant a trust fund. He didn't spend any of it on me, that's for sure.'

'Or on clothes or furniture, by the looks of his current place,' said Flowers.

'I can imagine,' Dawn said, rolling her eyes. 'He didn't bring much with him when we moved in together.'

'Did Art fly to Khancoban regularly or, for that matter, any other town?' Ryder asked.

Flowers mentally kicked himself for not thinking of that question.

'I have no idea. I'm sorry I can't help you more, but Art flew all over the place. He'd tell me when to expect him home, and that's all I needed to know really. I was always busy organising events for the bowling club where I work.'

Flowers nodded, then caught Ryder's eye. The sergeant gave a quick shake of his head indicating there was nothing else he wanted to ask. Flowers looked at his watch and smiled at Dawn. 'Thanks very much. We have a clearer picture of him now.'

They all stood, and Flowers and Ryder took a last look at Mabel. 'Good luck with her,' Flowers said. 'It's great to hear about animals being released back into the wild.'

As they left the house, he said to Ryder, 'So, Lorrimer didn't live like a trust-fund baby.'

'No, and neither do the others,' Ryder said. 'You can tell Ethan resents him and Heidi having to work elsewhere to supplement the family income.'

'I noticed the homestead was a bit run down. The window paint's peeling, and they spend zilch on heating.'

'It's not that unusual,' Ryder said. 'The countryside's green now but they've come through a long period of drought. They'll be hoping for a few good years of rainfall.'

When they reached the car, Flowers lobbed the keys at Ryder. 'If I'm going to make that flight to Canberra, Sarge, you'd better put your foot down.'

Eleven

By 4 pm daylight was fading fast, with angry dark clouds building up over Lake Jindabyne. Flowers strode into the Nuggets Crossing shopping centre, aiming to top up his food supplies and his badly depleted caffeine levels. The bakery would be closed by now, but he was confident someone would be serving coffee to the crowds returning to town after a day on the mountain.

When he reached the group of shops built around a courtyard, he spotted an *OPEN* sign in the window of the Brumby Cafe and Gallery. Inside, he followed his nose to the cafe at the back. Benches with charging stations were built along the walls where a couple in ski gear were perched drinking hot chocolates. On the other side, a man in a ski-patrol uniform like Vanessa's was typing on his laptop.

Flowers approached the counter where a tall woman about his age with shoulder-length dark hair was heating milk in the machine. She looked up and smiled.

'I'm pleased you haven't shut that down,' he said, watching.

'What can I get you?'

'Any chance of a turmeric latte?'

'Sorry.' She pointed to a coffee menu perched on a small easel atop the counter. 'I can make you any of those.'

Flowers scanned the list. 'I'll have the mint mocha and a pistachio slice, thanks.'

'Good choice. An energy boost is what you need at this time of the day.'

'It's been a long one.' And he still had the half hour trip to Thredbo ahead of him.

'Have here or take away?'

'I'll take it with me, thanks.'

He wandered over to the wall, absently running an eye over the paintings of snowy landscapes and sketches of landmark buildings and homesteads. Ryder's meeting with the inspector at headquarters in Sydney was a stroke of luck for Flowers. He could spend all night on the computer if he wanted to before jumping back on the case work in the morning. Anticipation was already building up in his body at the thought of tonight's excitement. So what if he was wrecked from lack of sleep? It was worth it.

'Can I help you with something?'

Flowers turned, recognising the elderly woman he'd seen at the Tooma Hotel a couple of days ago. She was refolding a pile of jumpers. 'I'm fine, thanks, just killing time while I wait for my coffee.'

Flowers turned back to look at the sketches, his gaze immediately locking on to a homestead he recognised. He swung around. 'Excuse me, is this the Lorrimer house?'

'That's right.' The woman put down the jumper she was holding and walked over to him. 'That's White Winter Station in its original splendour, before all the other bits were added.'

Flowers studied the sketch. 'There's a garage over this side now, isn't there?' he asked, pointing.

'Yes. The artist has sketched the homestead numerous times, and other parts of the property. It's a significant structure and was the original family home of one of the pioneering graziers in the area.'

'Who's the artist?' Flowers asked.

'John Gilbert. Have you been to his gallery in Thredbo?'

'No. I've been to the museum. I didn't know there was a gallery there.'

'It's worth a visit.' The woman smiled, and it was obvious she had a genuine interest in the subject. 'John has drawn hundreds of sketches over the years, but he's eighty-five now and his eyesight isn't what it was.' She reached for a cardboard box that was sitting on an antique desk. 'There are some smaller prints in here.' She began flipping through the prints before lifting one out to show him. 'This is a later one after the garages were built. That's mostly how it looks today.'

Flowers studied the sketch. 'I was only there a couple of days ago.' He looked up to find the woman watching him closely, a knowing smile on her lips. 'Did I see you having lunch in the Tooma Hotel? You had lots of Vinnies bags. You told the barman you were off to Tumbarumba.'

'Observant, aren't you? But then so am I. You were sitting with a man a little older than yourself with thick, dark hair. I was trying to work out if you were detectives or undertakers.'

'Undertakers,' Flowers said with a laugh. 'Wait until I tell the sarge that. I'm Detective Mitchell Flowers, by the way.'

'Wendy Buchanan.'

'Are you the owner?'

'The shop used to be mine. My niece, Cate, has taken it over. I help out when it's busy and I source some bits and pieces for her,' she said, looking around at the merchandise on display.

As Wendy wandered away, Flowers began looking through the various prints of pygmy possums, rivers, mountains, sandstone buildings and even a couple of elaborate tombstones. He pulled out a plastic-covered sketch for a closer look. John Gilbert's signature was scrawled below the drawing followed by the words 'White Winter Station'. What Flowers had assumed to be headstones in a local council cemetery were in fact the private family graves on the Lorrimers' property. He thought of Ethan tidying the area the other day, possibly in preparation for Art's interment.

Holding on to the print, he looked around for Wendy Buchanan, but couldn't see her.

'Large mint mocha,' the woman behind the counter called.

Flowers slipped the print back into the box and went to get his coffee.

Laden with his laptop case, his groceries and Art Lorrimer's old flight bag, Flowers stomped on the mat outside his apartment. Shaking the snow off his boots was the least he could do for the overly helpful owner who'd asked him on arrival if he'd like her to stock the fridge with the basics, change the towels every third day, and vacuum the floors. No, no and no. Thank you. She'd looked at him oddly, and he'd used the case he was working on as his reason for not wanting to be disturbed.

Inside the dark apartment he dumped everything on the floor as the door clicked shut behind him. Flicking on the light switch, his eyes went straight to the desk set against the wall. The high-speed computer, oversized monitor and related equipment were all there, their tiny coloured power lights blinking.

In the bathroom, the towels were still hung haphazardly on the rack, a few pieces of rubbish in the bin. Satisfied the owner hadn't been in, he put a frozen lasagne into the microwave and stacked the other meals in the freezer. The lofty goal of cooking from scratch had gone by the wayside now he was working days and half the night too. In a lone nod to healthy consumption, he sprawled on the lounge and twisted the top off a bottle of ginger kombucha. He scrolled on his phone for ten minutes, then decided to call Sterling and leave a message.

'Hi, Mitch.'

Flowers sat up and put aside his drink. 'Hey, Nerida, I didn't think you'd be home yet.'

'It was slow today. The most exciting thing was Elijah teaching me how to make cocktails.'

Lucky Elijah, Flowers thought with a sudden surge of longing that he swiftly shut down. 'Did you get to drink them?'

'Hah. He let me go early, actually, so I went for a snowboard this afternoon. Learn anything in Port Stephens?'

Flowers ignored the beeping microwave and recounted his trip to Lemon Tree Passage. 'Newcastle forensics are going through the house and fishing boat, and the car he left at the airport. We had a brief look through his personal papers and put his dentist in touch with Harriet.' He yawned. 'I'll go through the rest of the stuff in the morning while I'm waiting for Ryder to get here.'

There was silence at the other end of the line. Flowers picked up his kombucha and took a swig. 'Are you working tomorrow?' he asked.

'I am, thank goodness. Even when I was out on the hill, I couldn't stop those words running through my head.'

'You mean: *I wonder if this will delay the Lorrimers' plans . . .*' Flowers said softly.

'Yes, Mitch, *those* words.'

'Yeah, my brain's too dead to come up with anything.'

'You and me both,' she said with a sigh.

'I do have a good news story though.'

'Tell me.'

Flowers told her about the joey Dawn Fleming was caring for.

'Oh my God, I wish I could have met Mabel,' Sterling said. 'I'm *so* jealous.'

'We should check out the sanctuary when this is over.' The words slipped out before he could stop them. Flowers grimaced, bracing for her response.

'You're a big softie, Mitch,' she said with a low laugh. 'I remember you adopted one of the koalas injured in the bushfires.'

'I did,' he said quickly. 'I also cried when my Tamagotchi died in year two.'

Sterling snorted with laughter and Flowers relaxed, glad she hadn't made a big thing of his impulsive suggestion they visit the sanctuary. Erasing his memories of the night they'd spent together was proving harder than he'd imagined. But he would get there, in time. Sterling had admitted she would like to date him, but was prioritising her career. Flowers understood. Ryder's team was highly regarded, and Sterling had worked hard to get where she was. He knew that as Homicide's latest recruit, she feared she'd be the first one transferred out should Ryder twig that there was something going on between them and worry it would interfere with their work.

'What's that beeping sound?' Sterling asked suddenly.

'It's just the microwave,' Flowers said, glancing over his shoulder before jumping up from the lounge. It wasn't the microwave but the alarm on his computer announcing he had fifteen minutes before he needed to log on.

'Go and eat,' said Sterling. 'You've had a long day.'

And it was about to get longer. 'Okay. I'll call you tomorrow.'

Flowers hung up and switched his phone to silent before putting it on the desk beside the monitor in case Ryder or someone in his family called. Smiling, he rubbed his hands together in anticipation. He was young and fit, and more than capable of pulling a few all-nighters. While he was determined to make Ryder proud by doing outstanding work on the case, he wanted *this* too.

Moving swiftly, he turned off the lights, plunging the apartment into darkness. Then he sat in the chair, placed an expensive headset over his ears and logged on.

Twelve

Sterling woke at first light. Outside, frost had turned the grass white, the bracing air making her grateful for her beanie, mittens and merino-wool running gear. Starting at an easy pace, she avoided the slippery grass, keeping to the bitumen as the sky turned pink in the east.

I wonder if this will delay the Lorrimers' plans for . . .

Damn! If only the final part of that sentence hadn't been lost in the din of conversation.

Warm now, she increased her pace as the road turned downhill. She passed the pharmacy, the coffee shop, and the Snowy Hydro Information Centre, noting the usual cars parked along the street. Turning left onto the Alpine Way, she stuck to the gravel shoulder, away from the vehicles hurtling past on the road.

A kilometre on, she took the quiet access road that led to the pondage, her warm breath sending puffs of mist into the air. She didn't stop until she reached the parkland at the edge of the three-kilometre lake.

Hands on hips and sucking air into her lungs, she walked towards the boat ramp and stood looking across the water. An early-morning skier clad in a black wetsuit was bouncing across the wake.

She smiled, happy memories of her father teaching her to waterski coming to mind. These days her racing boat was stored at a friend's property on the banks of the Hawkesbury River, along with her caravan. While she no longer raced herself, she loved driving the boat for the next generation, and being involved in the sport she loved.

Reluctant to cool down too much, she turned away with a pang of longing and broke into an easy jog. Hugging the shoreline, she thought back to her meeting with Ryder when he'd pitched the idea of her coming to Khancoban.

'We think you're a good fit for this assignment. You're not known in the area, and you're a young-looking thirty-two, the perfect age to spend a season in the snow and mix with a lot of people. Have you ever spent time there? I know you're an ace waterskier.'

'Waterskiing's nothing like snow skiing. I've snowboarded a couple of times.'

'Any good? Come on, Sterling, don't be modest.'

'I found it pretty easy.'

'Do you think you could handle the weather?'

'Sure.'

'Good. Well, we're only talking about it at this stage, but you might want to think about throwing your hat in the ring if we decide it's a goer.'

She'd accepted the assignment, fearful of another sideways shift if she refused. Not that she thought Ryder would do that to her, the sarge was awesome, but he kept saying *we*, and she knew people higher up the chain of command were involved. People she didn't know or trust. Any one of them could be like her old boss, or her ex-police partner, Rob, in Taree.

Memories of that horrible day replayed in her mind.

'Sterling.' Rob hitched a thumb over his shoulder. 'The inspector wants you in his office.'

'What about?'

He shrugged and sat down at his desk while Sterling hurried to the inspector's office, tapping lightly on the door.

'Come in, Sterling. Look, what's happened here?' he asked, not inviting her to sit, just sliding a report across the desk to her.

Sterling picked it up and ran her eyes down the page. It was the report she'd written from the warehouse job Rob had given her. 'I'm sorry, Inspector, I don't understand.'

'There are cameras at that location.'

'No, Sir, there aren't.'

'I'm telling you there are,' he said insistently, his eyes on her. 'How do you explain it?'

Sterling's heart began to thunder. 'When we arrived at the warehouses, I asked my partner if he wanted me to go and locate the security cameras. He told me not to worry about it, that he knew the spot well and there were no cameras there.'

'Well, that's wrong, and you've written the report, Sterling. You've put your name to it.'

'I know that Sir, but I trusted what my senior partner was telling me,' she said, her body burning hot with a mixture of anger and embarrassment. 'Naturally, I assumed the information he was giving me was reliable.'

Sterling stopped running and crouched down to untie her shoelace. Taking her time to retie it, she covertly checked that she wasn't being followed.

'You stitched me up,' she said, standing beside Rob's desk and peering down at him.

'Don't worry about it,' he said softly, getting up from his chair and standing too close to her. 'Why don't you and I go out tonight, and we'll talk about it.'

Sterling shook her head and backed away. 'No, I'm not interested.'

In that moment she knew he'd done it deliberately, and in the days that followed he'd made it known to anyone who'd listen that she was hard to get along with. A surge of renewed anger welled up inside her. It had taken her three years to fight her way out of the dead-end team she'd been dumped in following the botched warehouse report, and another two years to become eligible for Homicide.

Straightening up, she took off again, determined to outrun the memories, only stopping when she heard the familiar roar of water gushing from the spillway. Wiping the sweat from her forehead with her sleeve, she stared at the Road Closed sign. Figuring the barrier had been put there to stop cars driving onto the spillway and the television crews from taking footage of the wrecked plane, she slipped around the barrier and with her hands on her hips walked the short distance onto the spillway.

A chill slid down Sterling's spine and it had nothing to do with the cold morning air or the freezing spray of water carried backwards on the wind and onto her face. Standing there looking down on the airfield, it was impossible not to imagine Art Lorrimer flying in over the water, and the plane touching down in the dark. Impossible not to imagine his horror when he realised he was staring death in the face.

Thirteen

Flowers sat on the floor of the apartment, his back propped against the lounge and Lorrimer's documents spread out around him. There were registration papers for the boat and plane, a printed copy of last year's electronic tax return, and a copy of his yearly physical from a Port Stephens clinic. There was insurance for the fishing boat, and numerous policies for the Cessna, though none for the car.

Flowers stood up, his muscles stiff from sitting in the same position for too long. Nothing here would advance the case, and the pilot's wallet, phone and laptop, and his passport if he owned one, were likely to have been incinerated in the crash.

Yawning, Flowers pulled on his boots and shrugged on the new ski parka he'd bought in Jindabyne. It was 10.45, and the heating was making him sleepy. What he needed was a barista coffee and fresh air. Ryder wasn't leaving Sydney for another couple of hours, and technically Flowers was off duty.

Outside, the sub-zero temperature brought him instantly awake. The day was still, the trees drooping under their blanket of snow, the lifts spinning overhead. Pulling on his beanie and gloves, he struck out in the direction of the village, dodging the throngs of excited thrillseekers heading up the mountain. When he reached a hole-in-the-wall cafe, he ordered a coffee, then strolled past the shops, his blood pumping with fresh alpine air.

He was tossing his cup in the bin when he noticed the Gilbert Gallery that Wendy Buchanan had told him about. Inside, soft white lighting accentuated the artworks hung on a purple wall, while pieces of wood-turned furniture filled the floor below. An elderly man with small, round glasses looked up from a desk at the rear of the gallery, murmured a quiet good morning, then left Flowers to wander around.

He unzipped his jacket, hot now from the coffee and central heating. The walls were hung with wintery landscapes of rivers and mountains, of brumbies and wombats in the snow. After a while, he came to a section displaying John Gilbert's work. A striking sketch of the Cooma courthouse displaying a mind-boggling price tag was hung high on the wall. Below it was another sketch of the main range, drawn from the Charlotte Pass snow gums boardwalk. A third sketch was centred above a console table. Flowers leaned in to read the information card: *Towards White Winter Station from Southern Cloud Lookout.*

'Let me know if I can be of help,' the man said, looking up from his paperwork.

Flowers wandered over to the desk. 'Mr Gilbert?'

The man removed his reading glasses. 'I am.'

'Detective Constable Mitchell Flowers.'

'Oh heavens.' Gilbert left his glasses on the desk and stood up. 'Is there a problem of some sort?'

'No problem. I was looking at some of your work in Jindabyne yesterday. Wendy Buchanan told me about the gallery.'

'Oh, dear Wendy.' Gilbert came out from behind the desk, walking with care as though he feared he might fall. 'She's been incredibly supportive of my work over the years, and she does so much for the community.'

Flowers nodded. 'I noticed her carrying an armload of Vinnies bags the other day.'

'Oh, she's always scouting about,' he said with a smile, deep grooves lining his face. 'When she first opened the cafe, she'd trawl through the second-hand outlets, and perhaps pick up an antique jug or a first edition book. She'd put them in the section of the shop where you found my prints.'

'She said she still sources pieces for her niece,' said Flowers.

'Cate, yes. Do you have time to hear how it all started, Detective?'

'Sure.' It seemed Gilbert was up for a chat, which suited Flowers. He might learn more about the Lorrimers.

'A woman came into the shop and was delighted to find a replica of a distinctive orange bowl, identical to one her late grandmother had given her, and which she had broken. It wasn't an expensive piece but it was of great sentimental value. Word got around, and people began asking Wendy if she could look for this and that when she was out and about, like a single crystal wine glass that had been broken from a set of six.' Gilbert shook his head. 'She has an astonishing success rate, but more importantly, she loves doing it.'

'She takes special requests?' asked Flowers.

'Absolutely, it's become a hobby of hers over the years. You'll often see her with a basket of vegetables from her garden, and some treasure she's found, on her way to visit a neighbour. She spreads her largesse far and wide, as C J Dennis wrote.'

'The world needs people like her,' said Flowers, going back to the sketch Gilbert had drawn from Southern Cloud Lookout. 'She said you've drawn White Winter Station a lot.'

'Yes, initially the old house, but as I became more familiar with the property I branched out into landscapes. Of course, the station is in the distance in that one.'

'You must know the family well.'

Gilbert hesitated. 'I'd describe us as acquaintances. It's terribly sad how they just lost Art. I'd never met him. I assume you know all about that.'

'We're investigating the crash,' said Flowers, then continued on in case Gilbert was inclined to ask questions. 'They had a great print of the cemetery in the cafe. I liked that one.'

'The original's right here,' Gilbert said, heading back towards his desk. 'I'm afraid it's not for sale though. It's my wife's favourite.'

Flowers followed then stopped to stare in awe at the sketch easily ten times the size of the print he'd seen yesterday. He recognised the jacarandas, and the tall hedge bordering the gravestones that he'd assumed to be a maze. One headstone towered over the others, a white angel with intricately carved wings perched on a column scattering rose petals.

'That's cool.'

'Thank you. It's a shame they've let the cemetery go in recent years.'

An image of Ethan Lorrimer tidying the area returned to his mind, but then something in the sketch caught Flowers' attention. He moved closer, peering at the name on the headstone that hadn't been visible in the smaller print.

'Herbert Buchanan?' he asked, turning to look at Gilbert.

'Yes, Herbert was Wendy's great-grandfather. Wendy was born in that house seventy-something years ago. She lived there until she was ten, I think.'

'She didn't say.'

'No, she wouldn't. There's been ill-feeling between the two families going back generations now.' Gilbert gazed at the sketch. 'I'll miss drawing the station though. I was due to go out there soon and do the final one.'

'Are you retiring?'

'Retiring, no, though I only manage to do one or two a year now.'

'Oh, sorry, I thought you must be hanging up your pencils, if that's the right expression.'

Gilbert chuckled. 'Artists are like musicians, Detective, we don't retire, we die on the job.'

'So, why won't you be sketching the station anymore?' Flowers prompted.

A middle-aged couple had just walked in. John Gilbert greeted them the way he had Flowers.

'White Winter Station has changed a lot over the years but, sadly, the biggest change is yet to come.' Gilbert's attention strayed to the couple who were showing particular interest in one of the paintings. 'The station is being subdivided. I'm not telling you anything that isn't public knowledge, Detective. The plans are on display at the Tumbarumba Council.'

'Really?' Flowers managed to say, his mind racing from the unexpected news.

'Yes, now you'll have to excuse me,' Gilbert said. 'I should speak to these people. It's the second time they've come in looking at that painting.'

'Good work, Flowers.' Ryder's voice buzzed in Flowers' ear as he walked past the frozen duck pond, snow crunching beneath his boots.

'It wasn't great police work, Sarge. It fell into my lap.'

'As I told Sterling recently, it's all about observation, whether you're interviewing someone or buying a coffee.'

'We need to talk to the Lorrimers again,' Flowers said.

'We do, but let's talk to Wendy and Cate Buchanan first. I'd like to know more about this bad blood before we ask the Lorrimers about it. I won't be back in Thredbo until after four, so we're not going to make it to the council today. Which shire is White Winter Station in?'

'Snowy Valleys in Tumbarumba.'

'Okay, how about you pick me up at six in the morning.'

'Sounds good, Sarge. How are things in Sydney?'

'Inspector Gray is happy enough with the progress report. I should get a forensic update from Harriet soon. I've also been through Lorrimer's logbook. It's pretty sketchy. Records aren't required for fun flights and there're no regular flights to Khancoban or anywhere else. Newcastle command have his car.'

'I couldn't find insurance for that, only rego.'

'Doesn't surprise me. It's a twenty-five-year-old Toyota in suspect condition. According to the guys at Cessnock Airport, Lorrimer was friendly and easy-going but a bit of an adrenaline junkie. They didn't know anyone he was close to, but that's not surprising, they all work independently out of there.' There was a pause. 'I can't shake the feeling that Lorrimer deliberately made it easy to pack up and disappear at a moment's notice.'

'I got that impression too,' said Flowers, his footsteps ringing as he crossed a steel-grate bridge. 'The family said he owed people money. Maybe he was still living in fear that they would find him.'

'Maybe,' said Ryder. 'I've spoken to the water police.'

'Oh yeah, what did they say?'

'They *were* patrolling around Lemon Tree Passage yesterday, but they were looking for stolen lobster traps. It happens from time to time apparently.'

A beep alerted Flowers to an incoming call. 'Hang on, Sarge. I have Collins on the other line.' He hit hold and accepted the call. 'Hello, Sergeant Collins?'

Collins launched straight into his reason for calling. 'Yeah. There were two others arrested along with Art Lorrimer all those moons ago. I've photocopied the details. Are you in Khancoban today, or should I email these to you?'

'I'm heading down there soon anyway so I may as well pick up the hard copies.' Flowers checked his watch. 'I'll be there around one.'

'Okay, well call me when you're ten minutes away and I'll let you know where I am.'

Flowers hung up and relayed the conversation to Ryder. 'I'll shoot down there now,' he said. 'Who knows, I might learn something more from a chat with Collins that I wouldn't learn in an email.'

'Good idea.'

They spoke for another few minutes before winding up the call and then Flowers headed back to his apartment, trying not to think about his conversation with Sergeant Collins. He hadn't gone more than a block before his conscience forced him to be honest with himself.

I'm heading down there soon anyway, he'd said, the lie shooting from his mouth before his brain had engaged. Angry with himself, Flowers kicked a large clump of snow on the side of the road, watching as it exploded into tiny pieces.

He wanted to see Sterling. There was nothing more to it than that. And Sergeant Collins had given him the perfect excuse to drive to Khancoban.

Fourteen

Flowers pulled into the hotel carpark, immediately singling out Sterling's four-wheel drive with the faded paintwork.

When he'd called Collins ten minutes out of town, the sergeant had told him he was having lunch at the hotel and invited him to join him.

Now that Flowers was here there was no turning back, despite the second thoughts swirling through his head.

When he opened the door, he saw Collins sitting alone at a table in the middle of the room with mostly empty tables around him. Sterling had her back to him, though she was close by, setting up some chairs near the entrance. Dressed in head-to-toe black, the first thing that struck Flowers was how much weight she'd lost while undercover.

He closed the door behind him, and she turned, the recognition in her eyes so fleeting it would have gone unnoticed by anyone not looking directly at her, as he was. But then she walked confidently towards him, looking reassuringly familiar and different at the same time.

'Hi.' She smiled. 'Here for lunch?'

Flowers forced himself to look past her to where Collins was devouring a hamburger. 'Maybe just a drink. I'm meeting someone.' He glanced at her, noting the winged eyeliner and red lipstick before pointing to Collins. 'He's right there.'

'Okay,' she said cheerily, 'I'll bring you over a menu in case you change your mind.'

Flowers headed towards Collins, reminding himself that Nerida was known as Ida here, having shortened her name to the last three letters.

'Ahhh, g'day.' Collins put his hamburger on the plate and wiped his hands with a paper napkin. 'Are you eating?'

Flowers sighed and pulled out a chair. 'I may as well.'

'Can I get you a drink?' Sterling was back before his butt had even hit the seat.

'I'll have a Coke, thanks,' he said off the top of his head, 'and I've changed my mind, do you make a chicken schnitzel?'

'Does a bear shit in the woods?' she said in a loud whisper to Collins, drawing raucous laughter from the sergeant.

Flowers blinked in amazement.

She cocked an eyebrow at him. 'Chips or vegies?'

'Vegies,' he said, glancing at Collins. Sterling had settled into a role he was unfamiliar with, and it was both unsettling and amusing.

'Gravy?'

'Gravy would be good, thanks.'

'Cool. I'll be right back.'

Flowers breathed a mental sigh of relief and grinned at Collins, who was still chuckling to himself.

'She's a great one, that one—a real character,' Collins said, watching as Sterling gave Flowers' order to someone in the kitchen. 'Runs rings around the others.' He picked up two sheets of paper from the table.

'The first guy is Kyle Worthington. Apparently, I arrested him along with Lorrimer but I confess I don't remember him. My notes say they were workmates at Perisher before Worthington moved to Canada. Unfortunately, he died in an avalanche while skiing in the back country.' Collins passed the sheet to Flowers.

Sterling returned with a huge glass of Coke and ice. Collins went back to his hamburger while Flowers sipped his drink and began reading through Worthington's charge sheet.

'Were there any charges laid against him in Canada, prior to his death?'

'Nope. I checked.'

'Thanks.'

Collins swallowed a mouthful of hamburger and slid the second sheet across the table. 'This is Rodney Garrett. He was in here the other day with Heidi.'

'Lorrimer?'

'Yep. He was a school friend of Art's. He was probably here visiting the family.'

'Sure.' Flowers glanced sideways at the sergeant. Was that when Sterling had overheard the conversation between him and the other man. What plans had they been talking about? Plans for the sale, for the subdivision?

Flowers itched to tell Sterling what he'd learned at the gallery this morning, but it would have to wait until tonight. She was so close he could smell her perfume, and yet she may as well have been in another galaxy. 'Has Garrett been charged with anything since then?' he asked.

'Nope. He lives near Jindabyne. His address is on the back of that sheet.'

Before Flowers could thank him, Collins' phone lit up. 'Khancoban Police,' the sergeant said, pressing the device to his ear. 'Right. Oh geez. Okay, I'm on my way.' He hung up and looked at Flowers. 'Prang on Swampy Plains Creek Road. Lucky I didn't order coffee, hey.'

Flowers thanked him, now regretting having ordered lunch. But it was too late to cancel, as moments later Sterling was on her way back with his schnitzel.

'Aw, you look like Nigel no-friends,' she said, putting his meal in front of him.

Bloody Nerida. She was enjoying this. 'Yeah, the sergeant was called away.'

'Hey, Ida?' a bloke summoned her from a nearby table.

Sterling planted her hands on her hips and swung around. 'Hold your horses, Gus. I know this is your second home, but you're not the only diner in here.'

Then she turned back to Flowers. 'You enjoy your lunch in peace, sweetheart, and let me know if there's anything else I can get you.'

Sweetheart? Flowers almost choked on a mouthful of Coke, the gas bubbles fizzing in his throat and up the back of his nose.

'*Sweetheart?*' Flowers said when Sterling called him that night.

There was a warm laugh at the other end. 'I thought you'd appreciate that one.'

'*Does a bear . . . ?*' Flowers stopped, shaking his head at the memory. 'How do you get away with *that*?'

'There was no one else within earshot—well, maybe Gus— and I knew *you* weren't going to complain to management. Sarge suggested I try and make a connection with Collins, so I've been working on him.'

'He's a fan, trust me.'

'Good. He won't be suspicious when I ask him to introduce me to his handsome mate if he comes in again. I want a name.'

'It would be good to know who he is, for sure.' Flowers stretched out on the bed and told her about what he'd learned at the gallery. 'The Lorrimers are selling up. The property is going to be subdivided.'

'Wow! That puts a different spin on things.'

'I know. I was thinking the guy with Collins could have said, *I wonder if this will delay the Lorrimers' plans for the subdivision,* or *for the sale?*'

There was silence on the other end of the line. He could imagine Sterling thinking.

'I've got it,' she said finally. 'It was *the Lorrimers' plans for White Winter Station.*' She groaned. 'It was so simple. I can't believe I didn't work it out. And it makes sense.'

'It does. Ryder and I are off to the council first thing in the morning.'

'Well, this widens the investigation into Lorrimer's murder, doesn't it?'

'Sure does,' Flowers said. 'I think a lot of people would be unhappy about that subdivision, sweetheart.'

'Oh, stop it, Mitch. You're talking to the real me now.'

'Am I?' he asked, feigning seriousness. 'Who's the act really for, Nerida—them, or all of us at Homicide? Which one's the real you?'

She groaned. 'You're so annoying.' But then she began to laugh, sounding more like herself. 'It feels good to laugh. I miss that, miss the camaraderie of the squad,' she added quickly.

Then before he had a chance to say anything, she went on. 'So, why were you in the pub with Collins?'

He told her about the two guys arrested for supply along with Lorrimer.

'Rodney Garrett?' Sterling said. 'And it was him at the pub with Heidi a couple of nights ago?'

'So Collins said. What's he like?'

'Surly. Not very friendly, a bit like Heidi. I only spoke to them long enough to give her my condolences.'

'Right.' Flowers stood up and walked into the living room. 'We should know more after tomorrow.'

'I can't wait to hear what you learn at the council.'

After a few more minutes they said goodbye, and Flowers hung up, his head spinning. The plane crash was the nucleus of the murder enquiry, but they were running this other job in the background, the death of Scruffy Freidman and the associated drug ring. Added to an already intriguing mix was the sale of White Winter Station and the past ill-feeling between the Lorrimers and the Buchanans, though he had no idea what that was all about or if any of it fitted together.

A message popped up on his phone. *Last chance to join us for dinner. Be here in fifteen if you want first course. Ryder.*

Flowers sat in front of his monitor and keyed in a reply. *Appreciate the invite but heading to bed early. Say hi to everyone. Pick you up at 6 am.* His thumb hovered over send. Ryder was the epitome of decency, and Flowers hated lying to him even about something as harmless as dinner. He stared at the computer monitor. There would be no early night for him, it was almost time to log on.

He hit send and picked up his headphones.

Fifteen

Only when the replete and weary guests at the Golden Wattle gathered by the fire for a final port or schnapps did Eva's family have the dining room to themselves.

Ryder looked around the table at the people who were now a huge part of his life. Vanessa, of course, Eva and her partner, Jack Walker, and their cute little girl, Poppy, who was asleep in her father's arms.

Ryder slipped his phone into his pocket and went back to his soup.

'Mitch not joining us?' Vanessa said, lowering her spoon.

'No. I've invited him a couple of times, but he keeps refusing.'

'That's strange.'

'Hmm.'

'Maybe he's met someone,' Jack said.

Ryder shook his head. 'I doubt it. He doesn't seem to have much luck with the ladies.'

'That's surprising,' put in Eva. 'He's attractive, all that dark-auburn hair.'

Vanessa dunked a piece of bread into her soup. 'Yes, Mitch is the real deal. He deserves somebody nice.'

'I'm worried about all the painkillers he's taking,' said Ryder. 'He could be suffering the after-effects of that concussion he got during the Hutton case.'

'Is it affecting his work?' Jack asked.

Ryder shook his head. 'Nothing like that. He's just a bit tired and headachy.'

Vanessa laughed. 'Maybe he has met someone. Why don't you ask him, Pierce?'

Ryder reached for another piece of bread. 'Because I don't want to know about that.'

'But we do,' she said with a cheeky smile at Eva.

Ryder wondered, as he did almost every day, what he'd done to deserve someone as happy and kind-hearted as Vanessa. She was the perfect antidote to all the bad stuff he dealt with daily, and he could tell by her glowing face how much she was enjoying working as a patroller again, and spending time with Eva and Poppy before they moved to the farm.

Ryder spooned soup into his mouth in an effort to ward off the empty feeling in his stomach. This was Vanessa's final season as a patroller and in eight weeks he'd be done with Homicide and back in uniform. Try as he might, he couldn't imagine enjoying the work out west, throwing drunks out of the pub on a Friday night and looking for stolen cattle. Then again, he couldn't imagine life without Vanessa, and he'd had plenty of time to get used to the idea of being a country cop. He'd known from the start that Vanessa was moving home when her parents retired, and it hadn't taken him long to commit to going with her. Now, that time had come. Her parents were moving on, and he had to do the same.

Poppy began to stir, and Eva rose from the table and went to put the weary pre-schooler to bed before she woke up entirely. Vanessa hurried out to check whatever amazing dish was being kept warm in the kitchen, leaving Ryder and Jack alone.

'You know these mountains like the back of your hands, don't you?' Ryder asked, pushing aside his personal thoughts and bringing his focus back to the case. 'You've trekked and camped all over them, right?'

Jack nodded slowly. 'Yep.'

'Did you ever hear anything, or see anything that made you suspect a drug ring was operating and controlling the turf down here?'

'No, but I was only here during the winter months. Everybody knew drugs were for sale in Jindabyne during the ski season if you wanted them. I assumed they would have been brought in by one of the city gangs.'

'Not necessarily,' said Ryder.

'I can run it past my contacts if you like? The army trains out in the back country. They spend a lot of time in the area.'

'That would be great—' Ryder began, then stopped as Vanessa came in carrying a heavy baking dish laden with lamb shanks and roasted vegetables. Ryder jumped up and took it from her. Leaning across the table, he set the main course on the large placemat in the centre as Vanessa sat down.

'I'll keep my eyes and ears open,' Jack said, low enough for only Ryder to hear.

Sixteen

A white sheet of paper pinned to a freestanding partition in the foyer of the council building read 'Pending Development Applications'. Ryder ran an eye down the list until he came to number eight, White Winter Station. Beneath the name was a web address where further details could be accessed.

'I can log in,' said Flowers, taking out his phone.

'Just make a note of the website. We can check it later,' said Ryder. 'I'd rather speak to someone.' That was the difference between him and his younger partner. Flowers would look online for everything. He wouldn't even make a dinner reservation if the restaurant didn't have a website, whereas Ryder still always picked up the phone and called.

'We'd like to talk to the person in charge of your subdivision team,' he said to a woman sitting behind an old-fashioned desk. 'I'm Detective Ryder.' He glanced at Flowers. 'This is my partner, Detective Flowers. Sydney Homicide.'

'May I ask what it's in relation to?' said the woman, looking a little taken aback.

'We have questions about the White Winter Station development.'

'Oh, yes.' She picked up the phone but kept the receiver in her hand. 'Mhanda Van Engelen, our town planner, has been heading up that application. She'd be the best person to speak to.'

'Great. Do you know if she's in?' said Ryder.

The woman pushed a button on the phone. 'I saw her in the carpark this morning.'

Mhanda van Engelen appeared in the foyer a few minutes later. Tall, with an athletic build and dark-blonde hair, she strode towards them with a vitality that suggested a serious love of exercise.

'Hello,' she said. 'We can use the meeting room over here.' She opened a door and invited them in. 'Please take a seat.' She put a bulky file and an iPad on the desk and sat down. 'What would you like to know?'

Ryder introduced himself and Flowers again and then said, 'We're investigating the death of Arthur Lorrimer, Junior. He was killed recently in a plane crash in Khancoban.'

'Oh, I'm so sorry to hear that.'

'You didn't know?' asked Flowers.

'No, I've only just come back from leave.'

'You'd be aware that the Lorrimers own White Winter Station,' Ryder said.

'Yes, though I've never dealt directly with the family—actually, I've never met them. They signed a consent form for the development company to lodge the application on their behalf. All my dealings have been with the company.'

'What exactly is proposed for the land?' asked Ryder.

Van Engelen rested her fingertips on the file but didn't open it. 'Well, the application is for the land to be subdivided into allotments of various sizes, including some larger ones to be used for agriculture.'

'And that's for the entire station?' asked Flowers.

She nodded. 'Including one small lot for the existing house and graveyard. There are terms and conditions that need to be put in place for those.'

'So, where are you up to with all this?' asked Ryder.

She looked down and tapped her fingertips on the file. 'The re-zoning's been approved and it's moving towards the subdivision assessment. I can show you a copy of the proposed subdivision if you want, or it's all on the council's website.'

'We've got the web address,' said Ryder. 'We'd like to talk more generally about it.'

'Okay.'

'How has the proposal been received?' Ryder asked. 'I can't imagine it being popular with the community.'

She smiled. 'There are always objections to every project, but particularly when farmland is being broken up into smaller portions.'

'Have there been any nasty repercussions?'

Van Engelen shook her head. 'Not at all. You'd be surprised how many people are in favour of it. Population growth is good for the area. In the past, employment was always the problem, but not so much these days with people being able to work from home. The regions are booming, and we have a greater demand from people wanting to use the land for a variety of purposes.'

'Have the Lorrimers suffered any personal backlash?' asked Flowers.

'If they have, I'm not aware of it.' She tipped her head to the side. 'I mean, the owners of the neighbouring properties are never thrilled about these things, but they often end up indirectly benefiting from the improved infrastructure.'

'Okay,' said Ryder. 'You've been immensely helpful. We'll look at the website and be in touch if we need anything else. Thank you.'

They all stood, and Van Engelen picked up her file. 'The person you really should speak to is the developer,' she said. 'His main office is in Yass, but he's set up a temporary space here in Tumbarumba.'

The office of Temple Developments consisted of a single room at the back of an arcade of shops looking out to an open carpark. Owen Temple answered their knock. He was around sixty, with a stocky build and a receding hairline.

'Come in,' he said, peering at them over the top of his glasses, which were perched on the end of his nose. 'Mhanda called and said you were on your way. That's Janet,' he said, pointing to a woman with curly grey hair who was working at a computer. He moved with the speed of a busy man, ushering them in the direction of a small, round table ringed by four chairs in a corner. 'Sorry, we're a bit tight on space.'

'No problem,' said Ryder as they all sat.

'You're here to talk about Art.' Temple whipped off his glasses and held them in his hand. 'It's a terrible thing, isn't it?'

Ryder nodded. 'It's been an awful shock for the family.'

'I didn't know anything about it until Dan cancelled an appointment we had the other day.'

'We hear you're handling the property development on the Lorrimers' behalf,' Ryder said.

'That's right, White Winter Station. I've done some big developments in the past, and this one's right up there.'

Ryder nodded. 'What does it involve?'

'You name it,' Temple said with a laugh. 'Take a look around. We're in the middle of commissioning roads, electricity, environment, heritage and water reports. That's why we set up this office, so we'd be close to the council. It makes things a hell of a lot easier.'

'So, you've bought the land already?' asked Flowers.

'We've signed contracts, but that's subject to subdivision consent. We're pretty confident it will come through. Everything's moving ahead.'

'Ms Van Engelen said she wasn't aware of any strident opposition to what's being proposed. Are you aware of any?' Ryder asked.

Temple paused for a second or two. 'A little, but not as bad as it could have been. People always put in objections. Mostly they have no merit. This is an environmentally sensitive, ground-breaking development. It will help a lot of people in the area and put more money into the council coffers. That flows on to better roads and services for everyone.'

'Art Lorrimer's death won't hold it up?' asked Flowers.

Temple shook his head. 'I can't see why it would. I have a consent document signed by the Lorrimers to lodge the application, so everything should keep rolling along.'

Ryder nodded. This was consistent with what Mhanda Van Engelen had told them.

'Who on behalf of the Lorrimers signed it?' asked Ryder.

'Dan was one. I can't remember who else.' Temple stood up. 'Hang on, I'll get it.' He went to a filing cabinet near Janet's desk, put on his glasses and pulled a file from the top drawer. 'All the legal documents are in here,' he said, flicking through the file as he walked back towards them. 'Here it is.'

Ryder took the document and quickly scanned it. At the bottom of the page, both Daniel and Ethan Lorrimer had signed in their capacity as directors of WWS Pty Limited.

Ryder handed the document to Flowers. 'What about the contract for sale?' he asked Temple. 'Did they sign that as well?'

'I'll have a look.' Temple sat down and put the file on the table. 'Here we go,' he said, pulling out the contract from under a bundle of correspondence held together by a metal split-pin.

Ryder looked at the front page. Again, Daniel and Ethan Lorrimer had signed as directors of WWS Pty Limited.

'Very good,' said Ryder, passing the contract to Flowers. 'I think that's all we need to know at this stage.'

'Not a problem,' Temple said.

'Thank you for your time.' Ryder stood up. 'Good luck with getting the subdivision approved if it's in everyone's best interest.'

'Well, you can never be certain of the outcome, but I'm fairly confident,' Temple said, walking with them to the door. 'One particular councillor has been supportive of this project from the beginning, and he's influential among a certain faction of the council, which is good for us.'

Flowers opened the door. 'What's his name?'

'The councillor? Lewis Buchanan.'

Flowers and Ryder reached Jindabyne later than they'd expected. The mid-afternoon storm had dumped snow on the mountains, making the Alpine Way so treacherous the traffic was reduced to a crawl around the hairpin bends.

Flowers brushed the snow off his jacket before stepping inside the Brumby Cafe and Gallery. Wendy Buchanan was behind the counter, talking to a young woman he didn't recognise.

'Hello,' she said, catching sight of him. 'Back for another coffee?'

'I think my caffeine levels are fine for now.' Flowers turned briefly to Ryder. 'Wendy, this is Detective Sergeant Ryder. Is now a convenient time to ask you a few questions?'

'Of course.' She glanced at the young woman. 'I shouldn't be too long.'

Wendy led them to a quiet corner of the shop then looked at them expectantly. Flowers got the impression it would take a lot to ruffle her feathers.

'I took your advice and called in to the Gilbert Gallery,' he said. He told her how he'd been shown the original sketch of the cemetery with Herbert Buchanan's grave. 'John Gilbert told me your family once owned the property, and you lived there as a child. We're just checking that he has his facts straight.'

Wendy smiled. 'He's right, Detective. Herbert Buchanan was my great-grandfather.'

'Okay, next question. We've heard that Lewis Buchanan is a councillor on the Snowy Valleys Council. Is he related to you?'

'Lewis is my nephew, he's Cate's brother. Cate made your coffee yesterday.'

'Ah, gotcha. Where can we contact Lewis?'

'He's head of science at the high school here. You just missed him, he came in to get his coffee mug filled up. He mentioned a meeting, but I didn't ask if it was at the council or the school.'

Ryder took a business card from his pocket and handed it to her. 'There's no urgency for us to speak to him, but would you ask him to call us, please?'

'Of course,' she said, looking at the card. 'I'll send him a message with the details.'

'There is one more thing,' Flowers said, lowering his voice. 'We've heard there have been tensions between your family and the Lorrimers in the past. Is there any truth to that?'

Wendy gave a resigned sigh. 'Yes, there were bad feelings in past generations. As for me personally, I don't know any of the younger Lorrimers, and I hold no ill-will towards them. They *are* the legal owners of my childhood home.'

Flowers nodded. He was looking forward to hearing the Lorrimers answer the same question.

'We'll let you get back to work,' he said, satisfied they'd managed to track down Lewis Buchanan so easily. 'Thank you for your time.'

Wendy walked with them to the door.

'Cate not in today?' Flowers asked, more to fill the silence than anything else. Wendy Buchanan wasn't one for small talk.

'She was in earlier. She's up at the hut now.'

'One of the alpine huts?' Flowers asked.

'Yes.'

'Sergeant Collins was telling me about them the other day.' He looked at Ryder. 'There are more than a hundred of them scattered across the mountains, apparently.'

Wendy nodded. 'They're so precious, and so historic. We take their maintenance and restoration very seriously. Cate's a volunteer with the Hut Association. She's passionate about the one my family built. She's gone up to re-stock the provisions and make sure the storm hasn't caused any problems up there.'

'That's cool,' said Flowers. 'I'd like to check out a few of them one day.'

'There's a company that run four-wheel drive tours. You choose the huts you'd like to see, and they take you out for a half day or full day. Of course, it's easier in summer than winter. We're lucky though, Buchanan Hut is close to the road.'

'Where is it exactly?' asked Flowers, noticing that Wendy was more comfortable discussing the hut than the old family homestead.

'It's just off the Alpine Way at Dead Horse Gap. There's a lookout there where you can park. You'll see the walking trails right away.' She smiled. 'You'll need skis as this time of year, though, or snowshoes.'

Seventeen

'I can't wait to try these out,' said Flowers, holding up the snow-shoes he'd hired from the rental shop.

Ryder's arms were crossed, his head bent against the wind as they hurried to the car. 'I think you're wasting your time.'

'You could be right, but if Cate's still up at Dead Horse Gap, I may as well talk to her today.'

'Fine, but drop me off at Thredbo on the way through,' said Ryder when they were in the car. 'I'll check in with the Sydney squad while you're stomping around in the snow.'

'Good idea. No point freezing in the car.'

Flowers pulled out of Nuggets Crossing and they travelled in silence for the next few minutes while they warmed up.

'How did Cate seem when you met her yesterday?' Ryder asked as they turned onto the Alpine Way, the chatter from the police radio white noise in the cabin.

'Friendly enough. She made my coffee. I'm going to ask her about the feud. Hopefully she'll tell me more than her aunt did.'

Ryder glanced over at him. 'I'm not sure that has legs. Wendy practically dismissed it, and Temple told us Lewis Buchanan was one of the subdivision's biggest supporters. If there was still bad blood between them, I can't see him doing the Lorrimers any favours.'

'You could be right,' Flowers said, 'but I'm intrigued, and anyway I want to see the hut.'

'Watch yourself out there. I won't be happy if I have to send in a search party.'

'It's five hundred metres from the lookout, Sarge. I'd have to be trying hard to get lost.'

'Make sure you take the two-way radio anyway.'

Twenty minutes later Flowers dropped Ryder at the bottom of the Golden Wattle driveway, then headed back to the main road. It had stopped snowing, and a pale afternoon sun cast a golden light on the Crackenback Range.

A short while later, Flowers pulled off the road at Dead Horse Gap, the highest point on the Alpine Way. A black four-wheel drive with numberplates that read CAB was parked close to the start of the track. Figuring they were Cate's initials, Flowers pulled on his beanie, grabbed his snowshoes and locked the car door. He set the snowshoes on the ground, then slid his right boot into the shoe. 'All the way in,' he muttered, recalling the surfie dude from the rental shop's instructions. Once he had the first shoe on, he leaned over and did up the bindings. The wide plastic frame of the shoes distributed his weight equally over the snow when he took his first few steps.

A wooden sign confirmed this was the beginning of the Cascade Hut Trail. A second signpost underneath said: Buchanan Hut 500 metres, Cascade Hut 10 kilometres. Breathing a sigh of relief that Cate wasn't working at Cascade Hut, Flowers set off, tentatively at first, then moving faster once he gained confidence.

The trail was wider than he'd imagined, and he began to enjoy the walk. The view across the valley was amazing, the alpine air invigorating. He picked up his pace a little, finding his rhythm. Maybe he could get into this.

Further on, he came to a fork in the track. Cascade Trail continued following the ridge line, while a narrower trail branched off to the left, another wooden sign pointing the way to Buchanan Hut. The smaller trail was less exposed, bordered on both sides by ancient snow gums. Flowers shuffled along in his snowshoes, wondering what the Homicide boys would say if they could see him now.

The first sign that he was nearing Buchanan Hut was the smell of smoke tainting the pristine air. He rounded a bend, and the hut came into view. The size of a single garage, it was a wooden structure with an iron roof. Smoke billowed from the chimney. Cross-country skis and poles, and several empty chaff bags, lay on the ground nearby.

Before he had a chance to knock, the door opened and Cate Buchanan stood before him, her blunt-cut fringe short enough to show off her eyebrows.

'Aunt Wendy called and said the mint mocha detective might show up.' Her gaze dropped to his snowshoes then tracked back up to his face. 'You're keen,' she said, arching one bold eyebrow.

'I don't know if you could call me keen,' he said, smiling as she lowered the eyebrow. He gave her the once over in return. 'We're based in Thredbo. It's five minutes away, and I wanted to see the hut.'

She stared at him long enough for him to notice the family resemblance. Wendy would have looked a lot like Cate when she was younger.

'Do you mind if I ask you a few questions?' he said, reminding himself why he was here. He was enjoying flirting with Cate Buchanan, and why the hell not? He'd been suppressing his feelings for Sterling for too long.

'I don't, provided you do something for me.'

'You're brokering a deal?' Flowers asked, not sure if she was serious.

The corners of her eyes crinkled. 'Now you're here, I may as well put you to good use.'

'Doing what?'

'Carrying a bag of wood down here. There are still two in the car, and there's only an hour of daylight left.'

Bloody hell, she strikes a hard bargain. He hadn't counted on this, but if it got her talking . . . 'All right. I need to catch my breath though. This is harder than it looks.'

'Much harder than hiking.'

'I just figured that out.'

She rolled her eyes. 'You'd better come in then, but leave those snowshoes outside.'

Flowers undid the bindings then stepped into the warm interior. A hurricane lamp cast a bright glow from where it stood on a cupboard near the sink, while two sets of double bunks lined the walls. A fire burned in a bush-rock fireplace down the far end of the room, and the bookcase beside it was stacked with wood. Two camp chairs were arranged in front of the fire while a large tree stump served as a coffee table.

'When was this built?' Flowers asked, looking at the wooden floorboards.

'It was built by one of my ancestors in the 1920s. It's been damaged by fire a couple of times, but we've rebuilt it using the original materials where possible.'

'It's amazing.'

'Thank you. Our family have looked after it for a long time.'

'What kind of timber is that?' Flowers asked, gazing up at the beams.

'Alpine Ash. The original bark roof was replaced with iron at some point.'

'It makes you wonder about the people who've passed through, doesn't it? And why it was built on this particular spot,' he said.

'I can tell you why. My ancestors owned one of the original snow leases up here. The road wasn't here then, just tracks made by First Nations people.'

Flowers frowned. 'What are snow leases?'

Cate picked up a fire iron and prodded a log, sending sparks into the fireplace. 'Leases the government granted so graziers could bring their herds up to the high country in summer, where the temperatures were cooler. This hut was built as a shelter for the stockmen.'

'They would have needed it,' said Flowers, moving to warm his hands in front of the fire.

'The horsemen were a tough breed. Some came from as far away as Hay. The stock route was a kilometre wide. But then National Parks and Wildlife banned cattle grazing in the park because it was destroying the alpine environment. The snow leases were phased out over time, not that it made any difference to our family. We'd already lost ours.'

'Lost it? How?'

Cate smiled, the firelight reflecting in her eyes. 'That's where the Lorrimers come in.'

Flowers' heart rate spiked.

'Wendy said you were asking questions about the old feud,' she said. 'That's why you're here, isn't it?'

'Yes.'

Before Flowers could frame his next question, Cate reached up and took her parka from a wooden peg on the wall. 'It's a long story. Come on, I'll tell you while we're bringing down the wood.' She stepped outside, and he quickly followed.

'My *great-great*-grandfather, Herbert Buchanan, discovered gold up at Kiandra in the 1800s,' Cate began as they set off from the hut. 'He used the gold to buy land and establish White Winter Station. That's how most people got their land around here.'

Flowers nodded. Orville Parish had told him the same thing. 'I've seen your great-great-grandfather's headstone in the cemetery, the one with the angel.' He didn't admit to only seeing it in a sketch.

'That's right. His son, James, my *great*-grandfather, added to the land holdings. He's also buried in the family cemetery, as well as their wives and the children they lost.'

Flowers nodded again. Cate was powering along the trail on her cross-country skis while he needed every bit of breath to keep up with her.

'The last Buchanan to be buried in the cemetery was my grand-father, Henry. He fought in World War Two and died a few years after he came home. Wendy and my father weren't even teen-agers then.'

'So, there were two properties in the family?' Flowers asked, relieved to see they were almost back at the carpark. 'White Winter Station and the land up here that was leased from the government and used in summer?'

'That's right.' Cate pointed her skis across the slope and walked up sideways.

Flowers, no longer caring about style, scrambled up using the crampons on his snowshoes, while grabbing handfuls of low vegetation sticking out of the snow.

Cate undid her bindings and straightened up, barely puffing. 'My grandfather was ill, and he let the snow lease lapse. My grandmother had managed to keep things going while he was enlisted, but when he came back, she was so busy caring for him and the children, as well as running the property—'

'That's Wendy and your father?'

'Yes.' Cate unlocked the car with the CAB plates. 'My grand-parents were appalled when they realised Arthur Lorrimer Senior had snapped up the snow lease.' Cate lifted out a hessian bag and dumped it at his feet. 'Arthur was the son of a wealthy brewer in Sydney. He'd been sent down to look for grazing land. I remember Grandma telling me she thought he had something to prove to his father.'

'So, that was the snow lease up here, but how did the Lorrimers end up with White Winter Station?' Flowers asked, picking up the bag while she locked the car. Cate had divided the wood into manageable bundles, and they weren't as heavy as he'd feared.

'They couldn't bring the stock up here in summer, so the herd lost condition.' Cate scooped up her poles and, to Flowers' confusion, deftly secured them around her waist using the wrist straps.

'Did that affect the cattle price?' he asked, stomping after her as she slid sideways down the slope.

'Yes, Einstein,' she said, waiting for him to catch up. 'Two years later, my grandfather died, and Grandma was forced to sell the property. Arthur Lorrimer bought it at auction, and Grandma, my dad and Aunt Wendy moved to Tumbarumba.'

'That's tough,' said Flowers. 'To lose the snow lease, then your grandfather, and finally the property.'

'I'm sure it was.' She shot him a sideways glance. 'Aunt Wendy and I have talked about it from time to time. While things were pretty lawless back in those days, it's not as though Arthur Lorrimer acted illegally. He knew prime land when he saw it. It was more an opportunistic business move on his part.'

'And that's how the feud started?'

'Yes, Grandma and my father were very bitter. To add insult to injury, the Lorrimers refused to let Grandma visit the family cemetery at White Winter Station.'

'That's a bit ordinary.'

'Yes. Aunt Wendy is different though, she's not one to hold a grudge. She feels there's nothing to be gained by hanging on to the past. She's left it where it belongs.' Cate slowed her speed to match his. 'It's strange, because she was the one who loved the horses and the land more so than my dad.'

'Are your parents still in the area?'

There was a slight pause. 'My parents died over ten years ago.'

'Oh, I'm sorry,' Flowers said.

'Thank you. It was tragic. Dad had worked his whole life as an engineer with the Snowy Hydro and had recently retired. They were on the trip of a lifetime when they were killed in an accident overseas.'

'Your family has had its share of tragedy.' He had no more words for Cate Buchanan that wouldn't have been said many times over, so he walked on in silence, appreciating the quietness of the trail.

When they reached the hut, they carried the wood inside and stacked it on the floor. As Flowers straightened, he caught sight of a visitor's book on the mantel. Taking it down, he turned the pages, reading some of the comments written by people who'd visited the hut, while Cate extinguished the fire and did a final check of the tinned food, blankets and other essentials in the cupboard.

She looked up as he put the book back in its place. 'Many of the huts are more remote than this one,' she said, 'but they're all public, and can be used by anyone who needs shelter. Often the mountaineering and skiing guides reserve a hut if they've taken a group into the back country.'

Flowers nodded. That would be people like Eva's partner, Jack Walker.

'But we mostly get tourists here because we're so close to the road.'

'Not that close,' Flowers said, wiping his brow. 'I'm going to sleep well tonight.'

She smiled but said no more.

Flowers went outside and slid his boots into the snowshoes again while Cate extinguished the lamp and closed the door. It was right on dusk by the time they got back to the cars.

'Tell me something,' she said as she stowed her skis in the back of the four-wheel drive. 'Why are you so interested in this old feud anyway?'

Flowers didn't answer. She was too smart not to have worked it out already.

She tipped her head to one side. 'I mean, it all started here at Dead Horse Gap, but do you really believe it has something to do with the Lorrimer twin's death in that plane crash?'

Flowers held her gaze as car headlights from the Alpine Way flashed across her face. 'The Buchanan name keeps coming up,' he said carefully. 'And I'm always interested in history, especially if there's bad blood going back.'

Eighteen

When Sterling arrived for her five o'clock to midnight shift at the hotel, she was surprised to see Heidi Lorrimer behind the bar.

'I thought Heidi had another week off,' she said to Elijah as she hung up her coat.

'She called in earlier and asked if she could work. Luckily for me—we're booked solid until nine.'

Heidi stuck her head around the corner. 'Can I get anyone a coffee?' she asked. 'There's a lull now. We mightn't get a chance later.'

'I'll have one, thanks,' Sterling said. She'd taken note of the two women perched on stools down the end of the bar, and the middle-aged couple chatting at a table. Otherwise, the place was empty.

Elijah shook his head. 'Not for me, thanks Heidi.'

While Heidi went to make the coffee, Sterling walked through the dining room, checking that all the tables were set in readiness for the first sitting.

'I didn't expect to see you for another week,' she said when Heidi handed her a mug.

Sterling was waiting for the other woman to make some flippant remark in response before taking her coffee out the back as usual. But Heidi went behind the bar and leaned a hip against the counter.

'It's so gloomy at home,' she said. 'I'd rather be here. They're starting to put things together for the funeral.'

'From what I've been told,' Sterling said carefully, 'you'll feel better once the funeral's over.'

Heidi looked her up and down, then gazed into the dining room, making Sterling feel as though she had never said anything less useful.

'If there's anything I can do, or if you need me to cover any more shifts . . .'

'Thanks, but I'm fine. They'll handle it all.' And with that Heidi put down her coffee, picked up two menus and went to greet a couple who'd walked in.

Sterling sipped her coffee, deciding not to press her for more information. She and Heidi had never spoken at length about anything, and her sudden interest could raise her suspicions.

They'll handle it all. Spoken in a tone that suggested *they* always had.

Sterling took a final mouthful of coffee as a group of diners arrived, and for the next four hours, she was so busy keeping up with the dinner rush she didn't have time to think about anything else. At ten o'clock, Elijah told them the chef had left dinner for them in the kitchen.

'You go first,' Sterling said to Heidi, smiling. 'You've been here longer than me.'

'Okay.' Heidi spun around, then stepped back as she came face to face with Rodney Garrett.

Sterling's smile faded. Garrett had come in without either of them noticing, but in that split second, she saw that Heidi was afraid of him.

'I've been looking for you, baby,' he crooned, slipping an arm around Heidi's waist and putting his face close to hers.

'Rod, I'm working.' Heidi jerked away in pain, as if he'd pinched her.

'You call this work?' he asked, his eyes cutting to Sterling, his expression suggesting that she push off.

Sterling didn't move. She recognised Garrett's type from her police work. Needy, controlling and intimidating.

'Ida,' she heard Heidi say.

Sterling didn't flinch. She held Garrett's cold-eyed stare until he finally turned away and walked over to the bar.

Heidi grabbed her arm, though her eyes were on Garrett as he started talking to Elijah. 'Don't do that.'

'What, stand up to him?' Sterling couldn't help saying.

Heidi let go of her arm. 'Stay out of it,' she hissed, before going and joining Garrett.

Sterling looked around to see if anyone had noticed, but the room had all but emptied out. In the kitchen, she heated her spaghetti bolognaise in the microwave before carrying it out the back where they ate their meals. How frustrating that just when she'd started making progress with Heidi, Garrett had shown up. And it appeared he was more than the old school mate there to support the Lorrimers as Sergeant Collins had thought.

Sterling ate half her pasta then pushed the plate aside. She wasn't afraid of Garrett, but she should remember to behave more like a woman on a working holiday and less like a cop.

'Where's Heidi?' she asked Elijah when she returned to the bar.

He looked up from the drinks he was mixing. 'She asked me if she could go early. They had a quick drink and left.'

'I get a bad vibe from that guy.'

'Elijah shrugged. We've only exchanged a few words here and there.'

Sterling frowned. 'She was planning on having dinner and working through to the end of her shift. What do you think of him?'

Elijah picked up the drinks. 'Honestly, Ida, I haven't spoken to him long enough to know.'

The next two hours crawled by, and when the clock finally struck midnight, Sterling was out the door. In the carpark, she listened for the hushed tones of underage drinkers lurking in the darkness, but all was quiet save for an eerie wind moaning around the snowy peaks of the main range.

She began her counter surveillance but quickly abandoned it. The roads were clear of cars, the houses she passed ghostly shapes in the fog.

Stifling a yawn, she pulled into the carport. A shower, a cup of tea and a chat with Mitch awaited her, then the oblivion of sleep. Switching on her phone light, she climbed out and locked the car. Maybe she'd write an online review and suggest a sensor light be installed.

Sterling was halfway to the door when a bird took flight from the shrubbery so fast it brushed her cheek. She froze, listening to rustles coming from the bushes that were too loud to be birds. Heart hammering, she swung her torch towards the sound, the light falling on a huge spider hanging from an intricate web strung between the branches.

A low growl had the hairs on the back of her neck standing up. She angled the beam downwards, illuminating the bared teeth, flat skull, and beady eyes of a dog. She took a step towards the door then stopped as the dog snarled, its body crouched in an attack position. Careful not to make any sudden movements, she took another step towards the door, the key in her hand poised to slide into the lock. The dog was shielded by darkness now, and it took every ounce of her self-control not to rush as she slid the key inside the barrel.

Another growl, close behind her now.

A low staccato whistle rang out.

The growling ceased. In the shaky light of her torch, Sterling watched the dog slink away.

'At first I thought it was a feral dog,' Sterling said. She was tucked up in bed, a mug of the sleep tea Mitch had recommended cradled between her hands. She'd taken the gun and her personal phone from their hiding place inside the gas heater the moment she was safely inside the rumpus room. Now, showered and warm, the scare had finally worn off.

'I've seen feral dogs around here,' she said. 'One ran across the road in front of the car the other day. You could tell she'd recently had puppies.'

'You didn't see anyone around?' Flowers asked.

'No, but I heard the quick whistle. I couldn't tell which direction it came from though.'

'What breed was it, apart from a dangerous one?'

'I think it was a hunting dog. It had a pale-coloured coat. I don't remember seeing a collar.'

'It shouldn't be too hard to find out who in Khancoban has a dog like that.'

Sterling sighed. 'I'm thinking about reporting it to Sergeant Collins. He might know who owns it, especially if there have been complaints before.'

'You're right. I'll tell Ryder in the morning too, he should know about this.' There was a pause, then, 'Are you okay?'

'Yeah, now I'm inside with my weapon.' Sterling took a sip of her tea. 'I'll record a report on my phone in the morning and upload it to the case notes. I just hope I don't have nightmares tonight.'

'Call me if you're worried or you can't sleep, doesn't matter what time it is.'

'Okay,' she said quietly, 'thanks.'

After saying goodnight, she put her mobile beside the phone Ryder had set up for her alter ego and slipped the gun beneath her pillow. She'd put them back in their hiding place first thing in the morning.

She stretched out her legs and lay back on the pillows, listening for any sounds from outside and thinking about Mitch's last words. *Call me if you're worried or you can't sleep.*

Did he think about their night together the way she did? The squad had hit the pub for a celebratory drink after making an arrest that had been a long time coming. O'Day and Brown had left after one beer, then Ryder and Benson stood up after two.

Sterling smiled at the memory.

'Oh, come on,' complained Flowers. 'Why aren't you two sticking around?'

'Sorry, Daisy,' said Benson, flinging his coat over his shoulder. 'I need to call and say goodnight to my kids.'

117

'*I'm heading off too,*' *said Ryder.* '*I want to be clear-headed for court in the morning.*'

'*What about you, Sterling?*' *Flowers turned towards her after the others had left.* '*Are you up for another one?*'

'*Sure am,*' *she said, enjoying the nice, buzzy feeling zipping along her veins.* '*I've got nowhere to be.*'

'*Me either, sucks to be them!*' *he said with a laugh. He stood up.* '*Same again?*'

She nodded, flushing as he deliberately swaggered off to the bar. She liked Mitch. He was single and around her age. They didn't often get the opportunity to spend time on their own without the others.

At some point the band came on, and they only stopped dancing when hunger drove them out onto the street in search of a cafe or restaurant with a kitchen still open.

Sterling turned onto her side and curled up in a ball, memories of them laughing on the kerb as they tried ordering an Uber to take Flowers home. In the end, she'd taken him back to her place, which was only three blocks away from headquarters.

Sterling groaned and closed her eyes. In the cold light of day things had looked very different, and she'd known what she had to do. Homicide was the pinnacle of the force, and she was the lone woman in Ryder's squad.

If she'd learned anything at all, it was to never make the same mistake twice.

Nineteen

The chemical odour of the science lab transported Ryder back to his high school days, as did the test tubes, Bunsen burners and petri dishes with flourishing live culture. Ryder waited with Flowers while Lewis Buchanan closed the door behind them. The lab was silent save for the metronomic tick from the analogue clock on the wall showing 8.02 am.

'No one's in here this early,' said Lewis Buchanan as they sat on stools around a high lab bench. Buchanan's dark hair was cropped short, and he had the lean physique of someone who loved cycling or running marathons.

'Do we have your permission to record our conversation?' Ryder asked, putting his phone on the benchtop.

Buchanan waved a hand. 'Go right ahead.'

Ryder stated the time and date and who was present. 'You would have heard by now that we're investigating the murder of Arthur Lorrimer Junior?'

'Of course. I know you've spoken to Wendy and Cate a couple of times, and Owen Temple had a quiet word with me at the meeting last night.'

'We'll come back to Mr Temple a little later,' said Ryder. 'How well do you and your sister know the Lorrimer siblings?'

Buchanan hesitated, as though it wasn't a question he'd

anticipated. 'Not at all really. They grew up on White Winter Station, Cate and I in Tumbarumba.'

'You didn't go to school together, or play on the same sporting team?'

Buchanan shook his head. 'We knew who they were, that their father had bought our grandparent's grazing property, but we rarely saw them. Mostly, it was when they came to Tumbarumba for the rodeo.'

'Did the Lorrimers compete?' asked Flowers.

'No, they weren't rough riders. The rodeo's a popular event though, it raises money for the hospital. I have a feeling Mrs Lorrimer could have been on the committee.'

'And more recently?' Ryder asked.

Buchanan shook his head. 'I hardly ever see them.'

'Okay.' Ryder looked up as two uniformed boys walked past the window. 'You said Owen Temple had a word with you last night. Did the subdivision go before council?'

'Unfortunately, we didn't get to it.' A thread of frustration ran through Buchanan's voice. 'We have so many issues clogging up the agenda at the moment, mostly right-of-way issues. In the old days, if someone owned a property which didn't have access to the road, the neighbours would just let them through. Those arrangements worked back then because everybody knew everybody, or they were related. Now, with city people buying in, it's a different story.'

'So, have you received any nasty objections to the proposed development of White Winter Station? Any threats or that kind of thing?' said Ryder.

'No, just the usual stuff.' Buchanan looked confused. 'Why would someone kill one of the Lorrimers because they've decided to sell their property?'

'That's what we're trying to find out.' Ryder paused for a moment. 'Detective Flowers has spoken to your sister at length about the strained history between the two families.'

Buchanan shifted his feet on the rung of his stool. 'The key word there, Detective, is *history* . . . that's exactly what it is.'

'I'm curious about something,' Ryder said. 'Why are *you* such an ardent supporter of the subdivision? Because that's what we've been led to believe.'

Buchanan took a deep breath. 'Well, there's a few reasons. I like the subdivision Temple's doing. He's a good developer with a track record of retaining the rural character of the land. And the Lorrimers need to get out, they're only just holding on.'

That's two reasons, thought Ryder, waiting for Buchanan to go on.

'Look, I'll be straight with you, Detective, there's a sweetener in there for me too.' He shifted his gaze to Flowers, then back to Ryder. 'I have an agreement with Temple that I have first rights on the purchase of the small block of land that has the old house and cemetery on it.'

Flowers' eyebrows shot up. 'You want to buy back the family's old homestead?'

'That's right.' Buchanan slid his hands back and forth along his thighs. 'Cate and I want it for Wendy, it was her childhood home.'

'Okay.' Ryder frowned. 'So, you're using your influence on the council to try and push this development through?'

'Absolutely. I'm more than happy to take it off Temple's hands. The house and cemetery are problematic.'

Ryder looked up as a loud bell rang throughout the building.

'Don't worry,' Buchanan said. 'That's the bell for rollcall.'

Voices started to filter into the lab as students began gathering in the quad outside.

'Why are the house and cemetery problematic?' asked Flowers.

'Well, a proper right of way needs to be established so the cemetery can be accessed by the public, and the house is heritage listed. Anyone who buys it will be stuck with an old house they can't demolish, and they're going to have to spend a bomb doing it up.'

'So, why are you taking it on?' asked Ryder.

Buchanan smiled. 'I knew you were going to ask that. Cate has all these lofty ideas of turning the house into a public gallery where she can show off all the antique bits and pieces Wendy has collected over the years. Wendy still has the original furniture her mother had in the house, and there's a trunk full of old black-and-white photographs. Cate has already chosen ones to be framed for a history wall.' He rolled his eyes in amusement. 'She's even talking about serving high tea and having organised tours of the gardens and cemetery.'

Flowers nodded. 'I can totally see that.'

Buchanan held up both hands, his fingers spread wide. 'I'm just trying to make it all happen, Detective.'

'It sounds like your sister has her heart set on it?' said Ryder.

Buchanan nodded. 'She does.'

'What about your aunt?' Flowers asked.

Buchanan shrugged. 'Wendy's very pragmatic. She'll be over the moon if we get it, but it won't be the end of her world if we don't.'

'How many on the council object to the development proposal?' Ryder asked.

Buchanan jigged his knee up and down, a bundle of nervous energy. 'Only a couple, and they routinely oppose everything. Everyone else is on board.'

'For the purpose of the recording could you state their names for me, please?'

Buchanan did as Ryder asked, and then Flowers enquired whether the remaining councillors had needed a lot of persuading.

'No, they feel the same way I do, that turning the house into a gallery, and preserving it, will help highlight the history of the area.' Buchanan leaned forward, his eyes sparkling with excitement. 'The house was built by our ancestors. They're the ones lying in the cemetery. Who better to own it and take care of it than us?'

When a second bell rang, Ryder decided they should make a move. He thanked Buchanan for his time and turned off the recording app.

'There will still be large tracts of land for grazing and forestry, as well as farm-stay accommodation and other things,' Buchanan told Flowers as they prepared to leave. 'Ethan Lorrimer is thinking of buying forty hectares. He's keen to stay on the land, and he'd be able to work a property of that size himself.'

'You've spoken to him?' Flowers asked.

'Not personally. Temple told me he's interested.'

'Thoughts, Daisy?' Ryder asked as they headed to the car.

'I liked the guy. He was upfront, and didn't apologise for what he's doing, and why should he?' Flowers zipped up his jacket. 'If I were a councillor, I'd support it. The Buchanans have maintained the hut at Dead Horse Gap for decades, and Wendy and Cate have a track record running the cafe. It's their relatives in the graveyard, and if they want to share all that history with the public, well, that's cool.'

'Yeah, I was thinking the same thing.' Ryder looked at his phone as a message came through. 'It's Harriet,' he said. 'She's sending through the forensics report.'

Ryder began scrolling through the main points of the report. 'They've identified Art Lorrimer from the dental records, so the body can be released.'

'We can tell the Lorrimers they can go ahead with the funeral now,' Flowers said, then groaned as they walked up the couple of steps to the carpark.

'What's wrong?' Ryder asked.

'I'm sore. All that snowshoeing yesterday. I swear, it doesn't look hard but every muscle in my body's screaming.'

Ryder chuckled. 'Now you know how I feel when I come in from skiing. Here, let me drive.'

'What else does the report say?' Flowers asked when they were in the car and Ryder had turned the engine over.

'I think we might have to scrap our theory of Lorrimer transporting drugs. Harriet found no trace elements in the plane wreckage.'

'And he hasn't been done for drugs since his prior. Damn it.'

Ryder thought for a moment. 'I think we'd better get Benson down here. Ring him and tell him to pack a bag. We need to interview the tourists at the caravan park, starting with the ones who have teenagers. The others can chase up any who've gone home in the meantime. And, Flowers, tell him to give the tractor analysis to Brown.'

Flowers nodded. 'Where are we going from here, Sarge?' he asked, the phone to his ear.

'We need to talk to the Lorrimers again, but I want to call into Khancoban first.' Ryder was worried about Sterling's close call with the dog last night.

They both were.

Twenty

Dressed in her running gear, Sterling crouched in front of the oil heater, put her gun and personal phone inside, then clicked the fascia into place. She'd woken at dawn, then dozed on and off before deciding to get up. A sunny winter morning awaited, and she was hoping a run would blow away the cobwebs.

Outside, the spider web glistened in the sunlight, the front lawn white from an overnight dusting of snow. With the snarling dog at the forefront of her mind, she patrolled around the carport and shrubbery, checking for prints or anything that could have been dropped. Next, she checked the old bird aviary down the side of the house, then walked further along until she reached the locked gate that led into the rear yard. But there was no sign of the dog anywhere on the property.

Out the front again, she pulled up her hood and worked her fingers into her synthetic gloves. Sticking to the bitumen, she took the downhill gradient slowly. At the intersection, she varied her route to the Alpine Way, pulling back her hood now that she'd warmed up. After weeks and weeks of surveillance, she knew every house in the town of three hundred, and the make and models of the cars that went with them.

At the Alpine Way, she lengthened her stride along the flat section before taking the road to the pondage. Stopping to slowly retie her laces, she noted that the barbeque area was deserted save for a car with a trailer parked close to the boat ramp. Sucking in some deep breaths, she did a few stretches. Out on the water, a lone fisherman sat hunched in a dinghy, his fishing rod in hand.

Sterling ran on, following the shoreline, birds twittering overhead. Frigid air gathered in her chest while oxygen flooded her brain.

She stopped at the spillway and stood with her hands on the back of her head, pleased to see that the road had been re-opened. After a while, she started to walk.

Someone wanted Art Lorrimer dead, and the most common motives for murder were gain, crimes of passion, revenge and concealment. This wasn't a crime of passion.

As his next of kin, all three Lorrimer siblings were the beneficiaries of his estate and stood to gain from his death. Motive right there.

Concealment? What damaging information did Lorrimer have that forced someone to murder him so it didn't become public? And revenge? Lorrimer owed people money, people so dangerous his parents purchased a plane so he could escape. Criminal gangs were notorious for having long memories, a fondness for exorbitant interest rates and a tendency to commit murder without a second thought.

Were these the same people Scruffy Freidman had intended to give up to the drug squad? Freidman had been turning informant, so concealment was definitely the motive for his murder.

Sterling walked on, the thundering water gushing from the spillway drowning out all sound. The *suspected* murder of Lorrimer had overshadowed the murder of Freidman, for now, and she could understand how those tendrils had become entangled, especially with Lorrimer's past drug convictions.

She stopped at the end of the spillway and stood looking out over the quiet airstrip. She'd taken this undercover job well before Lorrimer crashed on the runway below. Her assignment had been to gather information about a drug ring operating in the Snowy

Mountains with a view to finding whoever had killed Scruffy. She had to remember that.

She retraced her steps and started running again before she cooled down too much. She was due at the hotel in an hour.

She saw the dog first.

It was standing in the tray of a white Ford Ranger ute that she'd never seen parked on her street. She'd spotted the vehicle as soon as she'd turned the last corner, and immediately began her counter surveillance. Thankfully, the wind had become gusty on the way back and she'd pulled up her hood, the drawstrings tight around her face.

Sterling ran on, closing the gap between her and the ute, grateful she was on the other side of the street. Closer now, she refused to break stride or turn her head or acknowledge that she could see Rodney Garrett leaning against the car door, his arms folded, ankles crossed. He was here to intimidate her. She'd challenged him yesterday, and he was going to show her no one was allowed to do that.

Drawing level, she stared at the bitumen, her skin crawling as she ran past. She'd met numerous men like him in the course of her work, though normally she'd have her gun and handcuffs. The dog scared her more.

A car was reversing out of the driveway ahead, giving her the opportunity to cross the road. When her feet hit her driveway, she was already unzipping her pocket and feeling for her key. She resisted looking back, even as she let herself in.

'He knows where I live,' she told Ryder, pulling her work clothes out of the closet and tossing them on the bed. 'That's a bit disconcerting.'

There was silence at Ryder's end. She knew he and Flowers would be exchanging some form of silent communication in the car.

'I got his plate number.' She read it aloud, imagining Flowers plugging it into his phone. 'The thing is, I don't know whether Garrett's dangerous, or he's just being a dick.'

'You should report it to Collins,' Ryder said, 'and don't hesitate if you need to be pulled out, Sterling.'

'Yes, Sarge.'

'I don't like it,' she heard Flowers say.

'Let me see how I go today,' Sterling said, checking the time. She was due at work in forty-five minutes and still needed to shower. 'Heidi's rostered on, so it will be interesting to see how she is, and whether Garrett turns up at the pub. Hopefully he made his point this morning.'

Twenty-one

She had the wrong phone.

Shit! She must have mixed them up after calling Ryder.

Sterling made sure her personal phone was switched to silent then slid it into the front pocket of her jeans and left her shoulder bag in the cubicle. She needed to keep it on her person. Leaving it in her bag was too dangerous. She was *never* supposed to have her personal phone on her, only her Ida Stevenson phone, the one attached to her undercover identity.

Yanking down her shirt, she went into the staff toilet and locked the door. She could tell Elijah she'd forgotten something and go home. She could say she needed a prescription filled at the chemist. No, that wouldn't work, she was finishing at four and had plenty of time to do that, and it would be unlike her. She'd never missed a shift or asked for even the smallest amount of time off.

A noise outside alerted her to someone moving around. She ripped off some toilet tissue and flushed, anxiety making her heart skip. She could say she was unwell. Elijah would let her go without question. She turned on the tap and washed her hands, staring at her reflection in the mirror. She looked a picture of health, her eyes bright, her cheeks still flushed after her run and hot shower.

Best to stick it out, she thought as she dried her hands. What if Garrett came in and heard she'd gone home sick? He would think he'd won. Sterling balled up the paper towel and tossed it in the bin. No way was she going to let that grub think he'd got to her.

With a reassuring pat of her phone in her pocket, she pulled open the door and came face to face with Heidi.

'Hi,' she said simply, stepping around the other woman before heading out into the dining room. The lunch rush hadn't started, there were only a handful of people sitting around having a drink. Furious with herself for not taking enough care, Sterling touched her phone again, wishing the pocket were deeper.

'Hey, Ida,' Elijah greeted her. 'It's nice outside today, so we're going to offer a barbecue as well as the usual menu. Can you grab a few things from the kitchen?'

'Sure.'

In the kitchen, Sterling picked up a stack of dinner plates. Before long, Heidi joined her and soon they had everything set up on the picnic table closest to the barbecue.

'I'm going to run down the street and buy another gas bottle, just in case,' Elijah said suddenly. 'Ida, could you put the umbrellas up, and maybe bring a couple of bins out here? Heidi can look after the dining room.' He waved a hand. 'I won't be long.'

Alone on the narrow porch that ran the length of the building, Sterling touched the phone beneath her shirt and relaxed a little. Elijah was right, the day was bright and sunny, and with any luck Garrett and his snarling dog were miles away.

She stepped onto the grassed area and began opening the blue-and-white striped umbrellas. It was an exercise in restraint not to keep touching her phone, but it was vital she didn't draw attention to herself. With the job completed, she went back inside, cutting a path through the tables on her way to find the bins.

'Ida?'

She looked up. Heidi had a line of people at the bar. That was the unpredictable thing about hospitality. It could be quiet for no reason, then everyone walked in at once.

'Call Elijah,' Heidi said. 'We're short on tomato sauce.'

'Sure.' Sterling's stomach plummeted. Elijah's number was saved on her other phone, which was locked inside the oil heater. The one in her pocket was useless. She hurried out the back to the cubicles, relieved no one else was there. She paced the small area, her mind racing. Where the hell would Elijah's number be?

She stilled, her eyes shifting to the door of his office. Gathering her fears, she slipped inside and closed the door. Heart thumping, she hurried over to his desk. There was a stack of purchase orders and another of invoices he'd been working on. She flicked through them, searching for his number. She had a minute, two at the most, judging by how many people Heidi had to serve before she came looking for her.

She froze as a scuffing sound came from the other side of the door. Breathing hard, she didn't move, praying whoever it was would leave but expecting the door to fly open and for Elijah to walk in. She could imagine his shock. What could she say?

The sound of footsteps . . . receding.

Sterling held her breath.

Silence.

Leaning across the desk, she snatched up a card from the holder and scanned it, her hopes soaring at the mobile number printed on the bottom.

She straightened up, her elbow carelessly knocking the stack of purchase orders off the desk and scattering them across the floor. Sinking to her knees, she gathered them up, the blood pounding in her temples. Was it all about to end right here? Would she be forced to reveal who she really was if Elijah suddenly walked in?

Standing up, she put the papers on the desk and pushed them into a neat pile so they looked similar to how she'd found them, though they'd be out of date order. At the door, she listened for sounds from outside, but all was quiet. Slipping into the staff room, she closed the door and went to stand near her cubicle. With her back to the passageway, she reached into her pocket for her phone.

It was gone!

Shit! It must have fallen out of her pocket when she'd been crawling around on the floor.

Rushing back into the office, she found the phone under the desk. She scooped it up and quickly left, closing the door behind her. Back at her cubicle, she switched on her phone and tapped in Elijah's number, taking some deep breaths as she tried to slow her breathing.

'Hello?'

'Hi, Elijah. We're short on tomato sauce. Can you grab some while you're out?'

'Ida?'

Fuck! 'Yeah, it's me.'

'Oh, your caller ID's off. I nearly didn't pick up.'

Sterling closed her eyes. 'Really? I must have changed the settings somehow.'

'No worries, I'll get some now. See you soon.'

Sterling hit end call, sweet relief flooding her system. She slid the business card underneath her handbag and out of sight and switched the phone off again.

'Get on to him?'

Sterling spun around. Heidi was standing a little too close.

'Yep,' she said, sliding her phone back into her pocket, and hoping Heidi wasn't observant enough to notice it was a different make.

Heidi's eyes narrowed. 'Are you feeling okay? You're sweating.'

Sterling swallowed. She had one chance to turn this around. She wiped her forehead, making her fingers appear shakier than they were. 'I'm coming down,' she whispered. 'Where can I score a hit in this town? Do you know anyone?'

Heidi said nothing, just looked at her long and hard.

After a while, Sterling dropped her gaze. 'Forget it,' she muttered, taking a step away.

Heidi's hand shot out and grabbed her arm. 'Not now,' she said quietly.

Twenty-two

Flowers picked out Rodney Garrett's ute the moment he turned into the hotel carpark. The plate matched the one Sterling had given them that morning. Across the other side of the carpark sat Sterling's early-model Forrester.

Flowers swung into the space beside the ute, put the car in park and hopped out. Ten minutes ago, he'd left Ryder at the airport. Inspector Gray had issued the order while they were in transit to Khancoban.

'Speak to the press about this plane crash, Ryder,' Gray's voice had boomed through the cabin. 'At the very least give 'em an update.'

In the carpark Flowers walked around the optioned-up ute. He checked the tray first, then peered into the cabin. He was half expecting the dog to jump up at the window barking and snarling, but the cabin was empty. The ute had all the hunting accessories: a tough bull bar, a solid mounting behind the cabin for the rifles, and a powerful set of spotlights at the front. He'd been hoping to find large dents in the panels, broken tail-lights or bald tyres, but unfortunately the vehicle was in good condition. They'd already checked Garrett's registration and licence, and both were current.

Flowers banged his palm on the bull bar and strode towards the hotel. Rodney Garrett was a tool, and Flowers wanted to get a good look at him. He hoped he'd recognise him from the photograph on his licence.

As he neared the hotel, the aroma of meat cooking on a barbecue wafted through the air, but for once it failed to make his mouth water. He pushed open the door and stepped inside, noticing that only a handful of tables were occupied. Most of the patrons were outside, sitting at picnic tables along the verandah or on the grassed area.

From Sterling's description, the guy with the brown hair and beard pulling beers at the bar had to be Elijah. Sterling was beside him, arranging the drinks on a tray. Flowers moved further along the bar. He propped an elbow on the wooden top and surveyed the crowd. Sterling would see him soon enough.

The first person he recognised was Heidi Lorrimer with her pink-striped hair. She was near the barbecue, using tongs to serve salad onto a diner's plate. While Flowers watched, she held out a breadbasket for the diner to take a roll. Most people were dressed in jackets and beanies, making it impossible to tell if any of the men outside were Garrett.

When he looked back, Sterling was walking away with the tray of drinks. He turned and faced the bar so he wouldn't be looking right at her when she came back.

A movement in his peripheral vision made him look to the right. Rodney Garrett was sitting at a small table across from the end of the bar, his legs stretched out so they partially blocked the access way to the rest rooms. As Flowers watched, a woman with a small child was approaching him. She stopped, the child holding onto her hand. Only when she looked pointedly at Garrett did he slowly shift one leg out of the way and then the other.

What a dog act. Flowers' blood boiled. This guy was an absolute douchebag.

'What would you like?' the barman asked him.

Flowers looked up. 'Lemon squash, thanks.'

'Ice?'

'That'd be good.'

Ice clinked into the glass. 'The barbecue finishes at two-thirty,' the barman said as he filled the glass, 'in case you were wanting lunch.'

'Thanks.' Flowers reached over and tapped his card.

He chose a table where he had a line of vision to Garrett, as well as being a short distance from the glass doors leading outside. A family of five were between him and the door. He sat down and pulled out his phone, making a show of scrolling through as he took a drink.

'Hi there.'

His heart leaped at the sound of her voice, and he looked up to see Sterling standing by the table. She smiled, her notepad and pen at the ready. 'Are you having lunch today?'

'I only have time for a drink,' he said, putting his glass of lemon squash on a cardboard coaster.

'No worries, I'll clear some of this away for you.' She reached across in front of him before he could reply.

Flowers leaned back in his chair.

'Be careful.' The words were no more than a breath as she gathered up the fork, knife and bread plate on his table.

'Sure,' he said with a quick nod and a smile, hoping it would look liked he'd just thanked her.

Be careful? Was she warning him that Garrett was on the premises?

Sterling moved on to the next table to take the family's order. The youngest of the three children was writhing around on his mother's lap, clearly unhappy. The mum looked tired and stressed as she tried holding the child still while she ordered. The father seemed close to losing his patience, though he sat there refusing to help his wife. One boy reached out and punched his brother. The father snarled, then went back to ordering his lunch.

Flowers watched Sterling take their order into the kitchen. Beyond the bar, Garrett had disappeared, presumably into the men's rest room.

Flowers put down his glass and stood up, just as Heidi Lorrimer came inside. She stopped short when she saw him, her eyes cutting to the table where Garrett had been sitting.

'Excuse me?'

It was the woman at the next table, beckoning Sterling.

'Could we get a peanut butter sandwich for this one as soon as possible?' she asked as the child bounced up and down in her lap.

Wishing the father would take the child and give his wife a break, Flowers passed by their table. He approached the bar, where Heidi deliberately avoided making eye contact with him. Maybe Ryder had already spoken to her. They were heading to White Winter Station tonight, and Ryder had asked for all three Lorrimer siblings to be there. Or was Heidi nervous because she knew what her boyfriend had done to Sterling?

Flowers rounded the corner and Garrett was right there, playing a game on a retro console that was decades old. Their eyes met for two full beats before Flowers pushed open the swinging door and went into the rest room.

Sterling glanced at Flowers as he went back to his table. How long did he intend on staying, slowly downing his drink and not ordering lunch? A few of the staff had seen him in here before with Sergeant Collins, and knew he was the detective investigating the plane crash. One of the other girls had even commented on how hot he was.

'You think?' Sterling had screwed up her nose. 'I suppose he's okay. Like a taller Ewan McGregor.'

'*That's* who he reminds me of,' the girl had exclaimed. 'I've been racking my brain trying to think.' She frowned at Sterling. 'You don't rate Ewan McGregor?'

Right now, Sterling wished Ewan bloody McGregor would piss right off. She'd finally asked where she could get drugs, and Heidi had said *not now*. Of course, Flowers didn't know that, but nothing was going to happen with a detective in the dining room.

Sterling touched her phone for the briefest second, reassuring herself it was still there. 'Are you sure I can't get you something to eat?' she asked pleasantly, passing by Flowers' table. He shook his head and continued scrolling through his phone.

The father at the next table heard her and wheeled around in his seat. 'How about something to eat *here*?' he demanded, his voice so loud the youngster beside him started to cry. 'How long does it take to make a friggin' peanut butter sandwich?' He pushed back his chair and stood up. 'You don't have to cook it,' he said sarcastically. 'How about I come into the kitchen and make it myself?'

'How about you sit down and chill out!'

Sterling swung around, appalled to find Flowers on his feet. She held up her hand to silence him before turning back to the irate customer. 'I'm so sorry for the delay. I'll bring you the sandwich right away, at no charge.'

Then she turned back to Flowers, struggling to control her fury. 'It's okay. It's all under control.'

Twenty-three

The lights were on in the homestead when Ryder and Flowers arrived. They left the warmth of the car to step into a stinging wind roaring in from the Southern Ocean. They hurried towards the verandah, and the door opened seconds after their knock. A dog barked from somewhere at the back of the house. Ethan Lorrimer's tall frame stood silhouetted in the doorway.

'Apologies for having to arrange this so late,' Ryder said. 'We've been in Khancoban all day.'

As on the previous visit, they sat around the table. Dan's eyes were ringed with tired circles; Heidi's looked similar, though they were also smudged with mascara she hadn't washed off. Ethan's five o'clock shadow added to his swarthy appearance, his expression one of resigned tolerance. Only Kristin looked bright-eyed and energetic in her activewear and running shoes.

'The remains have been formally identified,' Ryder said, 'which means Art's body can be released. You can go ahead and hold the funeral now.'

Dan nodded. 'That's good news. We have the service organised and have been sorting through photographs. We may not have been close to Art for a long time, but we all have happy memories of him as a child.' He glanced at the others. 'That's how we're choosing to remember him anyway.'

'I'm sure,' Ryder said quietly.

Beside him, Flowers reached for his notepad and pen.

'We'll start with some general questions,' Ryder said, 'and then we'd like to get a clearer picture of your movements on the night of the accident.'

The Lorrimers exchanged glances. As usual, it was Dan who spoke first.

'You'll get full cooperation from us, Sergeant,' he said, his voice calm and direct. 'We have nothing to hide.'

'Thank you. What assets did Art have?' asked Ryder.

Dan's eyebrows shot up. 'I don't know what his assets were. There's a life policy, but that gets paid to the company.'

'How much is it worth?' asked Flowers.

'Just shy of two million dollars.'

The room grew quiet. Ryder looked at each of the siblings. Dan held his gaze. Ethan's eyes were fixed to a spot on the tabletop. Heidi fiddled with an earring.

'That's some serious money,' Flowers said.

Dan frowned. 'The company has similar policies on all our lives.'

'What about other assets?' asked Ryder.

Ethan looked up. 'He had the Cessna. I assume that was insured.'

Ryder nodded. 'He also had a fishing boat, but the house was rented.' The words of Art's former partner came to mind. *He once said something about family money.* 'Your parents are both deceased. Who owns this property?'

Heidi put her hands in her lap and looked at Dan.

'The company holds it on behalf of the trust,' he said.

'Do you have a copy of the trust deed here?' asked Ryder.

Dan shook his head. 'It's at our lawyer's office.'

'And the insurance policies?'

'In our safety deposit box,' Dan said sharply. 'Are we under suspicion for Art's murder, Detective?'

'Everyone's under suspicion until they're not,' Flowers said, his voice firm. 'We're looking at every possible motive.'

'And you think one of us murdered Art for his share of the

property and the insurance money?' Dan asked, shaking his head. 'That's ridiculous.'

'Money is a powerful motive,' said Ryder. 'Will you give us permission to speak to your lawyer? It shouldn't be a problem if you have nothing to hide.'

Dan looked enquiringly at his brother and sister. 'I'm fine with that, but I don't speak for all of us.'

Heidi rolled her eyes.

'What's that for?' Dan snapped.

Ethan ignored the other two and looked at Ryder. 'I have no problem with it.'

Dan was still looking at his sister. 'Yes or no, Heidi?'

'*Yes.*'

'All right,' Dan said, as though he were dealing with a five-year-old. 'I'll contact our lawyer first thing in the morning and give our consent.'

Flowers asked for the lawyer's details and jotted them down on his pad.

'We'll also need to look at those insurance policies,' Ryder said.

'That might take us a bit longer,' said Dan.

'I'll drive into Yass and pick them up,' Ethan said to his brother. 'That way you and Kristin can keep going with the funeral arrangements.'

Dan nodded, looking somewhat appeased.

'Thank you very much for all that.' Ryder cleared his throat. 'It's come to our notice that you're selling the family property. You didn't mention that on our previous visits.'

Dan frowned. 'I never thought it was relevant. In any event, it's being subdivided subject to the approvals coming through.'

'Yes, there's a long way to go yet,' Kristin said with a heavy sigh. 'I hope they don't find some endangered species of worm or something,' she said, rubbing her hand along her husband's forearm. 'You know how these things go.'

For a few seconds no one spoke.

Flowers shifted in his chair. 'So, what's brought about your decision to sell the property when it's been in the family for so long?' he asked.

Dan and Ethan looked at each other. 'You go,' Dan said.

Ethan took a deep breath. 'It's time. All of us have our own lives. Personally, I want to stay on the land, but I don't want a property this size. If the subdivision gets approved, I'll buy one of the bigger allotments for primary industry. If it doesn't, maybe I'll buy a small farm somewhere.' He looked at Dan and Kristin. 'It will be a big relief to these two.'

Dan reached out and squeezed Kristin's hand. Then he turned to Ryder. 'We have a young one with a few challenges. Kristin's back and forth from Sydney every month, but I can't leave this place.' He shook his head, looking somewhat defeated. 'We need to be closer to specialist doctors and a lot of other services that we just don't have out here.'

Ryder nodded at the unexpected revelation. 'That's tough.'

'It is,' Dan said. 'Kristin's from Sydney. Her parents are still there, thank goodness. They're a great support but they're getting older.'

'What about you, Heidi?' Flowers asked. 'Are you keen to move on?'

Ryder knew where this question was leading. Flowers had no time for Heidi's boyfriend and was sweating on what she was going to say.

'Yeah, this place was great when we were kids, but I don't think we should live here for the rest of our lives just because our parents did.'

'Okay,' Ryder said. 'Now, we haven't asked you this before, but can you tell us your whereabouts on the night Art flew into Khancoban? I don't care who starts.'

'Can I go first?' Kristin raised her hand as if she were in class. 'I need to check on the kids. I left them doing homework upstairs, but I bet they're playing video games.'

'Okay.' Ryder put his phone in the middle of the table as everyone watched on. 'Do we have your permission to record this?'

They all nodded, and Ryder asked Kristin where she was that night.

'I was home with the children, where I've been for the past three weeks. I haven't spent a night away from the property since I came back from Sydney the last time.'

'Okay, thank you.'

'Am I right to go now?'

Ryder nodded.

'I was here too,' Dan said when Kristen had left, 'not in the house, but in one of the far paddocks. We had a heifer in labour. I'd only come in about ten minutes before you arrived to tell us about Art.'

'I remember.' Ryder nodded then looked at Ethan.

'I couldn't tell you if I slept in my truck that night or not. I could have come home late and left early before anyone was up. That happens a lot. I'll have to check my roster.'

'That would be helpful,' said Ryder. 'We'll speak with your foreman or co-workers if necessary.' Finally, Ryder looked at Heidi. 'Where were you, Heidi, on the night your brother flew into Khancoban?'

'I worked earlier in the night and then I was at my boyfriend's place,' she said.

'You were there all night?'

'Yes, I had the next day off. He lives on a property near Jindabyne.'

'What's your boyfriend's name?' asked Flowers.

Ryder didn't miss the edge to his partner's voice.

'Rodney Garrett.'

Flowers slid his notepad and pen across the table to Heidi. 'Write down his address and phone number, please. We'll be talking to him too.'

The porch light was extinguished when they were halfway across the driveway, plunging them into darkness.

'That's a bit rude,' muttered Flowers, digging in his pocket for the key. He pressed the button to unlock the car, the hedges surrounding the cemetery lit up in the brief flash of light.

'Creepy,' said Flowers when they were inside the car. He started the engine then hit the button to lock the doors, just to make Ryder chuckle.

Flowers put the car in gear and pulled away, the headlights drifting across the building as they circled the driveway. A lone figure stood at the window watching them depart. 'Who was that?' he asked.

'I don't know. I couldn't tell.'

Flowers took it easy, cows mooing every now and then as they passed by the darkened paddocks. Only when he turned onto Tooma Road did he switch on his high beams.

'Well, that definitely fits with what Mhanda Van Engelen and Owen Temple told us,' he said.

Ryder nodded. 'About the subdivision, yeah. As for their alibis, we can't check Dan and Kristin's, but we can confirm Ethan's story with the salvage crew.'

Flowers stared at the narrow road illuminated by his high beams. 'And best of all, we get to talk to Rodney Garrett. I can't wait.'

'You'll have to. I'm meeting Sterling at Perisher in the morning. I know you said she seemed okay, but I want to judge for myself.' Ryder gave a heavy sigh. 'I need these cases solved before I transfer to regional, and I want Sterling out of Khancoban by then.'

Flowers glanced at Ryder, troubled at the worry in the sergeant's voice. 'She'll be out by the end of the ski season, won't she?'

'It depends. My replacement could leave her there if she's started making inroads into the drug ring, and we haven't made an arrest by then. That's why I'm counting on you to help me nail this. I don't want anything to happen to her.'

'That makes two of us,' said Flowers, hating the thought of Sterling being undercover indefinitely. 'You can count on me to do everything I can to try and find out who put that tractor on the runway.'

'I know I can, Daisy.'

The trust that Ryder was showing in him was gratifying, and Flowers thought how lucky he'd been to have had Ryder as his mentor.

'If we're not able to see Rodney Garrett tomorrow, Sarge, what do you want me to do?'

'Keep in touch with Benson. Remember, this is a *suspected* homicide. It could still be kids who moved that tractor. And chase up the Sydney squad. Tell them to get on to Art Lorrimer's service provider and see what the hold-up is. I want his phone log.'

'Yes, Sarge.'

They travelled in silence until they reached Khancoban half an hour later. Flowers slowed down, sticking to the speed limit as they crawled through the darkened town. He wasn't looking forward to his chat with Sterling tonight, not after the furious look she'd given him at lunchtime.

Leaving Khancoban behind, they began the winding ascent up the mountain. Towering alpine ash formed a canopy in places, and as they climbed higher snow flurries began to fall.

'It's dark through here,' Flowers said, steering through the hairpins. 'Thank God they've put these new double guard rails in with reflectors, it's a long way down on your si—Whoa!' Flowers stared through the windscreen. Across the road, close to the rocky cliff, a deer was racing along beside them, keeping pace with the car.

'Slow down in case it comes across,' said Ryder.

Flowers braked lightly, letting the deer pull ahead. Sure enough, it suddenly crossed in front of the car and with graceful ease flew over the guard rail to disappear down the steep embankment.

'That was freaking amazing,' Flowers said excitedly. 'A bit different to driving in Sydney traffic.'

Ryder chuckled. 'I reckon. I hear they cause their fair share of problems though.'

'I'm not surprised.'

For the next hour Flowers stayed focused on getting him and Ryder safely to Thredbo.

'Remember Thalia Cooper?' Ryder asked as Flowers left the Alpine Way and turned into Banjo Patterson Drive.

'The sergeant at Jindabyne?'

'Yeah. How about you call in and see her tomorrow morning while I'm with Sterling? She might know Garrett.'

'Good idea, Sarge. It would be helpful to know a bit about his background.'

'Especially if he's likely to set his dog on us,' Ryder said, stifling a yawn.

'I hope he does. Then I'll be able to arrest him.'

At eleven-thirty Flowers finally called Sterling.

'Hello?' she said. He could tell by her clipped tone how angry she was.

'Hi, Nerida,' he said, sounding pathetic even to himself. 'Sorry it's so late. Sarge and I just got back from the Lorrimers.'

She didn't ask what they'd learned, or enquire about his day like she usually did. She didn't say anything at all.

Flowers swallowed. 'Look, I'm sorry about today. I was out of line—'

'Out of line?' she said, her voice like ice. 'What were you even doing there?'

'Ryder sent me to check on you, after Garrett was in your street. His car was in the carpark. I knew he was inside.'

'And what, you thought he was going to set his dog on me while I was waitressing? God, why didn't you just leave when you saw I was okay?'

'I wanted to get a good look at him. I'd only seen the photo on his licence.' Flowers cringed. It had seemed like a good idea at the time. 'And then the bogan at the next table . . .'

'You caused a scene,' she snapped. 'You drew attention to yourself, and to me. People know you're a detective, some of them have seen you in the hotel with Sergeant Collins. And you've interviewed Heidi.'

'I didn't like the way that tosser spoke—'

'I can handle it! I've been handling it for thirty years!' She spat the words down the phone. 'You have no idea the kind of shit you have to deal with as a woman, *you've* never had to deal with it.'

'I—'

'Would you have acted like that if it were Ryder?'

She had him there. Flowers closed his eyes. 'No,' he said. 'I wouldn't have reacted like that if it were Ryder.'

For a long time, she didn't say anything, and he resisted the urge to try and explain further. She knew the reason, and he'd only make things worse.

'You compromised your judgement, and my position,' she said quietly.

And then she ended the call.

Twenty-four

Ryder sat in the armchair in the darkened suite, watching the snow build up on the windowsill outside. For safety reasons, Jack had installed lighting down both sides of the lodge, and with the curtains drawn back, the suites looked out at the softly illuminated snow gums.

'Pierce?'

He turned to see Vanessa sitting up in bed. He'd been so pre-occupied with his thoughts he hadn't heard her move.

Vanessa pushed back the covers and came over to him. 'Can't you sleep?' she asked, perching on the arm of the chair.

Ryder shifted a little to give her more room. 'No. I wish I could, I'm tired enough.'

'What's on your mind?'

Ryder rubbed a hand over his eyes. 'I'm worried about Sterling. I'm meeting her in Perisher in the morning.'

'Is she handling the job okay?'

Ryder lowered his hand and nodded. 'She's been going really well, but we've had two serious incidents in the last forty-eight hours.' He told her about Sterling's terrifying encounter with the dog, and then her shock at finding Garrett loitering in her street the next day. 'He had the dog in the back of the ute,' he said.

Vanessa grimaced. 'I agree, that sounds dangerous.'

'I know. I don't think Sterling will want to come out, but if I decide that she needs to, I might have to override her and extract her on the spot.'

'And she won't be happy about that?'

'I don't care if she's unhappy. I care if she's alive.'

Vanessa nodded, and for a few minutes they watched the snowfall together. 'Pretty, isn't it?' Vanessa said eventually.

'It's nice. Jack did a really good job. It's a lot safer out there now.'

'And, as a bonus, we get to enjoy the romantic view.'

Vanessa stood up and Ryder did the same. 'Come on, let's go back to bed,' he said. 'I'm keeping you awake.'

'Try not to worry,' she said a little later as they lay side by side. 'You have good instincts. You'll know what to do at the time.'

Twenty-five

Ryder was the only person sitting outside the Pretty Valley kiosk. He'd arrived in time to catch the first lift, then spent twenty minutes having a dodgy ski around, wondering why Vanessa was always so keen to get up for first tracks. Being the first one up the lift this morning hadn't enhanced his skiing style at all.

Now, as he waited, he kept his helmet and goggles on and looked down at the hot chocolate he'd bought for Sterling, complete with three marshmallows on a stick that looked like a snowman.

The scraping sound of a snowboard close by told him she'd arrived. 'Any problems on your way here?' he asked as she propped the snowboard against the bench seat.

'No. I thought one car was tailing me, so I pulled into the place that sells honey, but it didn't follow me in.' She sat down and looked at the hot chocolate in his hand. 'Nothing like an early-morning sugar rush, hey Sarge?'

He pushed the mug in front of her, keeping his eye on a couple of skiers loading onto the Pretty Valley chairlift. 'It's for you.'

'Thanks, I love these.'

'I know.' Ryder stretched out his goggles strap and lifted them onto the front of his helmet. 'Did you leave the car at Bullocks Flat?' he asked, squinting in the sudden glare. The day was bright and sunny with little wind, perfect conditions for snow sport enthusiasts.

'Yep. I caught the ski tube, then walked over from the terminal.'

'Good. I'm in the Perisher carpark.' Their separate arrivals gave him confidence they were safe here for a short while. 'Flowers is updating the case management file then he's heading into Jindabyne to talk to Sergeant Cooper. We're trying to get some history on Garrett. Then we're off to see the lawyer who acts for the Lorrimers.' Ryder told her about the trust deed and insurance policies.

'There's motive there,' Sterling said in a low voice. 'I only know Heidi a little. What are the two older brothers like?'

'Daniel comes across as pretty open,' Ryder said, keeping an eye on their surroundings as he spoke. 'His behaviour is typical first-born male. Ethan's cagier, harder to read. I get the feeling he's not a people pleaser. They're different, but they seem to be pretty much aligned on the sale of the property. Honestly, it's hard to tell. Anyway, we shouldn't stay here more than ten minutes,' he said, looking around at the almost deserted runs. 'Tell me how you are, Sterling.'

She picked up the snowman and bit the head off. 'I screwed up,' she said, swallowing the marshmallow. 'I mixed up the phones and took the wrong one to work.'

Ryder's hopes plummeted. 'Did someone borrow it?'

Sterling shook her head. 'I had to ring Elijah though, and I didn't have his number in that phone.' Sterling took two gulps of the hot chocolate. 'I had to search his office to find it. I was pretty worked up, a bit trembly, I couldn't help it.' She gave him an apologetic look.

Ryder nodded. 'Things go wrong, especially when you're under pressure.'

'Heidi came up just as I ended the call and asked me what was wrong. I must have gone white. I was definitely sweating.'

'What did you say?'

Sterling fiddled with the remains of the marshmallow snowman. 'That I was coming down and needed a hit. I know you didn't want me doing that, Sarge, but it was the only thing I could think of.'

Disturbed as he was by Sterling's news, Ryder was reassured by her quick thinking. 'That's high stress, and you acted on instinct. Maintaining your cover is difficult.'

Sterling nodded. 'I'm starting to realise that now.'

'What was Heidi's reaction?'

'She didn't answer right away, then she said "not now".'

'Well, what do you know?' Ryder mused quietly. 'Do you think Heidi Lorrimer is a user?'

'I'm not sure. She could know someone who is. Rodney Garrett?'

'Maybe. When she said "not now" was it like "not now, *maybe later*"?' Ryder asked.

She nodded. 'That's how I took it.'

'Okay.' Ryder paused. 'Can you see anyone behind me?'

Sterling looked past his right shoulder. 'Just a couple of skiers further on.'

'Anyone at the kiosk?'

'Only the girl behind the counter.'

'Okay, we need to get moving soon. So how are you feeling about things now?'

Sterling was quiet, as though thinking back over her horror day yesterday. 'Both dog incidents happened before the phone mix up, so that has more to do with me standing up to Garrett in the pub. He's taken a dislike to me.'

'Have you reported it to Collins?'

She shook her head. 'Not yet. I wanted to talk to you first.'

'Did Garrett cause a problem in the hotel yesterday? Flowers said he was in there.'

Sterling drained the hot chocolate. 'I don't think so. The guy's a tool, but whether he's a dangerous tool, I don't know.'

'Flowers wasn't impressed by what he saw.'

Sterling nodded and dropped the used toothpick into the mug. 'Yeah, I can't see those two getting along.'

'Okay, let's go,' said Ryder, pulling his goggles over his eyes and standing up. 'We've been here long enough.'

Sterling knew her way around Perisher better than he did, and she suggested they ride the Pretty Valley chairlift. 'Once we're at the top, you'll be able to take a green run all the way to the bottom.'

That sounded like an excellent idea to Ryder.

'I'll be honest, Sterling,' he said when they were safely on the chairlift. 'I'm tempted to bring you out because of the threat Garrett could potentially pose. This harassment could escalate. When's your next shift?'

'Tomorrow. I have today off.'

'That's good. Stay here as long as you can. That's an order.'

'It's a tough job, but someone's gotta do it,' Sterling said with a laugh.

'Hopefully we'll learn more about Garrett today.'

Sterling curled her hands around the safety bar. 'Can I ask you something? I feel like Art Lorrimer's death changed the focus of what I was sent here to do, which was to help find the person who killed Scruffy Freidman.'

Ryder nodded. 'Things have taken a turn that way because you're working with Heidi. And you're right, we're concentrating on Art Lorrimer's death because it was a plane crash, it made the nightly news and people want answers.'

'Yeah. I guess Scruffy's ending wasn't nearly as dramatic.'

'Scruffy died as Scruffy lived. Don't worry about our shifting focus. It'll come together at some point.' Ryder paused as the chair rattled past a pylon. 'You're a good detective, Sterling; you took a risk yesterday, and you picked the perfect time to do it.'

'Thanks.' She took off a mitten and tightened the chin strap on her helmet. 'I need to see if Heidi comes back to me with something.'

Ryder glanced at her. 'You're sure you want to go through with it?'

'I'm certain. There's a chance she could introduce me to someone in that drug ring.'

They were almost at the unloading ramp. Ryder removed one of his gloves and dug in his pocket for the single key. 'Room 10, Crystal Lake Motel, Jindabyne,' he said, passing it to her with great care. 'Put it on your key ring as soon as you can. It's a bolthole should you find yourself needing one.'

Twenty-six

Flowers was still in Sergeant Thalia Cooper's office when Ryder arrived at Jindabyne police station. Confident his partner would be getting the rundown on Rodney Garrett, Ryder found the bathrooms and hit the shower.

Ten minutes later, he turned off the water, rubbing the elbow he'd smacked on the wall and smiling ruefully at the cramped amenities. He was in for more of this when he transferred out west, not that *any* reservation he had about the move mattered in the slightest. It was a small price to pay for the chance to raise a family in the country with Vanessa. Ryder dressed, shrugged on his coat, and ran a comb through his hair. From memory, Thalia Cooper was a lot like Sergeant Collins. Collins seemed to have everything about rural policing worked out. He knew the townsfolk well, and while he was responsible for keeping Khancoban safe and orderly, he appeared to have struck the right balance of being able to successfully work and live in the community.

Ryder opened the bathroom door. Hopefully, he'd be able to strike that balance too.

'Sergeant Ryder, nice to see you again,' Cooper said when he emerged with his bundled-up ski gear tucked under one arm. 'It's good to see you making use of our facilities.'

'And very nice they are too, Sergeant.'

Cooper smiled and walked with him and Flowers to the entrance. 'I've just been telling Detective Flowers I know *of* Rodney Garrett, though he doesn't show his face around town very often. I understand he's a huntin' shootin' fishin' kind of guy—not into snow sports. We don't see much of the people who live on that property. It's very secluded, and they keep to themselves. I'd appreciate you letting me know how you go out there.'

'I will, though we won't get there until later this afternoon,' said Ryder. 'We have an appointment in Cooma first.'

'You sure get around, Sergeant.' Cooper opened the station door for them. 'Take care.'

They left Ryder's car parked in front of the police station and set off for Cooma together in Flower's car. 'How'd the meeting with Sterling go?' Flowers asked as he turned onto the Snowy Mountains Highway.

'She's staying undercover.' Ryder ran Flowers through his conversation with Sterling. 'All we can do is wait and see what Heidi Lorrimer does. It's unlikely to happen today. Sterling has the day off.'

'That's good,' said Flowers, 'we can relax for a little while.'

The law offices of Thomas and Associates were on the first floor above a local bank in Cooma. The receptionist showed them into a small conference room overlooking the main street and told them Mr Thomas would be with them shortly. Flowers poured himself a glass of water from a jug in the middle of the table while Ryder stretched and went to stand at the window. During winter, the normally quiet streets were bustling with tourists passing through on their way to and from the mountains, skis and boards strapped to their roof racks.

The door opened and a man came in. 'Good morning, sorry to keep you waiting,' he said, moving towards the chair at the head of the table. 'Let's all have a seat.'

Jeremy Thomas was softly spoken, of medium height with grey hair, grey eyebrows and a bushy grey beard. He took a silver pen from his shirt pocket and opened the file he'd brought in. 'Dan Lorrimer emailed this authority through to the office this morning,' he said, handing Ryder a sheet of paper.

Ryder looked at the authority. The signatures of Dan and Ethan Lorrimer were consistent with the signed documents the developer had shown him. Heidi's signature was there too, giving Jeremy Thomas the authority to speak to the police about their affairs.

'How can I help you?' Thomas asked, putting the authority back in the file.

'We're trying to establish what Art Lorrimer's assets are. Dan Lorrimer tells us White Winter Station is held in a trust.'

Thomas nodded. 'Yes, the property is owned by the company on behalf of the family trust.'

'Who controls it all?' asked Ryder.

'Any two directors can sign for the company. The trust requires that all the family members have to be in agreement when dealing with the assets, and that includes selling them.'

'Does that mean Art's quarter share will form part of his estate?' Flowers asked.

'No, Art's rights in any of the trust's assets cease upon his death.'

Ryder raised his eyebrows. 'So, the remaining three will get a third share each now?'

'That's correct.'

'Who made the decision to sell White Winter Station?' asked Ryder.

'They all did. I have a form signed by all of them saying they agreed to the sale.'

'How long ago was this?' asked Ryder.

'It would have to be going on two years now. My dealings have principally been with the two elder brothers. They arranged for the form to be signed and returned to me.'

'Did Heidi and Art not take an interest in their affairs?' asked Ryder.

'Well, Art has always kept to himself, and Heidi's been happy to leave all legal matters to Dan and Ethan to handle. They're a little older than the twins, and they've always taken the lead since their father died.'

'Are there other reasons for them wanting to sell up or is it purely a financial issue?' asked Ryder.

'They all have their personal reasons for selling, but in addition to that, the property itself is expensive to run and maintain. It's become a financial burden to the family.'

'So, once they sell the property, can they distribute the money among themselves?' asked Flowers.

Thomas rotated the silver pen between his fingers. 'Yes, and that could bring the trust to an end.'

Ryder nodded, absorbing what the lawyer had just told them. He glanced at Flowers in case his partner wanted to ask something more specific. Some time ago, Flowers had expressed an interest in becoming a police prosecutor, though he hadn't mentioned it lately.

The question Flowers eventually came out with was more general. 'How long is it since you've spoken to Art Lorrimer?'

'It's funny you should ask. I haven't spoken to Art for well over a decade, but I did receive a letter from a lawyer recently saying that she was providing him with some legal advice. The lawyer requested a copy of the trust deed.'

Ryder glanced at Flowers again. 'When was this exactly?' he asked.

'Three weeks ago.'

'Did you send her a copy?' asked Flowers.

'Yes, of course I did.'

'We'll need to get the lawyer's details from you,' said Ryder.

'Of course.' Thomas pushed back his chair and picked up the file. 'I'll get them for you now.'

Alone in the conference room, Ryder thought about what the lawyer had said. 'There seems to be more to this than first meets the eye.'

Flowers nodded. 'Yeah. If everyone's share ceases when they die, like Thomas said, then there's good reason for them wanting to get their share out now.'

Ryder nodded. 'Especially Dan who has a wife and two kids. If something happened to him, they'd get nothing.'

'Exactly.'

'Something else struck me,' Ryder said. 'Thomas said the form he has agreeing to the sale was signed by the Lorrimers two years ago, but they tell us they haven't spoken to Art for many years. Maybe they haven't been entirely truthful with us.'

'They could have an email address.'

'You're right, Flowers. Good thinking.'

The door opened and Thomas came back into the room. 'I've photocopied the letter I received from the firm in Sydney. Their details are on the letterhead.'

'Thank you for all your help, Mr Thomas. We may need to talk to you again at some point.' Ryder stood up, his thighs and calves already stiffening after his stint on the mountain.

'Let's grab an early lunch—I skipped breakfast,' he said to Flowers when they were back on the street. 'We can sit down and sort out our movements.'

They found an old-style cafe with internal archways and a row of booths down one wall. The first person Ryder noticed when they entered was Wendy Buchanan.

'You two certainly get around,' she said, putting her teacup on its saucer.

'The same could be said for you,' Flowers said with a big smile, giving Ryder the impression his partner had taken a liking to the Buchanan family.

'Treasure hunting again?' Flowers was asking.

'I've already been into Vinnies,' Wendy replied, 'but alas, no luck today.'

'Well, there's always tomorrow,' Flowers said, raising a hand in farewell.

They sat in the booth closest to the front window and ordered burgers and coffee.

'The legal office Art Lorrimer used is in Macquarie Street,' Ryder said.

'I saw that. Pity it's not in Campbelltown. It'll take us four and a half hours to get into the city.'

Ryder sighed. 'While we're waiting on our food, can you call ahead and make sure this woman can see us? Tell her we'll be there around five.'

'Sure.'

'And then call Benson. We need him to stay in Khancoban, at least until we're back in Thredbo.'

While Flowers went outside to make the calls, Ryder messaged Sterling explaining that they needed to travel to Sydney, and for her to call Benson or Sergeant Collins if she was worried. When he looked up, he could see Flowers outside talking on his phone. It wasn't long before he swung around and gave Ryder the thumbs up.

With a heavy sigh, Ryder picked up his phone and called Vanessa.

Flowers stood at the huge window in a conference room that looked down at the Hyde Park Barracks, finding it hard not to compare this modern glass tower with the humble offices of Thomas and Associates above the Cooma bank.

It struck him as strange that it was the frugal-living, black sheep of the Lorrimer family who had engaged Apin Law, one of Sydney's most expensive law firms, for independent advice on the family trust deed.

The door flew open and a woman rushed in, apologising profusely for keeping them waiting. 'Oh good, they brought you a cup of tea,' she said as they sat around the table. 'I'm Prudence Apin, pleased to meet you,' she said with a pleasant smile.

'I'm Detective Flowers and this is Detective Ryder,' Flowers began, 'and as I mentioned on the phone, we're here to talk to you about your client, Arthur Lorrimer, who was recently killed in an aeroplane accident in the Snowy Mountains.'

'Oh, I was so shocked to hear it was him,' Prudence said, her silver hair shining under the lights. 'I saw the plane crash on the news, but I don't think they mentioned the pilot's name in the report, so I had no idea it was my client until you told me on the phone.'

'So, how long have you acted for Art Lorrimer?' Flowers asked.

'He's a new client. I only saw him for the first time about three weeks ago.'

Flowers nodded. 'We were told by the lawyer who acts for his siblings, Mr Thomas in Cooma, that you requested a copy of the trust deed and that he sent it to you.'

'That's right. Mr Lorrimer asked me to prepare an advice for him once I'd read through the deed. He'd recently found out his siblings had entered into a contract to sell the family cattle station, despite him making it clear he wouldn't agree to it.'

Flowers glanced at Ryder then back at Prudence. 'Mr Thomas said he has a form, dated around two years ago, signed by all four siblings, agreeing to put White Winter Station on the market. He said there's a clause in the trust deed that says they all have to agree if they want to sell any of any assets.'

'That's right. I've been through the deed, and there is such a clause.' Prudence opened a file on the table in front of her and began flicking through the pages on the metal spike. 'I was led to believe that he had *never* agreed to the sale, but if Mr Thomas holds a signed document, then he must have changed his mind. I'm yet to see that document.' She paused and ran her finger down one of the pages on the spike. 'Here is an email I sent to him saying that I'd prepared my advice, and if he could make an appointment to come in, we could discuss how he was going to proceed. Then I have a file note that he rang and spoke to me. I told him that if his siblings had entered into a contract to sell the property, then they had broken the terms of the trust.' She looked up. 'Of course, I didn't hear anything more.'

'Ms Apin.' Ryder leaned forward and looked at the file. 'Would you have anything there that has Art Lorrimer's signature on it?'

'Yes.' She began turning pages again. 'He would have signed our cost agreement.'

'Would it be possible for us to get a copy of the signature page?' asked Ryder.

'Yes, of course.'

Prudence left the room and returned a few minutes later, photocopy in hand, with a black line through the cost of their legal fees.

'Thank you. You've been extremely helpful,' said Flowers as he and Ryder left the conference room.

Flowers looked at Ryder as they travelled down in the lift. 'That was good thinking, Sarge, asking for his signature.'

Ryder nodded. 'It will be interesting to compare it with the authority they gave to Jeremy Thomas two years ago.'

When they were back in the car, Ryder offered to drive. 'Call Thomas' office and leave a message saying we want to see that form. There's a good chance he has an answering machine. Tell him it doesn't matter what time he calls back if he wants to talk more about it.'

'Yes, Sarge.'

Thomas didn't pick up, so Flowers left a message then settled back in his seat. Alone with his thoughts while Ryder navigated his way through the traffic, Flowers gazed at the hordes of commuters scurrying down the hill towards Circular Quay. He'd been trying not to think about Sterling all day, but now, as he took in the sparkling city lights, he couldn't help thinking of her locked inside a dingy rumpus room under an empty house six hours away.

They were skirting the perimeter of the airport when a text message came through on Flowers' phone. 'It's Jeremy Thomas,' he said, opening the message and reading it aloud. '*Detective Flowers, the Lorrimers' authority stated that I assist you in any way I can, so I'm forwarding to you a photograph of the document you requested. Regards, Jeremy Thomas.*'

'Have a look at them and see if they're the same,' said Ryder, the air pressure inside the car changing as they entered a tunnel.

Flowers studied Art Lorrimer's signature on the copy of the cost agreement then compared it to the one Jeremy Thomas had sent through on his phone. His heart quickened. The more he looked from one to the other, the more convinced he was that they were not the same signature.

Twenty-seven

They met in Ryder's room at the Golden Wattle Lodge at nine the next morning. Ryder was sitting on the edge of the bed while Flowers stood with his back to the window. Benson was on speaker phone. They'd sent the signatures to Sydney for the handwriting expert to look at, but Benson had been keen to look at them as well.

Flowers shifted his feet impatiently. 'What do you think?'

'I think it's forged.' Benson's voice rang throughout the room. 'I'm no expert but the signature on the cost agreement flows naturally. The second photo, the authority to sell the property, looks like a cautious copy to me.'

Flowers nodded. 'That's what we think.'

'Okay,' said Ryder. 'So, what are your thoughts, are all three Lorrimers involved in this?'

'I've no idea, not having met them,' said Benson.

'They could all know,' said Flowers, stepping away from the window, 'although Thomas said he's always dealt with the brothers. Maybe they gave the form to Heidi to sign first, and then forged Art's signature.'

'I think that's the most likely scenario,' agreed Ryder, 'but we can't conclude anything until we get the expert opinion. Still, it's not looking good for the Lorrimers. The only reason to forge Art's signature would be because he refused to sell.'

'Yeah, a contract for sale only needs two signatures,' put in Benson.

Flowers nodded. 'We've seen it, signed by Dan and Ethan.'

'O'Day has the warrant for the call log now,' Ryder said, looking up from his phone, 'and Brown is still working through the tractors that have been bought and sold and, I'm told, going quietly insane.'

Benson chuckled. 'It's a hell of a job. I couldn't hand it on quick enough.'

'Benson, can you type up the progress reports and upload them so they're up to date for Sterling?' asked Ryder.

'Yes, Sarge.'

'Good.' Ryder stood as a strong gust of wind slammed against the windows. Outside, ravens were calling to each other and flying around between the trees, a sign that snow was on the way. Ryder moved to close the curtains. 'So, we know from our forensics reports there were no traces of illicit drugs found in the plane wreckage, or in Lorrimers' house, or the boat at Lemon Tree Passage. Our drug theory is weak.'

'It is.' Flowers shifted aside as Ryder went over to the wardrobe. 'And why wouldn't Art Lorrimer *want* to sell? The guy hasn't been near the place in years, you'd think he'd want his money. *I* would.'

'Let's follow up on Heidi and Ethan's alibis for the night Art flew in,' said Ryder, shrugging on his jacket. 'Starting with Rodney Garrett.'

'Sounds good to me,' said Flowers.

Flowers and Ryder stood side by side at a garden gate, staring at the rundown farmhouse at the end of a dirt road on the outskirts of Jindabyne. On their arrival, two guard dogs stood up from where they'd been lying in a patch of winter sunlight and began patrolling the dust bowl behind the fence that passed as a front yard.

'Heidi goes from the rolling pastures of White Winter Station to this,' said Flowers, shaking his head. 'I'll never understand the female mind.'

Access to the property via a driveway was also blocked by a locked gate. There were no cars to be seen, but the driveway led to a large iron shed built close to the house with its roller doors closed, so it was impossible to tell if anyone was at home.

One of the dogs, a black-and-tan mixed breed, bared its teeth and began to growl. The rumble started deep within its throat and grew louder the closer it came to where they were standing. Soon, the second dog, a tan-coloured boxer, was doing the same.

'Do your magic, Dolittle,' said Ryder.

'No problem, Sarge.' Flowers set off around their car's bonnet and opened the driver's door. The wail of the siren sent the dogs into a barking frenzy. Flowers turned it off and came back to stand beside Ryder. 'Now he'll know we're here.'

Sure enough, a curtain twitched at one of the windows.

'Rodney Garrett! Open up! Police!' Flowers shouted, only to see the curtain fall back into place. 'Somebody's home,' he said to Ryder.

They waited, an icy wind whipping through their hair and the dogs watching their every move.

Flowers pulled out his notepad and found the page where Heidi had written down her boyfriend's details. 'I'll give him a call,' he said, taking out his phone.

Flowers listened to the phone ringing at the other end. Eventually it went to voicemail, but Garrett's manners didn't stretch as far as him recording a greeting. 'Mr Garrett, it's Detective Flowers from Sydney Homicide,' he said with forced politeness. 'We'd like to talk to you in relation to our enquiry surrounding the death of Arthur Lorrimer. Please call me back on this number to arrange a time. Thank you.'

'Those dogs didn't look like the one Sterling described,' Flowers said when they were safely back in the car.

'Maybe it wasn't Garrett who was home. Cooper said she didn't know how many people live there,' said Ryder.

'I'm not surprised. She could have warned us about the dogs though.' Flowers braked as he came to a T-intersection then made a left-hand turn onto the road that would take them to Berridale. From there, it was a three-hour drive to Batlow, where Ethan Lorrimer was working on the bushfire salvage operation.

'If Garrett doesn't call us, we'll seek a warrant for his arrest and bring him into Jindabyne Station for questioning,' said Ryder.

Flowers nodded. 'Let's hope he calls, because only a SWAT team is going to get past those dogs.'

They'd stopped for a sandwich and a milkshake at Berridale when Flowers' phone rang.

'Maybe this is him,' he said, putting down his sandwich and hitting answer. 'Detective Flowers.'

'Hello, it's Cate Buchanan here.'

'Cate?' Flowers blinked in surprise. 'What can I do for you?'

'Have I caught you at a bad time?'

'Ah.' Flowers looked at Ryder, who'd stopping eating. 'Just having a bite to eat in Berridale before we head to Batlow.'

'Oh, I actually need to talk to you about something. I was hoping you'd be able to come up to the hut this afternoon and see me.'

Flowers frowned. 'Can you tell me what it's about?'

'Not over the phone. It's to do with your investigation. It's important.'

Flowers leaned across the table and mouthed the words *it's important*.

'All right, Cate,' he said when Ryder nodded, 'I'll see you soon.'

'Thank you. If you're leaving now it should take you about an hour to get here.'

'Do you have any idea what it's about?' Ryder asked, sliding the remains of his sandwich into its white paper bag.

Flowers shook his head. 'I have no idea.'

'Do you still have those snowshoes?'

'Yeah, they're in the boot.'

Ryder nodded at the black clouds hovering over the distant mountains. 'It looks like you're going to need them. Maybe I should pick some up too and go with you.'

'Oh, don't worry about it, Sarge, I can handle it.'

'I wonder why she asked to see you at the hut,' Ryder said as they threw the remnants of their lunch in the bin. 'It's like she doesn't want to be seen talking to you.'

'Or she wants to get me alone,' Flowers said with a laugh, thinking of his last meeting with Cate Buchanan. 'Nah, she said it was important.'

Ryder smirked as they walked back to the car. 'Only one way to find out.'

The storm came in fast, dumping snow as far down as Jindabyne, so an hour and a half had passed by the time Flowers parked at Dead Horse Gap. There were three other cars at the lookout, all covered in snow—one of them was Cate Buchanan's. At least she hadn't left.

Flowers zipped up his parka and pulled his beanie down as far as he could. He moved to the start of the track, the wind roaring through the valley with such ferocity it almost knocked him over. He stopped, raising a forearm to cover his face as snow, ice and wind hurtled into him.

When he'd dropped Ryder at the Golden Wattle, the sarge had told him to wait, then returned to the car a few minutes later with his goggles and neck warmer. *You'll need these*, he had said. *And keep the two-way radio on you.*

Flowers set off, surrounded by fast-moving clouds and fog. With his vision reduced to a couple of metres, he followed the path care-fully, warming up despite the freezing conditions. The hard-packed, icy trail from last time was now soft underfoot thanks to the fresh layer of snow. He stopped to pick up a small branch that had fallen onto the path. Roughly the length of a Nordic walking pole, he kept hold of it and tramped on.

The lack of visibility made him feel like it was taking longer than last time to reach the place where the trail forked in two. Flowers hesitated, realising he'd been looking down at the track the entire time, and had failed to look out for the signpost pointing the way to Buchanan Hut. He had no idea if he'd passed the fork in the trail or not.

Fog and mist engulfed him as another savage blast of wind roared up the valley. Gripping the branch with both hands, he dropped his chin to his chest and tried to stay on his feet. Tiny specks of ice stuck to the lens of his goggles, and he closed his eyes and thought of Sterling and how angry she was with him. For so long he'd been hoping that something would happen between them again, but he doubted it ever would now, after his stuff-up two days ago. *I shouldn't be worrying about this*, he thought. *I could die in a snowstorm right now.*

After a while, the wind eased considerably, and he was able to scrub the ice off his goggles with his glove. The improved visibility lifted his spirits, and he decided to go a little further before turning around and retracing his steps.

'Detective Flowers?'

Flowers stopped at the sound of Cate Buchanan's voice. He could see her standing on her skis up ahead at the juncture in the trail. She wore a knee-length, black padded coat with an oversized hood that she was gripping tightly in place.

'I was so worried about you,' she said as he joined her. 'The weather's gotten worse.'

Flowers leaned on his branch, puffing a little. 'I was worried too. I thought I'd missed the turn.'

'Lucky you didn't. Come on. I have the fire going inside.'

It was quieter on the more protected trail, and Flowers relaxed, relieved to be in the company of someone who was familiar with the terrain. After a few minutes, the recognisable smell of burning wood filled his nostrils and the hut came into view.

'This would have been a welcome sight for many people over the years,' he said when they reached the hut. He bent down and removed his snowshoes, leaving them at the front door. 'Hell, it's a welcome sight for me.'

'Come in and take off your jacket,' she said, preceding him into the hut and holding open the door.

Flowers stepped inside, shrugged off his parka and gave it to Cate. The hurricane lamp was again casting a soft glow from its place on top of the cupboards, and on the far wall the river-stone fireplace burned brighter than it had the other day.

As the hut creaked and groaned against the onslaught of the storm, Flowers peered into the dark corners where the glow of the lamp didn't reach, his intuition warning him that something wasn't right.

And then a hulking figure emerged from the shadows.

Twenty-eight

Ethan Lorrimer stepped into the light, looking twice as large and twice as menacing as he appeared in the formal dining room at White Winter Station.

Flowers swung around and looked at Cate. 'What's this about?' he demanded. His radio was in his parka and he would be unable to call for back-up. 'I thought I was here to talk to you.'

Cate came forward, brushing past him to join Ethan. To Flowers' amazement, Ethan put his arm around her waist and drew her protectively against his side.

'Oh! Okay, cool,' Flowers said, some of the tension leaving his body. 'So, you two are together?'

Cate nodded. 'I'm so sorry we dragged you all the way down here. The weather wasn't anywhere near as bad when I called.'

'No worries, I'm smashing the snowshoeing now.'

Cate gave an embarrassed smile, and Flowers thought the corner of Ethan's mouth twitched, though it could have been a reflection from the fire.

He moved closer to the heat, and the couple separated. 'So, what is it you wanted to tell me?' he said, though he could almost predict what she was going to say next.

'Ethan was with me the night of Art's plane crash. All night.'

'Here?'

Cate's eyes widened. 'No, not *here*.' She smiled at Ethan. 'Although this was where we used to meet in the beginning, wasn't it?' She turned back to Flowers. 'He was at my place in Jindabyne.'

'Is there anyone else who can corroborate your story?' Flowers asked.

Ethan shook his head. 'No.'

'Why bring me all the way down here to tell me this when I could have come into the shop?'

It was Ethan who answered. 'Because I wanted to be here when Cate told you. No one else knows about our relationship yet.'

'No one?' Flowers raised his eyebrows and looked from one to the other. 'How long have you been together?'

'A couple of years,' said Ethan.

'Keeping that under wraps must take a bit of work.' Flowers turned his back to the fire. 'Does this have something to do with the old feud I keep hearing about?'

'Yes,' Ethan said, and Cate gave a solemn nod.

'That's strange, because everyone I've spoken to, including you, Cate, has insisted it's ancient history, all forgotten.'

Ethan shoved his hands in his pockets. 'Feuds down here last for generations,' he said. 'It's never forgotten, especially when it's about land.'

'That's why Ethan comes to me,' Cate put in. 'Jindabyne's full of tourists and short-term accommodation. People are coming and going all the time. And the crowd up there are into adrenaline sports at the ski resorts. No one's bothering about land feuds from years ago.'

Flowers raised his eyebrows. 'So, you've never been to White Winter Station?'

Cate shook her head. 'No, I've only seen photographs. Dad would drive past and show Lewis and I where he and Aunt Wendy lived when they were little. But you can't see the house from the road.'

Ethan's eyes met Cate's and he gave her a sympathetic smile.

Excitement charged through Flowers' body. He had no idea how this new information fitted into the puzzle, but the fact that the feud simmered on was an important piece. 'So, who would be upset if they found out about you?'

'I don't think Dan would be too happy,' said Ethan.

'Why's that?'

'Our contract for sale is with Temple Developments and we deal with them through our lawyers. Temple deal directly with the council. Cate's brother has been behind the development from the beginning. We don't know for sure, but we suspect he might want to buy one of the allotments when the subdivision's done. I certainly do, it's a beautiful spot.'

Flowers looked at Cate, but she averted her gaze. *We don't know for sure. One of the allotments?* Lewis had specifically told him and Ryder that Cate had grand plans for the house and gardens, including the family cemetery. Despite their two-year relationship, it appeared Cate hadn't shared the Buchanan family's plans with her lover.

'We're getting closer to the subdivision being approved,' Ethan was saying, 'and if Dan found out now that Cate and I had been seeing each other all this time, he'd wonder why I didn't tell him.'

'Why didn't you? Because she's a Buchanan?'

Ethan nodded. 'I thought he might suspect us of colluding in some way, especially with Lewis giving the subdivision his support. My father bought the property from Cate's grandfather before any of us were born. Dad was a bachelor a long time; I don't think my parents had Dan until Dad was forty-five. But from that point on, the families have never really liked each other. And Dan's a control freak at the best of times.'

'Neither of us knew back then how long our relationship would last, Detective,' Cate said. 'Ethan's family had just signed the contract and he was adamant nothing should jeopardise it.'

'It sounds a bit over the top now,' Ethan said apologetically, 'but buyers don't come along every day, not for properties like ours.'

Flowers nodded, committing everything they'd said to memory. He'd been so surprised to find Ethan Lorrimer in the hut he hadn't even taken out his notepad. 'I get that.'

'I told Detective Ryder I couldn't remember where I was that night, but I knew *exactly* where I was,' Ethan said.

Flowers nodded again. What he'd like to know was *exactly* which Lorrimer had forged Art's name on the form agreeing to sell, but he needed to wait for confirmation from the handwriting expert before he could bring that up.

'Okay, I'll go back and type up a report for Detective Ryder. I can't see why the information you've given me can't stay confidential unless it somehow becomes relevant in the case down the track.'

'Thank you, Detective Flowers,' Cate said.

'No, thank you. I'd rather walk down here in a storm than drive three hours to Batlow,' he said.

'I'll walk back to the car with you,' Ethan said. 'The trail can get icy in this weather.'

'That's okay, I'll be fine,' said Flowers, with a sudden burst of mountaineering confidence. Then it struck him that Ethan might want to speak to him privately. 'But if you'd feel better coming along . . .'

'I would.' Ethan shoved an arm the size of a small tree trunk into his jacket. 'I don't want to be responsible for a member of the police force going missing in the back country.'

Ethan was using snowshoes as well—though he had proper walking poles—so they took the path back to the main trail at an easy walking pace.

'How are the funeral arrangements going?' asked Flowers, hanging on to his branch as a gust of wind ripped through the trees and showered them with leaves and snow.

'We're getting there. It'll just be a simple service, and then we'll go on to the local cemetery where our parents are buried.'

'Oh, they aren't in the cemetery at White Winter Station?'

'No. That cemetery caused our family a lot of problems. I don't think my parents wanted to be buried there.'

'What kind of problems? Sorry, but it's the first private cemetery I've seen, and I'm curious.'

They had reached the exposed main trail where the wind was stronger. Ethan had to raise his voice to be heard.

'It was all to do with Cate's grandmother. Her husband is buried in the cemetery, and she was always coming over to put flowers on his grave.'

'Right,' said Flowers, wondering why that would have caused such a headache for Arthur Lorrimer Senior.

'It went on for ten years,' Ethan said. 'I can't even remember where I heard the story, but as Cate's grandmother aged, Wendy began driving her mother over and, apparently, my mother became jealous. She thought Dad was developing feelings for Wendy, who of course was a lot younger than my mother. That's when my mother put a stop to them visiting.'

'Oh.' Flowers recalled Cate's words from the other day. *Yes, Grandma and my father were very bitter. To add insult to injury, the Lorrimers refused to let Grandma visit the family cemetery at White Winter Station.*

'That wouldn't have improved the situation,' Flowers said eventually.

They walked on in silence, stopping only when a particularly ferocious gust came hurtling across the range.

As they neared the carpark, it started to rain. Flowers looked at Ethan through Ryder's goggles. 'I saw you working around the cemetery the other day. I assumed you were getting it ready for Art's interment.'

'No.' Ethan stopped at the foot of the small rise that led up to the carpark. 'I'm doing it for Cate.'

Flowers frowned. 'For Cate?'

Ethan nodded. 'Once the sale goes through, I want to take her home and introduce her to the family. I'd like her to see the station before all the work starts and it changes for good.' Ethan dug his poles into the snow and turned his back to the wind. 'I don't think our family have shown enough respect for the people who established the property. I'd feel ashamed showing Cate the cemetery the way it is today.'

Twenty-nine

Eva hurried into the kitchen at the Golden Wattle Lodge, a folded blanket in her arms. 'Take off that wet jacket, Mitch,' she said, 'and wrap this around you. I've warmed it up in the dryer.'

Ryder watched as Flowers did as Eva asked, relieved his partner had stopped shivering. It was a miracle he'd avoided hypothermia.

'I think the Irish coffee is doing the trick,' Flowers said.

'Never fails,' Eva said with a smile. 'Jack's building up the fire if you'd rather sit in the lounge. There's no one out there at the moment.'

'I'm good. Thanks, Eva.' Flowers looked at Ryder across the table and picked up the tall, steaming glass.

Ryder waited until Eva had left the room. 'So, Cate and Ethan Lorrimer?'

'Yeah, that was a surprise. Almost worth freezing to death for.'

Ryder smiled. Despite Flowers' battle with the elements, he looked healthy and alert, like one of those guys swimming laps in the ocean baths in the middle of winter.

'So, how did they meet if this animosity still exists?' asked Ryder.

'I asked him that before I got in the car. They're both members of the Hut Association. Ethan was one of the volunteers who turned up to repair Buchanan Hut after it was damaged in a bushfire.'

'And no one knows about their relationship?'

'According to them, no.'

Ryder frowned. 'Okay, let's run through what we know. Two years ago, Cate Buchanan and Ethan Lorrimer begin a relationship, and around the same time, the Lorrimers' lawyer receives a form signed by the four siblings stating that they've agreed to sell White Winter Station. The form is to show they're complying with the terms of the trust, but we suspect Art's signature was forged.'

Flowers nodded.

'Art finds out the property is on the market and gets a copy of the trust deed sent to Prudence Apin. Her understanding was that at no time did he agree to sell. So, if his signature turns out to be a forgery, she's probably right.'

'Unless he did agree and then changed his mind,' put in Flowers.

'Correct. With a head of steam, and the knowledge the others have broken the terms of the trust, he comes home to confront them. Someone knows exactly when he's flying in because they drive the tractor onto the runway beforehand.'

'We need that call log,' said Flowers.

'We do. Now, we know the Lorrimers have motive. They will benefit from his death, receiving a third share rather than a quarter share of the sale proceeds, plus the company will get a serious injection of cash from Art's life insurance policy.'

'That's strong motive,' said Flowers.

'I agree, but we need to look at who else had motive. Who else could have got wind that Art was about to put a stop to the sale?'

'Lewis Buchanan,' said Flowers. 'He's supported the development from the start, and he has an ulterior motive. He wants the house and cemetery for Cate and Wendy, and probably for his own benefit too. Art could have called the council to try and find out what was going on and that tipped Lewis off. It's possible.'

Ryder didn't look convinced. 'Is it a strong enough motive for murder though?'

'People have killed for less.'

'That's true. What about Owen Temple?'

Flowers drained the last of his coffee. 'He has serious skin in the game.'

'He does.' In his mind's eye Ryder saw the office Temple Developments had set up in Tumbarumba. 'He's invested a lot of money. He'll lose big if the sale falls through.'

'And then there's Wendy Buchanan,' said Flowers. 'Her nephew says she's chill with things no matter which way they pan out. But she was considered a threat to the older Lorrimers' marriage, at least by Mrs Lorrimer—enough to ban her and her mother from visiting the grave. There could be motive, if Wendy thought Art was going to ruin her only chance of getting back the family home.'

'I get that,' Ryder said, carrying their mugs over to the sink, 'but she'd have to know he was flying in, and how would she go about moving the tractor?'

'An accomplice? What about Cate?' Flowers said. 'We haven't mentioned her. She's a direct conduit between Ethan and her brother and aunt.'

Ryder turned around, leaned on the counter, and looked at his partner. 'So, are Cate and Ethan lying when they say no one knows about the relationship?'

'My gut says Ethan's telling the truth. He's cleaning up the cemetery because he feels bad for Cate, and we've seen evidence of that. There was no mention of the Buchanans' grand plans for the house and cemetery when I was talking to them in the hut, just that Ethan had heard Lewis *could* be interested in buying an allotment. And we know for a fact that Lewis and Cate, and maybe even Wendy, have massive plans for that allotment. Cate said nothing about that.'

'Doesn't mean Ethan's not aware of it though,' said Ryder.

Flowers shrugged.

'Okay, let's change tack. What do we know about the drug ring?' Ryder asked, coming back to the table.

'Not much, only that someone murdered Scruffy Freidman for turning informant. And Heidi may, or may not, help Sterling get access to drugs. We need to wait and see.'

'Sterling said something interesting at Perisher. She said her focus had switched from Freidman's murder to Art's because Heidi's a workmate. She's consciously trying to keep in mind the job she was sent here to do, which is to try to learn something about the drug ring.'

Flowers hitched the blanket higher on his shoulder. 'I see what she means.'

'It got me thinking,' Ryder said. 'We know Art had a record, and he disappeared because he owed the wrong people money—dangerous people, people not afraid of showing up at the cattle station even when Art's parents were alive. We're familiar with crims, we know they have long memories. If they're still operating down here, this could have been long overdue payback.'

Flowers took a biscuit from the plate Eva had put on the table. 'Yeah, maybe it's the only chance they've had because he's never been back.' Flowers bit into the biscuit, and they were quiet for a while mulling over their thoughts.

'If you're right,' Flowers said, 'it would mean that the Lorrimers are innocent.'

'And everyone else.'

The door flew open, and Eva and Jack's daughter ran in. She pulled up short when she saw them, the small backpack she took to pre-school hanging from her shoulders. Clearly surprised to find them in the kitchen, she put her finger in her mouth and said a quiet hello.

'Hello, Poppy,' said Ryder, smiling down at the little girl. 'How was pre-school?'

'We read Bluey,' she said in a voice barely above a whisper.

'Bluey's cool,' said Flowers, picking up the plate. 'Would you like one of your mum's biscuits?'

Poppy nodded and took a biscuit as Eva came rushing in. 'Sorry, she got away from me. I'll just get her a glass of milk.'

Ryder stood up. 'We'll get out of your way, Eva. We can finish up in my suite.'

Eva gave him a grateful smile. 'Thanks. I should start prepping for dinner.' She glanced at Flowers. 'Would you like to stay and eat with us tonight, Mitch?'

Ryder watched as Flowers hesitated.

'Thanks for the offer, Eva, but I'll head off as soon as I finish up with the sarge. Once I get home and comfortable, I won't feel like coming out again.'

'No worries, I get that, but any night you feel like joining us.'

'I'll get around to it, I promise.' Flowers stood up.

'Why do you have that on?' Poppy asked, pulling on the blanket Flowers wore.

'He likes that colour,' Ryder said. 'Suits him, don't you think?'

Poppy giggled and looked at the lilac-coloured blanket. 'No.'

'See you a bit later, Eva,' Ryder said, standing up and giving Poppy's head a gentle rub.

'What time does Vanessa finish?' Flowers asked as they walked into Ryder's suite.

'She's always one of the last to come in.' Ryder checked his watch. 'Maybe half an hour. Okay, where do we go from here?'

Flowers sat on the edge of the bed. 'Should we try and contact Rodney Garrett through Heidi before we issue a warrant for his arrest?'

'Let's give him until the morning,' Ryder said as his phone pinged with an email alert. 'No longer than that though.' Ryder opened the email. 'It's the handwriting analyst,' he said. 'That was quick.'

Flowers stood up, shrugged the blanket off his shoulders and looked at Ryder expectantly. Ryder scrolled past the technical information until he reached the analyst's conclusion. He looked at Flowers.

'It's a forgery.'

Thirty

Inside his apartment, Flowers ran the shower while he stripped off his clothes. Before leaving the Golden Wattle, he and Ryder had arranged a meeting with the Lorrimers at their lawyer's office for the following morning.

Flowers stepped into the shower, the hot water streaming over his head and shoulders, soothing his tired muscles. Ryder had suggested he get a good night's sleep ahead of the meeting. *I need to organise a few things for this blasted court case*, he'd said. *Hopefully, I won't need to give more evidence, but if I do, you'll have more on your plate, so I want you fit.*

Fit? Aside from the case work and the severe exposure he'd experienced today, it was the continuous lack of sleep that was wearing Flowers down. He braced his hands on the wall behind the showerhead and closed his eyes, his chilled body finally beginning to warm up. Once again, his thoughts shifted to Sterling. He needed to ring her later. In all the time she'd been undercover, last night was the only one he'd missed. He hoped she knew it had been their early-morning arrival back in Thredbo that had prevented him from calling, and not because she'd hung up on him the night before.

Straightening up, he raked his hair back with his fingers and reached for the body wash, a fraction of his energy restored. Several minutes later, he turned off the taps, stepped from the shower and dried himself off.

Muscles stiffening up from his trek to Buchanan Hut, and with his core body temperature finally restored, he set his alarm for two hours' time and rolled into bed.

The storm that had raged across the mountains for much of the day had subsided while Flowers was asleep. Still groggy, he dressed in jeans and a hoodie and went into the living room. Beyond the windows, the night was dark and calm. As he pulled the curtains closed, he could hear the snow guns firing in the near distance.

In the kitchen, he put a frozen chicken fettuccine in the microwave and set the kettle to boil. Unable to delay it any longer, he rang Sterling on his way back to the lounge room. It was already 8.15.

'Hi, Mitch,' she said a little hesitantly, and he realised he wasn't the only one who was nervous.

'Hey, Nerida, how are things with you?'

She sighed. 'I don't have anything to report. Heidi wasn't rostered on today, so nothing more has happened there. What about you? I saw the case notes about the possible forged signature.'

'It's just been confirmed as a forgery.' He told her about the meeting scheduled for the morning. 'Sorry I didn't call you last night; I was in the car with Ryder. We didn't get back to Thredbo until three in the morning.'

'I knew where you were. Ryder messaged me.'

'Ah, I should have known he would have given you the heads up.'

'Look, Mitch, I want to apologise,' she said quickly, as though anxious to get the words out.

'For what?'

'For the way I spoke to you. I was so angry—'

'You had every reason to be angry. Anyway, it was my fault. The guy was a dipshit, but I shouldn't have let him get to me.'

'And I shouldn't have hung up like that. You've been so great, checking in with me every night. It was unfair.'

'I'll live, and I'm tougher than I look. I'm right into this mountain stuff now.'

She laughed, sounding more like her normal self. 'Tell me what happened today. The case notes haven't been uploaded yet.'

That was another thing he had to do.

Flowers told her about their visit to Garrett's property and his second trip to Buchanan Hut.

'Ethan Lorrimer and Cate Buchanan,' she said softly. 'Who would have thought?'

'Not me,' Flowers said with a chuckle. 'My chin hit the floor when he stepped out of the dark.'

'I bet.'

'So, what's tomorrow looking like?' he asked after a few moments of silence.

'I'm rostered on for lunch, so I'll probably go for a run in the morning. It's a bit like *Groundhog Day*, really.'

They talked for a few more minutes, and then Flowers said good-night, relieved that she was no longer angry at him. Life wasn't as enjoyable when things were tense between him and Sterling.

In the kitchen, he took his meal from the microwave and carried it over to the computer. He had ten minutes to eat before he was due to sign in.

Thirty-one

Sterling opened her eyes and stared at the blackness, struggling to orient herself for a few seconds before remembering where she was. Rolling over in the dark, she reached out and tapped her phone screen, then propped herself up on one elbow to look at the time. Ten minutes past midnight.

She lay back on the pillows listening for the sound that had woken her, unsure whether the noise had been real or part of a dream. She hated waking in the early hours of the morning when her mind was free of distractions and her tendency to ruminate strong.

The unmistakable sound of shattering glass had her sitting bolt upright and groping for her phone. Was someone breaking into her car? She threw off the covers and went to stand at the window, shifting aside the curtain so she could peer through the narrow slit. The night was clear, and she could see the outline of the carport with the Forrester parked underneath. She could even make out the wooden stairs leading to the porch above. She scanned the street but there were no cars outside or moving shapes in the front yard.

A creak from the floor above.

Sterling stepped away from the window, letting the curtain fall back into place, and waited.

Another creak.

Sterling crept through the darkened room, careful not to trip over anything or make a noise. Crouching in front of the oil heater, she listened to the floorboards creak and groan as someone moved throughout the house. Careful not to make a sound, she removed the fascia and laid it on the carpet. Ever since the phone mix up, she'd taken to putting her personal phone away as soon as she'd finished talking to Mitch.

With the Glock in her hand, and both phones within reach, she went back and sat on the bed, straining to hear more from upstairs. Did they think the house was empty? Were they even aware there was someone in the rumpus room below? Her car was out the front, but if they were used to seeing the owner's caravan and four-wheel drive parked there, and noticed it had been gone for some time, had they decided to take advantage of that now?

She cradled the gun, running through her options. She could sit tight and hope they would assume downstairs was under-house storage and leave without coming down. That would be the best outcome. Her cover wouldn't be blown, and she could pretend to Sergeant Collins that she'd slept through the whole thing.

If they broke in down here, and she needed the gun, that would be the end of her assignment.

She started at a sudden thump. The burglar had knocked into something. She felt guilty that she was sitting tight while an intruder was ransacking the owners' home, and then wondered if it really was a thief or . . . Rodney Garrett?

Sterling's scalp crawled. Garrett knew she lived here. It would be reasonable for him to assume she lived upstairs. Had he become suspicious of her after she'd asked Heidi for the drugs?

She groaned inwardly. She was thinking like a cop, not about how Ida Stevenson, the waitress on a working holiday, would react. Ida would call the police and report the break-in, or perhaps flee to the safety of a friend's place. Sterling had a key to a motel room Ryder had given her. *It's a bolthole should you find yourself needing one.*

Sterling stood up and shoved her feet into her furry, rubber-soled boots, glad that she slept in a tracksuit. Putting the Glock and phones inside her small backpack, she silently zipped it up then set about putting the fascia back on the oil heater. Wrapped in her warm coat, and with her keys her only weapon, she waited at the door and listened, more convinced with every passing minute that any young woman living here would flee rather than confront burglars in the house.

Another creak on the floorboard and she moved, sure now that the intruder was still in the house. Opening the door, she stepped out into the freezing night, every sense on high alert. She locked the studio then moved swiftly through the darkness to the car. The moment she was inside with the door closed she flicked the lock and held her breath as the engine spluttered to life. A flash of light from upstairs as someone came close to the window. Reversing out of the carport, she kept the lights off until she was safely out on the road.

Just before she turned onto the Alpine Way, she pulled over onto the gravel shoulder and unzipped her backpack. Double-checking she'd picked up Ida's phone, she called the Khancoban police station. As she knew it would, the call was diverted to Sergeant Collins' mobile.

'Collins, Khancoban Police,' he said in a gravelly voice.

'Sergeant Collins, it's Ida Stevenson, from the hotel.'

'Yes, Ida, what's the trouble?' he asked.

'Someone's in the house,' she spoke in a deliberately panicky voice. 'They smashed a window, I think. I could hear them walking around upstairs.'

'You're staying in the Johnsons' house, aren't you?'

'Yes. I'm scared it might be Rodney Garrett,' she said. 'He's been watching me lately.'

There was silence at the other end, then, 'Are you sure about that?'

'There was a vicious dog in the front yard when I got home the other night, and then I saw him in my street when I was coming back from my run. He was just standing there watching. The dog was in the back of the ute, and I'm sure it was the same one.'

'All right. I'll drive by and check it out,' he said with a weariness that suggested too many years on the job and too many late call-outs.

'Thank you. I'm really freaked out,' she said. 'I'm going to stay at a girlfriend's place in Jindabyne.'

'Okay.'

'Thank you. I'll phone you in the morning or come and see you.'

'You do that, and drive carefully,' he cautioned. 'That road is dangerous at night.'

Sterling killed the call and put the phone in the bracket on the windscreen. Collins didn't have keys to get into the house, but then neither did she, only to the rumpus room. Still, if a window had been broken to gain access, he shouldn't have any trouble checking out the place.

Sterling turned on the radio, keeping the volume low as she began to drive again. So far so good. There wasn't a single car on the Alpine Way.

She was twenty minutes from Thredbo when Sergeant Collins called. 'I've been around and had a look,' he said. 'They broke the laundry window and got in that way, that's probably what woke you up.'

'I think it was,' Sterling said.

'They left the laundry door unlocked when they left, so I was able to go in. I can't tell whether anything's missing, but they haven't trashed the place. Usually, they're looking for cash, jewellery and electronics. I'll brush the place for fingerprints tomorrow, and get that window fixed. And I'll call the Johnsons, see if they want me to get the locks changed.'

'What about Rodney Garrett?'

'I'll talk to him too.'

'I'm staying in the studio downstairs,' Sterling said. 'Did they break in there?'

'No, I tried that bottom door. It was locked up tight.'

'Oh, thank you, Sergeant,' Sterling said, piling on the gratitude. 'I wanted to do the right thing.'

'Nah, it's all good,' he said amicably. 'Look, this kind of thing isn't out of the ordinary. We have break-ins now and again when people are away on holidays. Even though your car was in the carport, they might have thought it was a neighbour's who'd been given permission to put their car in there.'

'I hope you're right, Sergeant,' Sterling said.

'Anyway, come in and see me at the station later in the day.'

'I will.'

Sterling ended the call. She was ten minutes from Thredbo, climbing up towards Dead Horse Gap. A handful of Snowy Hydro maintenance vehicles had passed her, travelling in the opposite direction, and a logging truck hauling timber had made her think of Ethan Lorrimer. A few minutes later she was at the spot where Flowers had snowshoed down to Buchanan Hut. She'd like to come back here in the summer, to hike the mountain trails, visit the huts and maybe take a small boat out onto the Khancoban pondage.

A sudden longing bloomed inside her, a longing for her normal life, for the squad, for Ryder's solid presence, Benson's joviality, and Brown and O'Day's dry humour.

The soft lights of Thredbo appeared on her left, the physical ache catching her by surprise. Ryder and Vanessa were so close, as were Eva, Jack and Poppy. And Mitch. Sterling slowed down, the thought of an empty motel room in Jindabyne suddenly depressing.

How are you, Sterling? Ryder always asked. *Your mental health is important.*

She was lonely. Despite Ryder telling her numerous times, she hadn't realised the toll it took to work undercover, and of all the things she missed about her real life, she missed Mitchell Flowers the most.

Flowers stood up and moved to the window. The car had come down the snowy dead-end road about a minute ago. He'd heard it idling outside as though the driver was looking for a particular lodge. Then it had moved off slowly, but instead of pulling into an allocated parking space, or heading back up the hill, the driver had pulled in under the deck immediately behind his garage door. Obviously Flowers wasn't going anywhere at two fifteen in the morning—only to bed, and he'd been looking forward to that after another busy night—but he was annoyed because now he was going to have to deal with a late arrival who'd turned up at the wrong apartment.

Unable to see the car, he waited for the driver to appear. A door closed quietly. Footsteps crunched through the snow and then a figure came into view wearing a long puffer jacket with an oversized, fur-lined hood. From the cut of the coat Flowers could tell the driver was a woman. She started up the ramp that led to his apartment, stopping halfway up when the sensor light came on. She looked towards the front door as though checking for the number, and in the wash of light Flowers glimpsed the woman's face and a lock of blonde hair. Sterling!

He froze. What the hell was she doing here? He hurried to turn off the oversized LED monitor, his gaze sweeping anxiously over the expensive headset, the keyboard and mouse, and the professional webcam. The room darkened as the screen switched off, and he waited in nervous apprehension for the sound of the doorbell. She'd obviously come here for a good reason, and he had to let her in. He pushed his hair back from his forehead and held it there. What the hell was she going to think when she saw all this?

Two raps came on the front door.

Flowers swallowed. 'Who is it?' he called.

Silence, then: 'It's me, Mitch.'

The sound of her voice propelled Flowers into action, and he quickly unlocked the door. '*Nerida*,' he said in a low voice, opening it wide enough for her to slip past him into the lounge room. 'What are you doing here? What's wrong?'

'There was an intruder, upstairs in the house.' She slipped her backpack off her shoulder, dumped it on the floor and unzipped her jacket.

'Are you okay?' He hurried over to the table near the lounge and switched on the small lamp. It lit up that side of the room but left his set-up mostly in shadow.

'Well, *I* was okay.' Sterling shrugged off her jacket and dropped it on top of the backpack. 'But I figured Ida Stevenson wouldn't want to stick around while someone knocked off the place.'

'That's true. Sit down.' He waved a hand towards the lounge and sat in one of the armchairs opposite. Any minute now she was going to look around and notice the set-up on the desk and wonder what on earth he was doing.

She sat down, crossed her legs, and looked at him. 'I'm sorry for turning up at this ungodly hour.'

'No problem. As long as you're all good.'

She nodded, glancing at him uncertainly as though she sensed something different about him. Flowers swallowed, his mouth dry.

'I was going to stay in a motel in Jindabyne,' she said. 'Ryder gave me the key to a room he has booked there; in case I needed a bolthole. It's a great idea and I'm glad I have it, but as I was driving past, you and the others were so close, and I've been isolated for so long . . .'

Flowers moved to sit beside her on the lounge. 'Hey,' he said, putting an arm around her shoulders and giving her a comforting squeeze. 'It's okay.'

She sighed. 'I know I shouldn't have come here. I needed to see a friendly face and I gave in to the temptation.'

He nodded. 'You've been undercover for a while now, and someone breaking into the place is a real worry.'

She leaned into him a little. He patted her shoulder, careful to keep the embrace impersonal, like he would with anyone in need of comfort. After that one night together she'd made it clear he shouldn't hope for more between them, and he'd taken her at her word. Flowers steeled himself. It wasn't easy, but if she could play Ida Stevenson for all that time, he could play 'good friend only' when she needed him to.

Sterling slowly straightened up, and he took his arm away. Any minute now she was going to look around.

But instead she looked at him and said, 'I'm sorry if I'm giving you mixed messages.'

187

Flowers frowned. 'You've always been straight up with me.' *Unlike me with you.* 'I know how hard you worked to make Ryder's squad, and I understand that you want to stay there.'

She nodded. 'It's usually the woman who gets thrown under the bus when there's any kind of work conflict.'

'Things need to change then.'

'They do.'

Flowers ran a hand up and down his jaw. 'I don't want you to feel bad about that night. What's the big deal, anyway? We kicked on after the others had left and one thing led to another. We were in a celebratory mood.'

'That's a nice way of saying we were on the way to getting hammered,' Sterling said with a laugh.

At any other time Flowers would have felt great having her rock up at his door unexpectedly like this. But he was on edge, his heartbeat quickening every time she turned her head.

When she sobered, he asked, 'Did you phone Collins and tell him about the break-in?'

'Yes, he's already checked it out. I'm going to see him tomorrow when I get back. I told him I was freaked out and going to stay with a girlfriend.'

'Anyone on the road?'

She shook her head. 'Hardly anyone.'

Flowers looked at his watch. 'It's two-thirty. Let's call Ryder at six o'clock and ask him to come over.'

'I think that's a good idea.' She stood up suddenly and looked down at him. 'Do you mind if I make a cup of tea?'

Flowers scrambled to his feet. 'I'll make it. You sit down.'

'No, I'll do it. Is the kitchen this way?' she asked, turning directly towards the desk against the wall. Flowers stopped and, as he knew she would, she swung around, the laughter gone, a watchful expression on her face. 'What's all the gear for?'

Thirty-two

Flowers waved a dismissive hand. 'Oh, it's just some extra stuff I'm doing after hours.'

'What extra stuff?'

'It's not important. Don't worry about it.'

'Is this to do with the case?'

Oh man, she was insistent. 'I'm not trawling through the dark web if that's what you're thinking,' he said a little defensively. 'I'm playing a game, though there's a bit more to it than that.'

'Is that why you're always up so late?' she asked, running her eyes over the equipment.

He nodded. 'That's when it all happens in the Northern Hemisphere.'

Sterling shook her head and stared at the expensive set-up. 'And you brought all this with you?'

'It's actually pretty compact once it's tidied up, except for the monitor. I just pack it in the boot and throw a blanket over it. I had it with me in Queanbeyan when I was there for that court case, before I was sent here.'

'I just toss a novel in my backpack,' she said with a smile.

Flowers relaxed a little. 'I've never been much of a reader, and growing up on the coast, most of my mates were surfers, but with this skin, it was burn, peel, burn and peel again.'

'All that Celtic colouring.'

'That's it.'

'So do you play against other people online?' she asked. 'Is that the reason for the big camera?'

'Yep.'

'Are you addicted? You said there was more to it.' She looked right at him, and Flowers could tell she was keen to know more. Sterling was a good cop. She knew how to ask the right questions.

'I'm not addicted.' He took a deep breath. 'I'm good at it. I've actually accepted a job offer, testing games for one of the big companies in Japan.'

Sterling's eyebrows shot up. '*What?*'

'Yeah. Pretty crazy, hey?'

'Are you leaving the force?'

'I am. That's why I've been staying up so late. I had to do all these exercises where they tested my skills, and now I'm doing the in-house training.'

For a while Sterling just stared at him, and he could tell how shocked she was. 'Does Ryder know?' she said eventually.

Flowers shook his head. 'He thinks that old concussion is giving me headaches, but it's just the intense concentration.'

'And lack of sleep.'

'Yeah, that too.'

She continued to scrutinise him intently, as if she was seeing him for the first time. 'So, what does the job involve?'

Flowers raked his hair back from his forehead and glanced at the desk. 'I have to look for flaws in the game, mark down which sections are too easy so they can make them harder; note if there's an audio noise coming in at the wrong time or from the wrong direction, those sorts of things. Quality assurance, I guess. This all happens while the game is still in the development stage.'

Sterling was shaking her head. 'I didn't even know that job existed.'

'Yeah, it's pretty cool that I can earn money doing something I love. The money is really good too.' Flowers looked down and flexed his fingers. 'I'd still like to be a police prosecutor one day, but there's plenty of time for that later. I want to take this opportunity now, before my fine motor skills slow down.'

'That is fantastic,' she said, and he could tell by the warmth in her eyes that she was genuinely excited for him. 'You're a dark horse, Mitchell Flowers. But, come to think of it, you *do* whip everyone's butt at target practice.'

'And to think I haven't discharged my weapon in the line of duty yet . . . Not that I want to.'

Sterling looked back at the equipment and shook her head again.

'Would you like to see it?' Flowers asked, keen for her to know more about it now his secret was out. 'We've got three hours to kill before we have to ring Ryder.'

'Yeah, that'd be mad,' she said, following him over to the desk and watching while he switched everything on. 'This is so cool. Am I the only one who knows about it?' she asked excitedly.

'You and my family.' Flowers shifted a chair next to the one he was using and sat down. He touched the mouse, and the oversized LED monitor sprang to life.

'Wow! Look at the colour.'

Buoyed by her excitement, Flowers picked up his headset. 'Hold still,' he said, careful not to pull her hair as he placed the cushioned headphones over her ears. He turned back to the monitor. 'Now, this is a first-person shooter game,' he said, knowing she'd be listening to the rousing symphonic score coming through the headphones. 'This is the one I'm testing now, and we're on the side of the law, so we are the *good guys,* just like in real life.'

She nodded enthusiastically.

'Can you hear me over the music?' he asked.

She gave him the double thumbs up, blue eyes shining.

'Okay then.' Flowers showed her which character he'd chosen, and the weapons he had at his disposal. 'As I move though this historic building, which has multiple floors and balconies, bad guys will come at me from everywhere. I'll start the game and we'll choose to do level five,' he said.

191

The game began and Flowers pointed to his character. 'Okay, here I am walking through this room and someone's going to come out from behind that wall real soon. There he is!' He shot the enemy and moved on, already looking for the next one. 'Around this corner, we'll see a guy on the staircase. There!' he said, glancing across at Sterling before he shot the guy.

Flowers worked the mouse and keyboard simultaneously, striking deftly at the keys, his eyes focused on the screen. He'd played this game so many times he could imagine the music and audio effects that Sterling would be hearing through the headset. He played for another five minutes, pointing out distinctive features along the way.

'Watch this,' he said, glancing over at her before taking down five enemy soldiers in a row. 'Bam!' he said, and then exited the game before he really started showing off. It was a lot of stimulation for someone who'd never played video games before.

'You're amazing,' Sterling said, taking off the headphones and handing them back to him. 'I don't know much about gaming but even I can see you're pretty pro.'

'Thanks.'

'How did they find you?'

'From my gamer handle. I've competed for years.'

'I've seen the stadiums packed out with people watching gaming competitions.'

'Oh, that's the league. Those guys are really young, in their late teens. This would be all desk work for me.'

She put her hand over her mouth to hide a yawn. 'That's incredible. I'm still kind of stunned.'

'Go and lie down in my room, Nerida. I'll put my alarm on for six. I'll stretch out on the lounge.'

'Are you sure? I just hit the wall all of a sudden.'

'I'm surprised you've lasted this long. The bedroom's at the end of the corridor, the bathroom's on the right.'

'Thank you,' she said, though she made no attempt to move. She hesitated for a moment, then said, 'You have to tell Ryder.'

'I know I do, but not yet.'

'Are you worried how he'll react?'

Flowers had already thought about this long and hard. 'Not really. I think he'll understand why I'm doing it. I just don't see any point in telling him before I need to. In the meantime, I'm working my butt off trying to help him clear as much of his caseload as I can before he goes.' As Sterling released another yawn he took hold of her shoulders and turned her around. 'Go.'

'Thank you.' She picked up her coat and backpack from the floor and wandered off down the hallway. It was then he remembered she'd been going to make a cup of tea before getting distracted by all the computer gear.

Hearing her go into the bathroom, he hurried to the kitchen to boil the kettle.

It seemed no sooner had Flowers closed his eyes that his phone alarm went off, the annoyingly cheerful ringtone jolting him awake. Hanging an arm over the side of the lounge, he picked up his phone and turned off the alarm. 5.45 am.

Still dressed in yesterday's clothes, he stood up, stretched and then walked down the hallway to his bedroom. Nerida was curled up under her coat, her blonde hair spread out on his pillow. She was sleeping so peacefully it seemed criminal to wake her, but they had to ring Ryder and they needed to be ready by the time he got here.

He picked up the empty teacup from the bedside table and shook her gently by the shoulder. 'Nerida.'

She woke up straight away, turning quickly to look at him before relaxing back on the pillow when she remembered where she was.

'It's only me,' he said. 'It's almost six.'

He heard her take a two-minute shower and eight minutes later, as he was unplugging the cords and cables from his computer, she walked into the living room. 'I'm putting this in the bedroom,' he said.

She nodded. 'I'll help.'

For the next five minutes they wound up cords and carried all the components of his system into the bedroom. 'I'll just put everything in the bottom of the wardrobe. I was originally going to set it all up in here but the wi-fi is marginally stronger out there.'

'I'm sorry,' Sterling said, as Flowers closed the wardrobe doors. 'If I'd gone into Jindabyne like I'd planned, you wouldn't have had to do all this.'

'Don't worry about that,' he said. 'I enjoyed having you here. I can set that up again in about five minutes.'

'Great. Now I know who to call when I have tech problems.'

He smiled and checked his watch. 'It's just gone six. We should call Ryder now.'

'Mitch,' she said, before he had time to bring up Ryder's contact in his phone. 'I'll keep your secret for as long as you need me to. You can trust me.'

'I know I can.' He shouldn't have doubted her, shouldn't have worried about her finding out about a part of his life he hadn't shared with anyone at work. But he had worried, knowing she was all about the force.

'I missed you,' she said simply. 'That's why I came here. I had no idea how much I was going to miss you.'

He reached out and touched her cheek. 'I missed you too. But you already knew that.'

Thirty-three

'I'm glad you told Sergeant Collins about Garrett,' Ryder said to Sterling when he arrived. 'If he's been messing with you, a stern word from Collins might make him pull his head in.'

'What if his behaviour escalates?' said Flowers.

'I'll be on the lookout for that, don't worry,' said Sterling. 'Collins is brushing for prints. Surely he'll run a match with the prints on Garrett's record, particularly as I've singled him out.'

Ryder stood up and paced back and forth in Flowers' living room. 'He should, and we're going to have to leave it up to him to do it, otherwise we'll blow your cover.' He looked at Sterling who was sitting on the lounge beside Flowers. 'Any problems on the way here?'

She shook her head. 'I didn't run because I was scared, Sarge. I ran because I decided that's what Ida would have done.'

Ryder nodded. 'You need to make your own decisions and trust your intuition when you're undercover, because you don't have anyone else to rely on. And you did that.' Ryder hesitated. This was the bit he was unsure of. 'Is there any particular reason why you chose to come here?'

Sterling glanced at Flowers, and Ryder's mind began to race. Was there something going on here that he needed to know about?

'It was impulsive, Sarge,' Sterling said. 'I was heading to the motel room in Jindabyne, but when I reached the turnoff into Thredbo and you were all so close, I couldn't resist. I didn't go to the Golden Wattle because Eva has guests there as well as you guys. I knew Flowers was on his own; we've been catching up each night as you know.'

Flowers nodded, his expression serious. 'That's been working well. I've been able to fill in the gaps for her that aren't always in the case notes.'

Sterling gave Flowers a grateful smile then looked at Ryder. 'I think I needed to talk to someone from my real life, Sarge, and Flowers was the closest, and he's the one I know best. I've seen you at our meetings, but that's different, we're on limited time.'

'How do you feel now?' Ryder asked.

'Better.' She looked him straight in the eye. 'Honestly, I feel better.'

'Ready to go back?'

'Yes, I want to see this out.'

'In that case, let's get you out of here before people start to wake up.'

Thirty-four

'Sterling's back in Khancoban,' Ryder said, looking at his phone as they walked towards the offices of Thomas and Associates. 'A message just came through.'

'That's good,' said Flowers.

Ryder glanced at his partner. He'd been quiet during the forty-minute trip from Thredbo to Cooma. 'She did the right thing coming to see you.'

Flowers hesitated, his hand on the door of the legal office, and looked at Ryder. 'Despite the risks?'

'Yes, she recognised she needed to do something for her own wellbeing. That's healthier than ignoring it.'

Flowers nodded and opened the door, and they climbed the stairs to the first floor.

The Lorrimer brothers were in the reception area. Ethan nodded from the other side of the room where he was casually flicking through a magazine. Dan stood up immediately and made a beeline for Ryder.

'Detective, are you any closer to finding out who put the tractor on the runway? We're all looking over our shoulders at the moment.'

'I can assure you we're doing everything we can to find out.'

Dan nodded and glanced towards the stairs. 'Heidi didn't come home last night, and we haven't been able to get hold of her. We've left her several messages. Hopefully, she just hasn't bothered to respond and will turn up anyway.'

Ryder looked around as Jeremy Thomas came into the reception area and beckoned them into the conference room. 'That's unfortunate,' he told Dan, 'but I think it's more important that the two of you are here.'

Dan and Ethan glanced at each other as they filed in and took seats around the table. Ryder put his phone in the middle and asked for permission to record. Flowers took out his notepad and pen.

'We appreciate your cooperation in allowing us to speak to Mr Thomas about the legal structure the family has in place,' Ryder began. 'During our discussions, Mr Thomas mentioned that around three weeks ago, a lawyer acting for your brother, Art, emailed this office and requested a copy of the family trust deed.'

Dan Lorrimer frowned. Ethan's eyes narrowed.

'Did you send a copy?' Dan asked, turning towards Thomas.

Thomas turned a silver pen over in his hands. 'I did. I was required to.'

'Why didn't we know about this, Jeremy?' Ethan asked.

'I act for the family, Ethan, and that included Art. I acted on his instructions the same way I'd act on yours.'

'But it had been so long since we'd heard from him, I assumed you would let us know.' Dan gave a disappointed shake of his head.

A tense silence ensued. Ryder wondered how long Thomas and Associates would continue to represent the Lorrimer family.

'The lawyer acting on Art's instructions gained the impression your brother had never agreed to the sale of White Winter Station,' said Ryder, 'and yet Mr Thomas holds a document that appears to have been signed by all four of you two years ago.'

Thomas put down his pen. Dan was staring straight ahead at the wall. Ethan shifted in his seat.

Ryder turned to Jeremy Thomas. 'Could we see your copy?'

'Yes, sure.' Thomas opened the file, located the form and put it on the table.

Flowers picked it up and handed it to Dan. 'Can you both confirm that these are your signatures?'

They both looked at the page, then nodded and said yes.

'Where were Heidi and Art when they signed the form?' Ryder asked.

'Heidi signed it at home, and we emailed it to Art.'

Ryder looked at both brothers. 'Well, this is where we have a problem,' he said. 'We've had Art's signature on this agreement compared to another document he signed, and it's been confirmed by our analyst that the signature on this document is not your brother's.'

The room turned silent, save for the sound of reversing sensors coming from the street below.

Ryder waited. In the end, Dan looked at his brother. Ethan gave a slight nod.

'Oh, look, we were all in a bind because of Art,' Dan said. 'He'd taken off and it was always difficult to contact him. We emailed him the form. He rang, all fired up, and said he wouldn't sign. He said his share of the property was his superannuation, and that if the people he owed money to found out the property was to be sold, they'd come after him and try to extract it.'

Ethan nodded. 'He's always been the hothead, and we've often had to talk common sense into him.'

'So, the reason for Art's objection was to keep his money out of the hands of the same people who used to come looking for him?' said Flowers.

Dan nodded. 'Yes, but we think his objection came from a lack of understanding of how the trust worked, rather than any genuine desire to hold on to the property. Ethan and I have always managed the finances, Heidi and Art never took an interest. We didn't think that Art fully understood.'

'Understood what?' said Flowers.

'That even if we sold the property, his share could stay safely within the trust, for as long as he wanted it to.'

There was a pause in the conversation, and then Ethan spoke.

'I'll admit, we were pretty confident that when the time came for another conversation with him, that we'd be able to talk him around, and that he'd understand. The developer was threatening to withdraw his offer, but it was an opportunity that the family couldn't pass up.'

Dan nodded. 'We were under intense pressure, so I signed for him, and sent it back to Jeremy.'

'Then you two signed the contract with Temple Developments?' said Flowers.

'Yes,' said Ethan, 'but that's perfectly fine. We're both directors of the company.'

Dan rested his elbows on the table and clasped his hands. 'Look, we were never going to do anything but liquidate the property and make it easier for everyone to take their share and live their separate lives.'

Ethan stared at Ryder. 'Surely you don't seriously suspect any of us of murdering our brother?'

'Nothing's been discounted,' said Ryder. 'It's a line of enquiry that's part of the ongoing investigation into your brother's death.'

Dan turned to his lawyer. 'Jeremy, are there any repercussions from what you now know?'

The lawyer, who'd been silent the whole time, stroked his beard and contemplated Dan's question. 'There doesn't appear to be financial loss to anyone arising from your actions. The money is still there, but your suitability to continue as directors of the company could be brought into doubt should a complaint be made by an interested party.'

Ryder pushed back his chair and stood up. Beside him, Flowers was pocketing his notepad and pen. 'Well, that's a civil matter, it doesn't involve us.' Ryder leaned over and picked up his phone, switching off the recording. 'Thank you,' he said with a nod at the other men.

When they reached the car, Flowers stopped and looked at Ryder across the bonnet. 'What interested party is Thomas talking about? Only the family is involved in this.'

Ryder looked back towards the building on the corner. 'Exactly. Nothing is going to happen there.'

Thirty-five

Sterling locked the Forrester, straightened her work clothes and walked towards the entrance to the Khancoban police station. Before leaving home, she'd phoned ahead to make sure Sergeant Collins was in.

She pushed open the door and stepped into the waiting room. Though tiny compared to the Parramatta station where she normally worked, a wave of something akin to homesickness washed over her at the familiar working environment.

Sergeant Collins stood behind the counter directly in front of her, an imperceptible crackle of voices coming from the police radio.

'Here you are,' he said. 'Come through.' He led the way down a short hallway then stopped to let her go ahead of him into a room on the right. 'Take a seat,' he said, coming around the desk and sitting down heavily.

Sterling perched on the edge of an upright chair. It felt bizarre being on this side of the desk.

'Did you manage to get any sleep?' he asked, peering at her.

'A little,' she said.

'I haven't been up to the house to brush for prints yet. It's been one thing after another this morning.' Collins looked at his watch. 'I'm going to head up there in about ten minutes; Orville Parish is coming around after I've finished to put a bit of plywood over the broken window until we can get it fixed.'

Sterling nodded. 'Do you have any idea who broke in?'

'No, not yet. As I said on the phone, this happens from time to time, especially if people think the property is empty. It could have been someone looking to squat there. We've had that happen. Now, what's your full name?'

'Ida Stevenson, with a "v", not a "ph".'

'Okay. I've got your telephone number from when you called me and I know the address.' Collins put down the pen and looked at her. 'That's all I need for now.'

Sterling frowned. 'What about Rodney Garrett? Have you spoken to him about the complaint I made?'

Collins took a long, hard look at her, long enough to make Sterling nervous. 'This is about you seeing him in your street?' He gave her a dubious look. 'Have you seen the size of this town? We're always running into each other here.'

'So, did you speak to him?' she asked, again reminding herself not to sound too cop-like.

'Yeah, I spoke to him.' Sergeant Collins looked at her as if he was seeing her through fresh eyes and didn't quite like what he saw. 'He said he was nowhere near your place last night, and he also told me something else that I found interesting.'

Get to the point, Collins, Sterling thought. Whatever it was, it wasn't going to be good.

'He told me you're a user, that you asked Heidi Lorrimer for drugs at the hotel. Is that right?'

Shit! Garrett had turned this around onto her. Sterling looked at Collins across the desk, at the light reflecting off his bald head and his bushy porn-star moustache. Should she come clean and reveal who she was? What if Collins was bent? He'd been stationed up here for decades, and yet when Ryder had been investigating Scruffy Freidman's death, Collins had denied any knowledge of a crime syndicate operating in the area. Maybe he was on their payroll. Paid to look the other way.

'Yes, I did ask,' she said, trying her hardest to look contrite.

'Hmm. Well, I suggest you take a good, hard look at yourself before pointing the finger at other people.' He stood up. 'Now, I'll type up a statement of what you've told me, and I'll get you back in here so you can check it before you sign, okay?' He turned around and grabbed his hat from the top of the filing cabinet. 'And I'll be watching you, Ida.'

Thirty-six

Ryder and Flowers decided to drive past Rodney Garrett's place on their way back to Thredbo. They parked the unmarked four-wheel drive halfway down the dead-end road. From where they sat, they had a clear view of the house, but so far the only sign of movement had come from the dogs guarding the perimeter.

'Every time I feel like we're tightening the net around the Lorrimers, they give us answers that make sense,' Flowers said, his elbow resting on the centre console. 'We knew it would be Dan or Ethan who had forged Art's signature, and after hearing their reasons, I can understand why.'

Ryder nodded. 'They might not have acted ethically, but they didn't try to embezzle him out of his money. The money's still there. They haven't committed a crime just because they want their share. The sale of the property hasn't even settled.'

'Yeah, it sounds to me like they've been doing their best to deal with a difficult brother who's only ever thought of himself.'

'Ethan gave me that impression the first time we met him. Dan was defending Art's reasons for leaving, but Ethan sounded fed up.'

'And they planned on talking to him again, and felt he'd be okay with it once he had all the facts. Sounds to me like he was the type to go off half-cocked.' Flowers shook his head. 'There's one in every family, isn't there?'

'Yep. Your mother was saying that to me the other day.'

Flowers gave a short laugh. 'Okay, I know I'm having a whinge. I just hate sitting around like this.'

'For God's sake, ring Garrett again, and if you can't get on to him, call Heidi.'

Five minutes later, after Flowers had left a message asking for Garrett to present himself at Jindabyne police station, he started the car, drove to the end of the road, and swung slowly around in front of the house. The dogs stilled and stood looking at the car.

Flowers' phone rang.

'Here we go,' he said, reaching for the phone and putting it on speaker. 'Detective Flowers speaking.' He held his breath, waiting.

'It's Orville Parish here.'

Flowers' hopes plummeted. 'Yes, Orville. How are you?'

'Oh, I can't complain. Listen, I've been thinking about that tractor key. I don't know whether this is significant or not, but I thought I'd better tell you.'

'Okay, go on.'

'Well, there was a day, a long time ago now, when I turned up to cut the grass at the airport and Ben couldn't find the tractor key. It hadn't been put away in the drawer, and he was looking everywhere for it. After he'd been searching for about ten minutes, I said that I'd go home, and he could ring me when he found it. And that's when he said, "Look, it's no big deal if we can't find it, Dan has a spare key at his place."'

'He meant Dan Lorrimer?' Flowers said, glancing at Ryder.

'That's who I thought he meant. They're good mates.'

'So, what happened then?'

'I hung around a bit longer. One of the other pilots had turned up by then and not long afterwards they found the key. We didn't need the spare. As I said, it might be nothing . . .'

'Thanks very much for that information, Orville. You did the right thing telling us. We'll follow it up now.'

'Don't get me wrong, I don't like saying anything about Ben,' Orville went on before Flowers could hang up. 'He can be a bit disorganised, but he's a good bloke.'

They said goodbye and Flowers turned and looked at Ryder. 'Well, that's a turn-up. I wasn't expecting that.'

'Neither was I,' said Ryder. 'C'mon, let's get going.'

They made good time and arrived in Khancoban just before one. The airport was back in operation, a small plane Flowers hadn't seen before parked close to the shed. They found Ben Hoff standing at the copier, watching sheets slide into the collator.

'Hello,' he said, pausing the machine and waving a hand towards the table where Flowers had sat with Zane Alam and Sergeant Collins the morning of the crash. To Flowers, Hoff looked as if he was coming down with something; his lanky frame seemed thinner, his face drawn and his eyes tired.

'Are you feeling okay, Ben?' Flowers asked. 'You're looking a little dusty.'

'I'm fine.'

They sat down and Ryder held up his phone and asked for the usual permissions. Hoff agreed, then they waited as Ryder ran through the preliminaries.

'How well do you know Dan Lorrimer?' Flowers asked when they were set to go.

'I know Dan really well,' Hoff said, his eyes flitting between Flowers and Ryder. 'We've been good mates since primary school. Why?'

'How often do you see each other now?'

Hoff shrugged. 'Not as often as we used to. We both have families and commitments. We try to catch up for a beer and dinner when we can.'

Flowers nodded and told him what Orville Parish had said about the misplaced tractor key. 'Do you recall that particular day?'

Hoff frowned as though he was thinking back.

'Do you remember that day or not?' prompted Flowers, reluctant to give him too much time to frame an answer.

'Not really, but if Orville said it happened . . .'

'He remembers it clearly. He said you told him it was no big deal, that Dan had a spare. Was the Dan you were referring to Dan Lorrimer?'

'It would have been. I'm not friends with any other Dan.'

Flowers bit back his frustration at Hoff's constraint. 'Does Dan Lorrimer have a spare key to the tractor?'

Hoff shifted in his seat. 'I don't know if he still has it.'

'Why did he have the spare in the first place?'

Hoff looked as if he was going to be physically sick. 'I hate this. I feel like I'm dobbing in a good mate.'

Flowers leaned forward, excited for what they were about to learn. 'Just tell us,' Ryder said.

There was another lengthy silence while Hoff gathered his thoughts. 'Ten years ago, I bought that tractor from Dan Lorrimer. We were having a beer, and he said he was looking at upgrading the one he had. I was after a second-hand one for here. Our ride-on mower was on its last legs, so I asked him what he wanted for it.' Hoff raked his hair back with his fingers then shook his head. 'He gave me a price, and I bought it.'

He hesitated, and Flowers waited, wondering what was coming next.

'The thing is, I'm pretty absent-minded. I'm always losing my sunglasses and misplacing little things, you know, like the automatic buttons for those roller doors. It drives my wife mad. She reckons I need a handbag. I lose stuff—wallets, keys, you name it. That's me.' Hoff gazed outside to the airstrip where green shoots were sprouting through the patch of burnt grass, then he looked back at the policemen.

'So, when Dan delivered the tractor, he gave me two keys. Knowing what I'm like, I asked him if he'd hold on to one as a spare for me. Now, in all the time we've had the tractor, not once have I needed that spare key, which must be some kind of record. But that's because it's always in the drawer, and I'm not carrying it around with a whole lot of other stuff.'

'I remember asking you if that was the only key you had,' said Flowers, 'and you confirmed that it was. Then Detective Ryder and

I made it clear that we were looking for people in the area who owned similar models. Are you saying that the spare key you'd given Dan Lorrimer didn't cross your mind?'

Hoff shook his head. 'It's been worrying the hell out of me. Art had been away from this place for so long, and then the one night he flies in after dark, the family's old tractor is blocking the runway. I didn't want to think about who might have done it. I was hoping it was kids.'

Hoff sat back in his chair looking relieved that he'd finally unburdened himself of the information. 'I'm not sure if Dan even has the other key now. For a while, I thought about going there and asking him if he realised how it looked, or if he even remembered me asking him to look after the spare key. But I couldn't bring myself to do it. And I want to make it clear that not for one minute do I believe Dan Lorrimer had anything to do with his brother's death.'

'And yet you said you've been worrying yourself sick about it?' said Ryder.

'I know Dan, but I don't know the rest of his family that well. And as Detective Flowers said, anyone with a similar tractor could have started it. I'm hoping it's an awful coincidence that it was their old tractor in the way.'

There was another pause, then Hoff spoke again. 'Will I be charged for withholding information?'

Flowers looked at Ryder, who leaned over and turned off the recording. 'We'll get this statement typed up, then you can look over it and decide if anything needs changing before you sign.'

Hoff nodded, his face pale, and they all stood up.

Outside, Ryder and Flowers hurried to the car, which was parked on the other side of the gates where the crowd had gathered that first morning.

'We're only thirty-five minutes from White Winter Station,' Ryder said. 'Give Dan Lorrimer a call and see if they're back at the property yet.'

'Yes, Sarge.' Flowers tossed Ryder the car keys.

'Oh, and Flowers? If they *are* there, tell them not to leave.'

Thirty-seven

The lunch shift at the hotel was slow, with only a handful of tables occupied. Elijah had retreated to his office to do paperwork, leaving Sterling alone behind the bar with her thoughts.

Sergeant Collins had dismissed her complaint against Garrett simply because Garrett had told him that she'd asked Heidi for drugs. Presumably he now thought she wasn't trustworthy in any respect. So, the only way to change Sergeant Collins' mind was to reveal her true identity, but she needed to check with Ryder before she did that.

Sterling turned around and began organising the bottles of spirits on the shelf behind the bar. She had to admit she was a little nervous. Heidi was coming in to work the next shift, and Sterling wondered if Garrett would be with her. She checked her watch. She'd know soon enough. Only twenty minutes to go.

Reaching up, she turned a bottle of gin forty-five degrees so its label was facing outwards, thoughts of Flowers worming their way into her mind. His revelation in the early hours of the morning still had her head spinning. He was her biggest ally in the squad, and while a part of her was sad he was moving on, she couldn't deny the sense of anticipation she felt about what it might mean for their relationship. The chance that she and Flowers might be able to freely explore their feelings for each other meant that even

Rodney Garrett, and the shitty conversation she'd had with Sergeant Collins, couldn't dampen her excitement.

'Ida.'

Sterling turned around to see Elijah. 'Yes?'

'Could you leave that, and come into the office, please?' Without waiting for a reply, he turned around and headed back down the corridor.

Sterling frowned and, wiping her damp hands down the side of her jeans, followed him. The door to his office stood open.

'Come in.'

Oh no, she thought, closing the door behind her. Had he learned she'd been in here the other day, going through his papers when she'd been searching for his phone number? For the second time that day she perched on the edge of the visitor's chair, wondering just what he knew.

'I had a call from Sergeant Collins this morning. He said you'd been up at the station.'

Sterling nodded. 'I had a break-in at my place last night.'

Elijah frowned. 'He didn't mention a break-in, but he felt I should know that you were trying to procure drugs here, while you've been working in the hotel.'

Shit! She hadn't expected Collins to do that. She should have told him who she really was.

'Did you?' Elijah asked, his kind eyes full of disappointment.

Sterling's mind raced. The Ramshead was a great establishment. Elijah was a decent guy. No way was he involved in a drug ring. Determined not to make the same mistake as she had with Collins, Sterling licked her lips.

'Not exactly—'

Elijah raised both hands as if to cut off her excuse, cementing Sterling's belief that he had zero tolerance for drugs. 'Just answer the question: did you tell Heidi you were looking for drugs?'

'Yes, but—'

'I'm sorry, I have to let you go, Ida,' he said. 'I can't have you bringing this hotel into disrepute. The place will get a bad name and I'll lose business. I can't take the risk of you having access to money either. I'm sorry.' He pulled open a drawer and took out an envelope.

Sterling's heart sank, guessing what was inside. Elijah had already made up his mind before he'd asked to speak with her.

'That's the money I owe you, including for today's shift. I think it's better if you leave right away.'

'Just let me say something—'

This time Elijah stood up. 'You're a great worker, and we got on so well together. I can't tell you how disappointed I am.'

Sterling's heart ached for causing this lovely guy pain. Despite being undercover and playing a role, it still hurt deeply having Elijah think badly of her. But she had to accept that it was all over now. She couldn't stay undercover if she lost her job.

'Elijah, listen to me. My real name is Nerida Sterling. I'm a detective with the Sydney Homicide Squad, currently undercover in Khancoban investigating the murder of Scruffy Freidman and Arthur Lorrimer.'

Elijah's mouth fell open and he stared at her in amazement. Then he walked over to the door and yanked it open. 'Do you have any idea how ridiculous that sounds?'

Thirty-eight

Ryder and Flowers had time to kill after parking the car at White Winter Station. The Lorrimer brothers were still on their way home; they'd stayed in Cooma to talk to Thomas following the meeting that morning.

'Kristin's at home,' Dan had told Flowers. 'I'll call her and tell her to expect you.'

'Would you mind if we had a look around the grounds?' Flowers had asked.

'You can look at anything you want, Detective, just don't let our cattle out.'

Now, as Flowers and Ryder walked towards the high hedges surrounding the cemetery, they could see Kristin standing at the top of the verandah steps. Flowers raised a hand in greeting. She gave a half-hearted wave before turning and going back inside the house.

When they rounded the end of the hedge, the cemetery opened up in front of them, the air cooler in the shade cast by the old jacarandas.

'Wow,' said Flowers, heading for the white angel headstone which was the centrepiece of the graveyard. 'This is bigger than I thought it would be.'

'Herbert Charles Buchanan, born 1842, died 1907, sixty-five years,' read Ryder.

Flowers nodded. 'Yes, that's Wendy Buchanan's great-great-grandfather. He discovered gold in Kiandra and bought this land,' said Flowers, looking at the intricately carved angel's wings.

'There's his wife's grave.' Ryder pointed to a smaller, more conventional arch-shaped headstone. 'There's an infant child's beside hers. It's the same date of death. She obviously died in childbirth.'

Flowers moved on to a pedestal-shaped headstone made of sandstone. 'James Buchanan,' said Flowers. 'He's Herbert's son. Cate told me he added to the landholdings here.'

'This one looks more modern, it's made of terrazzo,' said Ryder, pointing to a box-shaped headstone with a chunky cross on the top.

'That's Henry Buchanan.' Flowers moved to stand beside Ryder. 'He's Wendy's father and Cate and Lewis' grandfather.' This time Flowers read out the words engraved on the headstone. 'Henry Buchanan, born 1917, died 1954, thirty-seven years.'

'Wasn't Henry the one who lost the snow lease?' asked Ryder.

Flowers nodded. 'He was never the same after the war, apparently. He's the last Buchanan buried on this land.' Flowers looked at the grave, trying to imagine how Henry's wife would have felt, visiting her late husband's grave on the family property she been forced to sell. And then the later blow when Mrs Lorrimer, wife of the Sydney brewer's son and mother of the four Lorrimer children, had banned the Buchanans from visiting at all.

'You can see where Ethan has been tidying up,' said Ryder, wandering around the remaining headstones. James Buchanan had married again after the death of his first wife. Both wives' headstones were located close to his grave. 'It's very overgrown towards the back.'

Flowers nodded. 'I can understand Ethan wanting to clean it up before Cate sees it, and I totally get why the Buchanans would want the allotment with the house and cemetery. There's a lot of history here.'

'I didn't realise you were such an historian,' said Ryder.

'I'm not usually. But I don't know, there's something about this whole area. The mountains, the alpine huts, the snow leases and this grazing land.'

'Man from Snowy River country,' Ryder said as they turned and began retracing their steps. 'Jack Riley's grave is just across the border in Corryong if you want to visit that one too.'

'Settle down,' Flowers said as they skirted around the hedge and headed back to the driveway. 'I'm just curious about this one because Cate told me the family history, and I've seen the sketches.'

As they began walking towards the front steps, Kristin Lorrimer came back out onto the verandah to greet them. When they reached the top, a car was winding its way down the hill towards the homestead.

They gathered on the verandah and it was obvious from Dan and Ethan's concerned expressions that they were expecting un-pleasant news.

Flowers turned to Kristin first. 'Has your sister-in-law been home today?' he asked, taking out his notepad and pen.

Kristin shook her head. 'I haven't seen Heidi for the last few days. Dan told me she was supposed to be at the meeting with you this morning.'

'We haven't been able to contact her,' Ryder said, watching as Flowers took a seat so it was easier for him to take notes. Everyone else remained standing. 'We'll call in to the hotel on our way back and see if we can catch her there.'

Ethan stood, his hands braced on the back of a cane chair. 'It's unusual to see you twice in one day,' he said, clearly keen to get things underway.

'We were in Khancoban,' Ryder said. 'We've just taken a state-ment from Ben Hoff.' He shifted his gaze to Dan. The eldest Lorrimer sibling was standing with his arms folded, his back against the wooden verandah railing. 'We understand you know Ben.'

Dan nodded. 'Yes, we grew up together.'

'Would you regard him as a close friend?' Ryder asked.

Dan hesitated a little. 'Yes, I would.'

'Do you recall him buying a tractor from you some time ago?' Ryder asked.

'Some time ago?' Dan mused, looking confused. 'I remember selling him a tractor ten or twelve *years* ago.'

'From our enquiries, we know that the tractor you sold to Mr Hoff was the same one driven onto the runway the night your brother flew in,' Ryder said.

Dan's eyebrows shot up. 'Was it?'

'You didn't think that was strange?' asked Ryder.

'No, why would I? I never fly out of Khancoban Airport. I wouldn't have a clue what equipment Ben has there now.'

'Okay.' Ryder waited until Flowers had finished writing before he continued. 'Is it true that Ben Hoff asked you to keep one of the tractor keys here as a spare?'

'Yes.'

Ethan swung around to look at his brother. 'I didn't know we had a spare key to that old tractor.'

Dan sighed. 'Remember how useless Hoffy was at keeping track of his stuff? He still loses everything. There were two keys on the keyring. He handed one back and asked if I could keep it as a spare.'

'Where is it?' asked Ethan.

Dan unfolded his arms and rested his hands on his hips. 'With all the other spare keys. I'm sure it's still there.'

'Where do you keep them?' Ryder asked.

'In Dad's old roll-top desk,' said Ethan. 'There are spares for the cars, the tractors, my truck, the quad bikes.' He looked at his brother. 'What else?'

'All the feed sheds, the house—'

'Okay,' said Ryder. 'Can you just show us the desk, please?'

Ryder and Flowers followed the family into the wide hallway. At the far end, a steep staircase led directly to the floor above. Dan stopped about halfway along and threw open a door on the right.

The office was a spacious room with wood-panelled walls and a huge wooden desk with a green leather captain's chair. Even the filing cabinets were wood veneer. Dan went to a small, antique roll-top desk set against one wall and opened it.

'God, I don't remember what's in half of these,' he muttered as he pulled out one mini envelope after another, read what was written on the front, and then shoved them back in their place.

'This might be it,' Dan said, 'the envelope's fairly old.' He stilled, looking down at the envelope in his hand. 'It's open.'

'Are the others sealed?' asked Flowers, peering around Ethan's bulky frame.

'Yes, of course,' Dan said, 'otherwise the keys would fall out and get mixed up.'

'Is the key in there?' Ethan demanded.

Dan nodded. He shook the envelope and the key fell into his palm. 'That's really strange. It's not as though the glue has dried up and the seal has come unstuck.' He held it out so they all could see. 'Someone's torn off the top of the envelope to get to it.'

Ryder held up his hands in a signal to stop. 'Just hold on to it, Dan, while Detective Flowers gets an evidence bag ready.' Ryder peered at the envelope Lorrimer was holding. *Ben Tractor Key* was written on the front in the same handwriting he'd noticed on the others.

'That's your handwriting, Dan?' he asked, just to be sure, as Flowers snapped on gloves and took a plastic evidence bag from his pocket.

'Yes, it's my writing.' Dan dropped the envelope and key into the bag then watched as Flowers sealed it.

Ryder looked at the Lorrimers. Dan's face had gone pale, and Ethan's was set in grim lines. Every so often the brothers exchanged a troubled glance.

'Who has access to this room?' Ryder asked.

Dan frowned. 'We all do. You could see it was unlocked. Any of us can go in.'

'Oh, just a minute,' Kristin said softly, bringing her hand up to cover her mouth.

Dan eyes widened in alarm, and he turned to look at his wife. 'Kristin, what's wrong?'

Kristin slowly lowered her hand. She gazed at Dan and Ethan, then turned to Ryder and Flowers. 'I was here with the children. There was no one else in the house at the time.' The woman looked close to tears.

'When was this, Kristin?' Ryder asked gently.

'The night Dan was out in the paddock.'

'Dan's always out in the paddock,' said Ethan brusquely. 'Which night?'

'Cut it out,' Dan snapped, rounding on his brother. 'Watch how you speak to my wife.'

'If you both wouldn't mind, please?' Flowers said, giving Ethan a hard look.

'What night, Kristin?' Ryder asked. 'Take your time.'

'The night he was delivering the calf. You came here the next morning and told us about Art.'

'That's right. What happened?'

'It was around eight-thirty. I'm sure of that because it was the children's bedtime. I was upstairs reading them a story.' She turned to her husband and grasped his hand. 'I heard someone come in. I thought it was you.'

Dan nodded and squeezed her hand.

She looked back at Ryder. 'I told the kids to stay in bed, and I'd come right back and tell them if we had a new calf.'

'It wasn't Dan?' Ryder asked, his heart a heavy beat in his chest. All eyes were on Kristin now, including Ethan's.

Kristin shook her head. 'No, it wasn't Dan. I only remembered when you asked who had access to the study that . . . Heidi came home briefly that night.'

For a few moments no one spoke.

'What did she want?' Ryder asked, breaking the loaded silence.

'I don't know, but . . . I heard someone go into the study. That's why I thought it was Dan.'

'Did you go downstairs?'

Kristin shook her head. 'No, everyone's always coming and going. I got up, and when I reached the kids' door, she was already coming out of the office. You can see over the banister and down into the hall from the doorway without going onto the landing. I went back to the kids and told them it wasn't Dad, it was Auntie Heidi.'

'Can you show us exactly where you were, please?' said Ryder.

Kristin nodded and they filed back into the hallway.

'Could you two stay in the office doorway?' Ryder asked Dan and Ethan before following Kristin to the foot of the stairs. He began to climb, his left hand curling around the smooth banister rail. Flowers followed along behind them, the steep wooden stairs creaking beneath their combined weight.

At the top, Ryder crossed the landing and joined Kristin in the doorway of the children's room.

'You're taller than I am,' Kristin said, 'but even I can see the study door down there.'

She was right. Dan and Ethan were clearly visible in the doorway below. Ryder moved aside for Flowers to take a look, and then they all traipsed downstairs again.

'How long was Heidi in there?' Ryder asked.

'Not long. I heard the door, thought it was Dan, spoke to the kids and got up. As I said, I was at the door when she came out, so she was in there for no longer than a minute. I assumed she'd forgotten something to take to Rodney's place.'

Ethan laid a hand on his brother's shoulder, his eyes shocked.

'She could have gone in there for anything,' Dan said defensively. 'We shouldn't jump to conclusions.'

'That's right,' said Ryder. 'At this stage, our investigation is ongoing. We'll talk to Heidi and find out exactly why she came home that night.'

Thirty-nine

Sterling let herself into the rumpus room and sat on the edge of the bed. Garrett had told Sergeant Collins that she was a user, and in no time at all Collins had warned Elijah that he had a junkie on staff. It seemed increasingly unlikely that Collins would run Rodney Garrett's prints against any he might have found upstairs in the house. It appeared a local's word carried far more weight around here than that of an outsider.

Not that she could blame Elijah for what he'd done. He ran a great establishment that he'd spent years building up, and he was popular with the locals. Apart from having to call Ryder and Flowers to tell them her assignment was over, the disappointment in Elijah's face was the thing that hurt the most.

Sterling stood up and dragged her suitcase out from under the bed. Despite things ending badly, she'd done her best. Ryder had been supportive when she'd told him she had asked Heidi for drugs after the phone mix up, even though, as he'd warned her, that was the thing that had ultimately brought the assignment to an end. *Don't try and make things happen*, he'd said.

Sterling opened the wardrobe and began taking clothes off the hangers. She'd learned a lot during this time, and though the desired outcomes hadn't been achieved, she refused to see the the time she'd spent undercover as a failure—which she'd been inclined to do when she was younger, whenever anything went wrong. Ryder had taught her it was okay to fail every now and again. *You'll learn more from your failures than your successes, Sterling*, he'd said.

Sterling slid a work shirt off a wire hanger. She'd miss Ryder. His imminent transfer was a loss to Homicide and had been a factor in her decision to take on this roll. Working closely with the sergeant and learning everything she could from him had been too good an opportunity to pass up. With a disappointed sigh she glanced at the old oil heater. She'd take ten minutes to pack a few things and regain her equilibrium, then she'd phone the sarge and Mitch.

It was time to get out of the bunker.

Forty

'I've got a terrible feeling in my gut it's Heidi Lorrimer,' Flowers said as he turned onto Tooma Road. 'She wasn't at the meeting this morning, and she hasn't got back to anyone on the phone, not even her family. And then after what Kristin said . . .'

'Your instincts are spot on.' Beside him, Ryder was riveted to his phone. 'O'Day has the call log. He left a message while we were in the house. Art Lorrimer made a call to Heidi Lorrimer's phone during the afternoon, and then again at seven-forty-one the night of the accident.'

'Ben Hoff said he spoke to Lorrimer that day and told him not to land, that the weather was too bad,' Flowers said.

'That was probably his first call to Heidi, and the second one to say he was coming in anyway,' said Ryder.

'I agree,' said Flowers. 'He was probably giving her his estimated time of arrival so she could be at the airport to pick him up.'

Ryder nodded. 'If she was working at the pub that night, and she asked if she could leave early, which Sterling said she does sometimes, she would have arrived at White Winter Station around eight-thirty.'

'Which is the time Kristin saw her go into the study.' Flowers glanced at the dashboard clock, his hands a little clammy on the wheel. 'We're thirty-five minutes from Khancoban. I'm pretty sure Sterling's at work.'

Ryder glanced at him. 'Switch on the police lights.'

Flowers did as he asked then put his foot down. The car surged forward.

'It's a shame Benson's in Queanbeyan,' Ryder said. 'I need to make sure we have the manpower if we're going to arrest Heidi at work.'

Flowers tightened his grip on the wheel. 'Especially if Garrett's there too. We already have a warrant out for him.'

'Oh, we'll arrest them at the same time, but we need to give Sterling the heads up,' said Ryder. 'She'll tell us if Heidi's there.'

'Try her phone, in case I've got her shifts wrong.' Flowers accelerated past a truck that had pulled over to the left in response to his lights.

'Sterling, it's Ryder here,' he heard the sergeant say. 'Call me immediately when you get this message.'

Ryder hung up and dialled another number. 'I'm calling the hotel's landline to see if I can speak to her.'

Flowers kept his eyes on the road, anticipating the scene to come. Mid-afternoon patrons having a drink and maybe some bar food, Sterling and Heidi moving between the tables, Elijah serving drinks behind the bar. Garrett sitting at the table closest to the rest rooms, his legs stretched out into the passageway. Flowers accelerated around a car, thinking of the access points to the hotel. He hoped Garrett was there. He really hoped he was there.

'Yes, may I speak to Ida Stevenson, please?' Ryder was saying. 'It's Detective Sergeant Pierce Ryder. It's urgent that I speak to her.'

Flowers braked. Up ahead, a large logging truck was turning onto the road, taking up both lanes of the single carriageway.

'She doesn't?' he heard Ryder say. 'Are you sure?' A pause, then, 'What about Heidi Lorrimer?' Another pause as Ryder listened to what the person on the other end of the line was saying. 'Okay, thank you.'

Flowers slowed to a crawl, glancing at Ryder as he hung up. 'What?'

'He said Ida Stevenson isn't employed there anymore.'

'What the hell?'

'I know.' Ryder glanced up at the truck. 'The good news is, Heidi starts her shift in five minutes.'

'Sterling must be at home,' said Flowers. 'Strange she hasn't got her own phone turned on though.'

'I'm going to call Sergeant Collins,' Ryder said. 'We could use his help at the hotel. He can go around to the house and stay with Sterling until we get there.'

Flowers switched on the siren, keeping to the right as the line of cars in front moved off the bitumen and onto the gravel shoulder.

'Sergeant Collins,' he heard Ryder say, 'Detective Sergeant Ryder here. Are you in close proximity to Khancoban right now?' A pause. 'Fifteen minutes. We have a situation here. We've had an undercover detective working in Khancoban, you know her as Ida Stevenson, the waitress at the hotel.' Ryder paused while Collins replied. 'I need you to go around to the house where she's living, you know the place, she's just been in to see you about an intruder. She's in the studio downstairs.' Another pause. 'Yes, could you have her ring me immediately, and wait with her until we arrive? I'll explain everything when we get there.'

Flowers was finally clear of the dust kicked up from the cars pulling onto the gravel shoulder. 'Not many questions from him?'

'I think he was too shocked to say much.'

Flowers glanced at the dashboard. 'Seventeen minutes. We'll be there just after Collins.'

Forty-one

Sterling looked at the suitcase lying open on the bed, filled to the brim with the clothes she'd brought with her. She only had her hair products and toiletries from the bathroom to go in now, and she needed to sort through the food. Not that she kept any more than the basics. She usually ate her main meals at work.

Work. Her daily routine had ended more abruptly than she could have imagined, but now it was time to pivot and return to her old and familiar life. Crouching in front of the heater, she wondered how officers who'd been undercover for many years coped when it was time for them to return to normality. She'd only been in Khancoban eight weeks, and yet she felt torn, as if she were standing with one foot in each life.

Was that the way Mitch felt? Torn between two worlds, one in the digital space, the other very much grounded in real life? Maybe he'd combine the two in the future and join a cybercrime unit, or become a spook with the Feds in Canberra.

Sterling took her gun from inside the heater and turned on her phone. While she waited for the screen to light up, she slipped the gun between the piles of clothing in her suitcase and clicked the fascia back into place. She looked at her phone as it buzzed with two alerts. A missed call from Ryder, and a text. *Call immediately.*

Ryder picked up straight away.

'Sterling, listen closely.'

'Yes, Sarge,' she said, perching on the edge of the chair.

'We have enough circumstantial evidence to charge Heidi with the murder of her brother. Flowers and I are about ten minutes away. I called the hotel when I couldn't get on to you. Heidi's due to start her shift there soon.'

'That's right.' If Ryder had called the pub, he would know by now she'd been put off. But that could wait.

'I clued Collins in when I couldn't get hold of you. He should be there any minute with a message for you to call me. We're going to need Collins' help arresting Heidi in a public place, especially if Garrett's around.'

'Right, Sarge.' Sterling sprung to her feet, too full of nervous energy to sit any longer. *Heidi?* Everything had been pointing to one of the Lorrimer brothers, or maybe both. But not Heidi.

'So, you and Collins sit tight,' Ryder was saying. 'When we get there, we'll work out the best way to take them into custody.'

Sterling swung around as a loud knock came at the door. 'He's here's now, Sarge.'

'Good. Can I have a word with him?'

Sterling put the phone on the benchtop and hurried to the door. Turning the deadlock with one hand, she grasped the knob and pulled the door open.

A powerful shove in the chest sent her careering backwards. Her spine struck the corner of the bench, pain reverberating through her trunk. She cried out, grappling for the benchtop, and somehow managed to stay upright. Dazed, shocked and winded, she dragged air into her lungs, watching as Heidi came towards her brandishing a syringe.

Sterling pushed away from the bench, dropped her chin to her chest and charged, ramming her cranium into Heidi's stomach with such force it jolted the syringe from her grasp. Heidi howled. Sterling dropped to all fours, crawling away and searching the floor for the lethal dose meant for her.

She spotted it by the bed and clambered towards it, reaching, stretching; fingertips almost touching the small, plastic cylinder before cruel fingers tightened on her skull like a vice. A scream of rage burst from Sterling's throat as she twisted her body, striking out with her legs again and again, hoping to kick the syringe under the bed.

Then Heidi hauled her up by two handfuls of her hair. Sterling cried out as strands of hair were ripped from her scalp. Heidi's arm hooked around her throat, the pressure of her bicep almost crushing Sterling's windpipe. Lightheaded, Sterling reached behind her, feeling the bones of Heidi's forehead with her fingers before plunging her thumbs into her eyes. With a roar of agony Heidi released her.

Gasping for air, Sterling staggered away. And then a shove from behind sent her sprawling on top of the open suitcase, the wind knocked out of her as the metal rim of the hard case dug into her stomach. Sterling's arm was trapped beneath her. She moved her fingers, feeling for the Glock she'd packed between her clothes. And then the lid of the suitcase rammed into her, striking her on the shoulder over and over and over.

Sterling lay prone, her fingers curled around the grip of the Glock, sensing Heidi looming over her.

A rustle of clothing told her that Heidi had moved away. And then the other woman's knees cracked as she crouched down to pick something up. Fear of what was in the syringe drove strength into Sterling's body. She wheeled around before the other woman could rise from her crouched position.

'Don't move,' she said between gritted teeth, holding the barrel of the Glock flush against Heidi's temple. 'Drop the syringe . . . *DROP IT!*'

Only then did Sterling become aware of anything else; of people racing into the room. Her head was spinning, and her arm was beginning to shake, but not for a single second did she take her eyes off Heidi Lorrimer.

'Sterling, did you get a needle stick?' she heard Flowers ask, and it was the slight tremor in his voice that made her eyes sting and blur.

She shook her head, the gun still pressed to Heidi's temple.

'Drop the syringe,' she heard Ryder say. 'Don't make this worse.'

Heidi lobbed the syringe onto the carpet, and in her peripheral vision Sterling saw Flowers step forward, pick it up and put it into an evidence bag. Flowers retreated and then Ryder was next to her with a set of handcuffs.

'Sterling?' Ryder said quietly. 'We have her covered.'

Only then did Sterling turn her head and look towards the door. Both Flowers and Sergeant Collins had their pistols trained on Heidi. She didn't know what kind of a shot Collins was, but she had no doubt Flowers would hit the mark.

She lowered her gun and passed it to Ryder. Then she took the handcuffs from him, waiting while he took hold of Heidi's arm and helped her to her feet.

Sterling snapped the cuffs around the woman's wrists. 'Heidi Lorrimer,' she said. 'I'm arresting you on suspicion of the murder of your brother, Arthur Lorrimer Junior. You have the right to remain silent, but anything you do say, can and will be used as evidence against you in court . . .'

Forty-two

Flowers watched the paramedics leave, then Sergeant Collins guided Heidi into the back seat of his police car. Across the road, a small group of neighbours were gathered in a huddle, curious to see what all the commotion was about.

'I'll go with Collins,' Ryder said, coming back to join Flowers where he was waiting outside the studio for Sterling. 'There's no major damage to Heidi's eyes. One is badly scratched from Sterling's nail, the other has a broken blood vessel. They've given her antibiotic eyedrops.'

Ryder dug in his pocket and handed Flowers the car key. 'I grabbed my things from your car. Look, if Sterling decides she's not up to coming, take her back to your place. You have plenty of room, don't you? Or there's a room at the Crystal Lake Motel, Jindabyne where she can stay. She has the key.'

'Yes, Sarge, I'll ask. I think she intends on coming, though. She's getting changed.'

Ryder glanced at the door. 'It's three-and-a-half hours to Queanbeyan and we might not even charge Heidi tonight.'

'Then again, she might decide to talk,' said Flowers.

'It's hard to know if she'll insist upon a lawyer.' Ryder glanced over his shoulder. 'It looks like Collins is ready to go. Let me know what you decide, okay?'

'Will do, Sarge.'

Flowers watched Collins and Ryder drive off and the neighbours start to disperse, and then Sterling came out with her suitcase. She'd changed into black pants, a white ruffled shirt and a black blazer. She looked more like the Sterling he knew, except she was slightly unsteady on her feet.

'Let me take that,' he said, pointing to her suitcase.

'Thanks,' she said, letting him take hold of the handle. 'I'll come back for the car and the rest of my things later.'

'Do you feel all right?' he asked, his stomach still churning from listening to the attack on the phone. It was the worst ten minutes Flowers had ever lived through, not knowing what they were going to find when they got there. Of course, they had no way of knowing that Heidi had brought a syringe with her.

'I'm hanging in there,' Sterling said, giving him a wry smile. 'The medics made sure nothing was broken and the shower helped. There's a couple of areas where I have bad bruising.'

'And that's going to be really painful for a while. Okay, just take your time getting in the car.'

'Excuse me.'

Flowers looked up to see a woman crossing the street.

'I noticed how gingerly you're moving, love,' she said to Sterling. 'Would you like an icepack? I have plenty in the freezer. Both my sons do snowboard cross.'

'Oh, that's thoughtful of you,' Sterling said. 'Yes, an icepack would be great.'

'I'll be back in a jiffy,' the woman said.

There was a sudden gleam in Sterling's eyes that looked like tears to Flowers, but before he could say or do anything, she quickly blinked them away. 'I keep reminding myself there's more good people in the world than bad,' she said.

Flowers lifted her suitcase into the boot. 'This job can make you doubt that sometimes.'

'Heidi's prepared to answer some questions,' Ryder said, leading the way down the brightly lit hallway at the Queanbeyan police station. 'She's already in the interview room. One of the junior officers has put food in the viewing area so you'll be able to watch from there.'

When they reached the viewing room, he opened the door for Sterling to go in first.

'Thanks, Sarge,' she said. Despite the long car trip, there was colour in her face again.

'How are you feeling?'

'Better.'

'She slept in the car for a while,' said Flowers.

Sterling nodded. 'A nice neighbour gave me two icepacks, so I feel as though some of the swelling has gone down. I probably look more beaten up than I am. Honestly, I'm just relieved it's all over.'

Ryder nodded. 'Collins admitted he was the reason you lost your job, telling your boss you were a junkie. He feels bad about it.'

'Well, technically Garrett wasn't lying when he told him about my conversation with Heidi. Where is Sergeant Collins?' she asked.

'On his way back to Khancoban. Benson's just around the corner if we need him, so I told Collins to get going.'

'Hey, this takes me back,' said Flowers suddenly, walking over to the window and looking down at Heidi sitting at the table in hand-cuffs. 'I haven't been in here since the Charlotte Pass case.'

'Wasn't that the start of your bromance?' asked Sterling, picking up a biscuit and taking a bite.

Flowers swung around, his eyebrows raised. 'I think she's had a head knock, Sarge.'

Ryder gave him a brief smile and went to the door. 'Come on, Daisy, let's get this party started.'

Heidi Lorrimer looked up as Ryder and Flowers came into the room. Ryder took a deep breath in an effort to rid himself of the rage burning in his chest that this woman had attempted to murder Sterling with methamphetamine.

On the way down from the viewing room they'd decided that Ryder would go in hard on the attempt on Sterling's life. The evidence they had against Heidi regarding her twin brother's death could wait.

Ryder turned on the video-recording equipment and recited Heidi Lorrimer's right to silence. After she'd confirmed her name and address, he ran through the rest of the formalities.

'You've agreed to answer some questions without a lawyer being present. Is that correct?'

She stared at him, her left eye blood red, her right eyelid half closed. She'd lost an earring in the struggle. The cuffs rattled as she shifted her hands from the table onto her lap. 'Yes.'

'Were you due to start work at the hotel in Khancoban this afternoon?' Ryder asked, impatient to get to the more crucial details.

Heidi responded, but the single word was inaudible. She cleared her throat and tried again. 'Yes,' she whispered hoarsely.

'What time was that?' Ryder asked.

She swallowed. 'Th . . . Three o'clock.'

'You never arrived at work, did you?'

Heidi didn't answer, her inflamed left eye focused on an imaginary spot on the table.

'What made you detour to the residence of the woman you know as Ida Stevenson instead of going to work as you had intended?'

Heidi licked her lips. 'My boss called and asked me to come in early. He told me he'd put Ida off. Apparently, she'd been trying to find out where she could buy meth.'

'Did she ask *you* where she could buy it?'

'Yes, once, but we didn't talk about it again.'

'So, why did you go to her place and not to work?'

Silence.

Ryder changed tack. 'How did you get to Ida's place?'

'By car,' she said, her cuffed hands rattling in her lap.

'Your car wasn't parked on the street,' said Ryder. 'Who drove you?'

'A friend.'

'What's your friend's name?'

Nothing.

'When I was at White Winter Station investigating the death of your brother, you said you were at your boyfriend's place the night your brother flew into Khancoban.'

She nodded.

'Could you speak aloud for the benefit of the recording, please?'

'Yes, I was there that night.'

'Is Rodney Garrett your boyfriend?'

She hesitated. 'You could say that.'

'Did he drive you to Ida Stevenson's residence?'

'Yeah, he was waiting for me in the car.'

Ryder paused so Flowers could come in. They'd worked together for so long now that their questioning style was in sync.

'Garrett didn't wait,' said Flowers. 'The neighbours saw his car speed away from the scene as soon as Collins arrived.'

Heidi stilled, then slumped in the chair, one eye completely closed.

'You know there's a warrant out for his arrest,' said Flowers. 'Why didn't you or Garrett answer our calls? He's yet to turn up at Jindabyne police station.'

Again, Heidi remained silent.

'Why did you bring a syringe with you?' Ryder asked.

She swallowed, licked her lips, said nothing.

'It's been confirmed there was a fatal dose of crystal meth in the syringe you took to Ida Stevenson's place. Did you prepare that syringe with the intention of injecting Ida Stevenson?'

Heidi was staring at the table, her chest rising and falling from her rapid breathing. 'You don't understand,' she said eventually. 'You couldn't.'

'I want to understand, Heidi,' Ryder said.

'I want protection,' she said suddenly.

Ryder leaned back in his chair and exchanged glances with Flowers.

'What sort of protection are you talking about?' Ryder asked.

She looked up and stared at Ryder with her blood-reddened eye. 'I've got information, first-hand information about the murder of Scruffy Freidman, and the important members of the drug syndicate.'

Ryder almost caught his breath. *Finally*, they were getting somewhere.

Beside him, he sensed Flowers' tension. Ryder turned and looked towards the viewing room. He could only imagine Sterling's reaction.

He turned back to Heidi, who had followed his line of sight to the window. Ryder leaned forward and clasped his hands together on the table, bringing her attention back to him.

'We don't give protection for just any information. It has to be material we don't have, and admissible in court. It also has to lead to a prosecution of a criminal activity for us to even consider it.'

'What does all that mean?' Heidi cried out, startling Ryder for an instant. 'I'm in fear of my life here.' She grimaced as she moved her cuffed wrists. 'I'm not saying any more until I get protection.'

'It won't hurt as much if you keep your hands still,' said Flowers.

'I can certainly put it to those above me,' said Ryder, 'but I can't guarantee anything. It will depend upon what you tell us, and how significant that turns out to be.'

Ryder waited, giving her as much time as she needed to consider what he'd said. Any moment now she'd refuse to say more until she'd seen a lawyer.

Eventually she looked up. 'Okay,' she said, 'but I want Ida in here.'

Forty-three

Sterling was on her feet in the viewing room. She'd gone under-cover hoping to get a lead on Scruffy Freidman's killer, and now Heidi Lorrimer was saying she knew who that was. Despite her body aching all over, nothing was going to stop Sterling being in that room.

A few minutes ago, Heidi had requested a rest room break, and Sterling was anxious for Ryder and Flowers to join her. Finally, Ryder and Flowers left the interview room and moments later she heard them coming up the stairs.

'I hope she doesn't have second thoughts while she's in the bathroom,' Flowers was saying as they came in the room.

'It's a shame we had to stop, but she asked for Sterling, and she's entitled to her breaks.' Ryder looked at Sterling while Flowers closed the door. 'Are you up for it?'

Sterling nodded. 'Yes, Sarge. Do you need to call Inspector Gray about the protection she's asked for before we go back in?'

'Let's see how much she gives us first.' Ryder walked over to the table and pulled a couple of grapes off the bunch. 'She'll be charged with assaulting a police officer and the attempted murder of a police officer. She knows that. What she doesn't know is that we have evidence of two phone calls where she spoke to Art on the day of the accident, and her sister-in-law witnessed her going into the study at White Winter Station and then leaving a minute later. A partial print of hers on that tractor key would be good.'

'Or better still, an outright admission of guilt,' said Flowers, sprawling in one of the chairs. 'I'm refusing to get my hopes up until I hear it with my own ears.'

The door of the interview room below them opened. It was the female police officer who'd accompanied Heidi to the rest room. They watched as she stood holding the door open, and then Heidi Lorrimer walked into the room.

'Here we go. Are you ready, Sterling?' said Ryder.

'Sure am, Sarge.'

Ryder tossed a few more grapes into his mouth then held the door open for her to go ahead.

Sterling's stomach tensed as Ryder started the recording equipment. He stated the date and time and full names of all present, then looked at Heidi. 'You can start when you're ready.'

'Rodney Garrett is a paranoid control freak,' Heidi said, looking at Sterling. 'Ida can vouch for that. He didn't like her because she recognised him for what he was. Oh, sorry, should I call you *Nerida*?'

Sterling stared at the woman across the table, her body aching from the injuries Heidi had inflicted on her. If she hadn't grabbed the Glock in time, she'd be lying on a slab in the morgue right now. 'You can call me Detective Sterling,' she said coldly.

'What can you tell us about this drug ring?' asked Ryder.

Heidi hesitated. Her lips parted, then closed. Finally, she said, 'Rodney Garrett . . . is the drug lord of the mountains.'

Sterling's heart pumped faster, causing her back and shoulder to throb. Steeling herself against the pain, she looked at Ryder. While he showed no reaction to Heidi's words, she could imagine Flowers cheering in the viewing room. Like her, he'd taken an instant dislike to Garrett.

'You picked the wrong person to stand up to, *Detective Sterling*. You'll have to watch your back in future.'

'You're in enough trouble already,' Ryder said. 'Do you want me to add threatening a police officer to the list?'

Sterling could imagine Heidi rolling her eyes at that statement, if she'd been able to.

'We've been to the compound with the dogs,' said Ryder. 'Is that the headquarters of this drug ring?'

'Yes. He won't be there now, that's for sure.'

'There's a general warrant out for his arrest,' said Ryder. 'The whole state is on alert. He won't get far.'

When Heidi said nothing, Ryder went on. 'How did you become involved?'

Heidi inhaled sharply, as though Ryder's words alone had caused her injury. 'Well, you can thank my twin brother for that,' she said quietly.

'What was Art's involvement?' Ryder asked.

'He got mixed up with them when he was young. He was friends with Rod, and then Rod started going out with the younger sister of one of the guys in the gang. They started using, and it got a hold on them. Then they started supplying. He and Rod were on the bottom rung of the ladder back then.'

'Was this around the time they were done for supply?'

'Yes. After a while my twin brother decided he'd had enough. He wanted to buy a plane and shoot through, so he began skimming money off the top of his sales, the idiot.' Heidi did little to disguise the venom in her voice.

Sterling leaned forward in her chair, her curiosity piqued by the hatred in Heidi's voice when she spoke of her *twin brother*. The woman couldn't even bear to say his name.

'So, you knew these people who were coming to your parents' property looking for Art?' said Ryder.

'*I* knew. I wasn't going to rat them out to my parents and brothers, though. I would have ended up getting the whole family into trouble. They were having a hard enough time at that point making the station pay for itself. They didn't need the extra hassle my twin was causing. I was back and forth from school anyway. In the end it got so bad my parents helped him buy the plane and off he went.'

'The people who used to come to the house, are they still involved in the organisation?' Ryder asked.

'Some are.' She looked at Sterling then. 'Others have met an unfortunate end.'

Sterling held Heidi's gaze, refusing to let the other woman intimidate her. She'd been unable to establish any real connection with Heidi at the hotel, always finding her standoffish and surly. Even now, it was difficult to get a read on her personality. She was threatening towards Sterling, venomous towards her twin, while managing to sensibly answer Ryder's questions.

Eventually, it was Heidi who broke eye contact, focusing her bloodshot eye on the viewing window.

Ryder sat back and gave Sterling the nod, a sign that she could ask a few questions of her own.

Sterling swallowed, the muscles in her throat sore from Heidi's chokehold. 'What exactly is your role in the organisation?' she asked.

Heidi brought her gaze back to Sterling. 'I'm a distributor. Rod cuts the shit up, and I take it to my suppliers and collect the money. I have my areas. There are others, enforcers and the like, but I'm not giving you names now.'

'Did *your twin* ever bring drugs into Khancoban Airport?'

Heidi glared at her, and for several fraught moments Sterling feared she'd gone too far and the woman was going to clam up.

'I don't know when he would have done that, he's never been home,' Heidi said quietly.

'So where does Garrett buy the ice then?' Sterling asked.

'From a manufacturer, and then he brings it to the compound. All that hunting gear on the car, it's a cover for what he really does.'

'Who's the manufacturer?'

'I don't know. I've never known.'

Sterling glanced at Ryder. She didn't have any more questions for now.

'Okay,' Ryder said, before pausing for a few seconds. 'I want to circle back to Art. I understand his involvement back then, and how he managed to get away. But you haven't told us how *you* got involved, Heidi, or were you involved from the beginning?'

Heidi shook her head, and her chest began to heave. She took several deep breaths as she struggled to bring her emotions under control.

'I didn't have a *choice*, they forced me into it. I used to smoke some weed with Rod and my twin when we were younger, I wasn't an angel. But that's as far as I ever went.'

'How did they force you?' Ryder asked.

'They said I had to take over the job he'd been doing, otherwise they'd never stop looking for him. They were going to kill him if he ever set foot in the place again. I had to work with Rod because we were friends.' She paused for a bit, breathing heavily. 'I said I'd do it, and I told my twin to stay away.'

Sterling caught Ryder's eye.

'You never thought of going to the police with this information?' Ryder asked.

'Are you crazy?' Heidi shouted suddenly, and Sterling couldn't help jumping, the attack in the rumpus room still fresh in her mind. 'You know what happened to Scruffy Freidman, and he used to be one of the enforcers.'

'Who murdered Freidman?' Ryder asked.

Heidi shook her head. 'I'm not telling you that unless I get protection. I've told you Garrett's the ringleader. He worked his way up, and he's kept me tied to him the whole time.'

'Why didn't you tell your older brothers?' Sterling asked.

Heidi hesitated. The only sound in the room was the hum of the video-recording machine. 'They never did anything wrong. They always tried to protect me, their little sister.' Heidi's voice cracked. 'And Dan has kids, and though Ethan looks scary, he's really a big teddy bear.'

'So, you kept distributing the drugs to keep your twin brother safe?' said Sterling.

'In the beginning. Then I was trapped.'

'Did you ever try getting out?' Sterling asked.

Heidi shook her head slowly. 'I was at Rod's beck and call, terrified I'd be next if I put a foot wrong. That's how it ends for all of us. It's just a matter of time.'

Sterling thought back to the time Garrett had come into the hotel and pinched Heidi.

Heidi grabbed her arm, though her eyes were on Garrett as he started talking to Elijah. 'Don't do that.'

'What, stand up to him?' Sterling couldn't help saying.

Heidi let go of her arm. 'Stay out of it,' she hissed, before going and joining Garrett.

Sterling frowned, the glare of the fluorescent lights making her head ache, but there was a question she needed to ask. 'So, you were living in fear, tethered to this cruel individual,' she said, 'and then your older brothers break the news that they want to sell the property, and share the money between all four of you. It must have seemed like a ticket to freedom.'

Heidi stared at her before falling forward on the table. A torturous sob burst from her lips as though wrenched from the very depths of her soul. And then a series of violent sobs shook her body, her shoulders heaving, her forehead resting on the tabletop.

Ryder suspended the interview.

Forty-four

Sterling looked up as Flowers came into the viewing room carrying a cup of tea.

'Oh, thanks, Mitch.' Sterling gratefully took the takeaway cup from his hands. 'Do you have any more of those painkillers?'

'Yep, I do.' Flowers reached into his pocket and pressed two capsules out of the tab for her. 'Are you feeling any better? That was hard going in there, you did well.'

'I'm okay.' Sterling was able to swallow the painkillers because the tea wasn't piping hot. The warm liquid felt good sliding down her sore throat. 'What's going on down there now?'

'The same officer is in with Heidi. She's getting her coffee and something to eat, and they're putting more drops in her eyes. Hopefully, she'll be okay to keep going when she's more comfortable. I don't know where Ryder went. Maybe he's calling Vanessa, or Inspector Gray.'

'Who would have thought she'd be forced to take her brother's spot in a drug gang?' said Sterling, shaking her head. 'It's a horrible story.'

'I know, but aren't they all?' said Flowers.

They were quiet for a while. Sterling drank her tea, hoping the painkillers would kick in before she had to go in there again. 'You know, I was a coffee drinker before I met you,' she said.

He smiled, reached out, and gave her back a comforting rub between her shoulder blades. 'Have I turned you?'

She nodded, and the sweetness in his eyes was enough to make her throat ache even more.

The door flew open and Ryder strode in. Flowers removed his arm, and if Ryder noticed, he didn't say anything. 'We're not driving back to Thredbo tonight,' he said, giving them each a room key. 'I've booked us into the motel a few doors down. The clothes we have on are going to be pretty rank by tomorrow.'

'I'll be fine,' said Sterling, trying not to sound too self-satisfied. 'My suitcase is in the car.'

'You'll be right then, Daisy,' Ryder said, 'you can borrow some of Sterling's clothes.'

'Hilarious, Sarge.'

Ryder grinned. 'Okay. I'm off to call Vanessa to tell her not to expect me tonight. It's after ten already.'

When the door closed, Sterling looked at her key. 'Room 11. Which one are you in?'

'Room 13.'

'Oh, that's bad luck.'

Flowers frowned. 'I don't believe in all that superstitious stuff.'

'That's not what I meant,' she said with a smile. 'I was thinking Sarge is probably in the middle.'

Forty-five

'I was working at the hotel, and I was giving most of that money to Dan to help with the bills, and I was working for Rod for *nothing*. Almost everyone else has a habit. They get paid in junk, but I refused to get hooked. That made Rod uneasy.'

Heidi's right eye was now covered with a soft pad, and the redness had cleared a little from her left eye.

'So, getting back to what Detective Sterling was saying before the break,' Ryder said, glancing at Sterling, 'how did you feel when your brothers, Dan and Ethan that is, suggested you all sell the property?'

Heidi swallowed. 'I felt like I'd been thrown a lifeline, like there was hope.'

'You agreed to the sale?'

'Yes. I was willing to go along with whatever they wanted to do. A quarter share of the property is still a shitload of money. With that, I could disappear, like my twin brother did.'

'Did you tell Garrett about the sale?' Ryder asked.

'No. I knew he'd find out though. Everyone found out in time.'

'How did he react?'

'He became clingy, coming into the hotel when he never had before. I ended up telling him my share was tied up in a trust fund and that my brothers and the lawyers had full control of that. I told him the property was mortgaged to the hilt, and there wouldn't be much left over after the sale, which was bullshit, but it got him off my back.'

Ryder opened the file he'd brought with him and took out a copy of the call log O'Day had emailed through. Two calls were high-lighted in yellow.

'Art rang you during the afternoon on the day of the accident, and again around seven-thirty that night. Why did he call you?'

Heidi froze.

Ryder pointed to the two calls. 'Can you confirm that this is your mobile phone number?'

She nodded.

'Could you please speak up for the record—'

'*Yes*, it's my number.'

'He called to tell you he was flying in, didn't he? I mean, someone had to get him from the airport. And he was furious with your brothers for going ahead and signing the contract to sell the property, so he wasn't going to call them. He called you, his twin sister.'

Heidi looked at the call log. 'He called to say he was coming in. But then the storm blew up.'

'Did he say anything else during that call?'

'No.'

'He didn't mention the sale of the property to you?'

Heidi shook her head. 'No.'

'And the second call?'

Heidi said nothing.

'Okay.' Ryder gave a heavy sigh. 'Did you call in briefly to White Winter Station on the night of your brother's accident?'

Heidi frowned, and Ryder could almost imagine the panicked thoughts going through her mind. 'No, I didn't.'

'Your sister-in-law, Kristin, told us that the night Art flew in she was upstairs reading the children a book, when she heard you come in around eight-thirty. Dan had been out in the paddock delivering a calf and she thought it was him. She went to the door, but it wasn't her husband who came out of the office. It was you, Heidi. Why did you go into the office, and then leave straight away?'

Heidi's lips turned white.

'Did you take the tractor key from the office? The spare key Ben Hoff asked your brother to hold on to because he was always losing things?'

'No, Kristin must have made a mistake,' Heidi said, though she was openly weeping now.

'Forensics are confident they'll be able to lift a print off the envelope and possibly the key,' Ryder told her. 'We're pretty confident of getting a match with a partial print on the syringe you brought to Detective Sterling's residence today.'

'Heidi,' Sterling said suddenly.

Ryder sat back so Sterling could ask her question.

'You said you wanted protection. You told us that you fear for your life. You won't get any kind of leniency if you continue to lie to us.'

'Did you take the key and move the tractor onto the airstrip?' Ryder asked, looking at Heidi.

She was distraught and exhausted, caught off guard by the evidence they'd presented that implicated her in her brother's death.

'Did you start the tractor with the spare key from the office at White Winter Station and drive the tractor onto the airstrip?'

'Yes!' she bawled out the word. 'He was going to ruin everything. I told him years ago what Rod had made me do, what I'd done for *him*, but he did nothing to help me. His twin sister. He didn't care.'

Ryder stayed quiet, letting her words sink in, trying to imagine what it would be like to be caught in such an intolerable situation. To glimpse freedom, and then have someone who only thought of themselves snatch it away.

Heidi blinked away her tears. 'He said the property was his superannuation and that he needed to keep it safe from the people he'd ripped off. The heartless bastard had destroyed my life once before, and now he was going to ruin the only chance *I* had of getting out of all that shit.' She hiccuped then coughed. 'Rod was scared of him too.'

Sterling turned bewildered eyes on Ryder.

'Why was Garrett scared of Art?' he asked.

'Because he's paranoid. All of them are, they're always looking over their shoulders, waiting for the next one to double cross them like Scruffy Freidman did. They don't trust anyone, even the people closest to them. My twin brother was flying in, and he could name almost all of them if he wanted to. Rod kept on and on at me, saying if the drug ring was brought down, I'd be going down with them. We'd all end up in jail.'

'So, you went to the airport under the cover of darkness and used the spare key to start the tractor. Then you drove it onto the runway where you knew the plane would come in?' Ryder asked carefully, for the benefit of the recording.

She nodded, then remembered to speak up. 'Yes,' she said, her one maniacal eye fixed on Ryder. 'You don't understand. There was no other way. He was going to stop the sale. I did it for Dan and Ethan too. I was there when Rod bashed Scruffy Freidman to death and threw him into the river. From that moment, I was living on borrowed time.'

Forty-six

Sterling had never come so close to losing her life before, and as she let herself into the motel room just after one in the morning, she realised she had indeed lived to see another day.

It was a shame the room's exposed-brick walls and nondescript carpet were depressingly similar to the rumpus room in Khancoban, save for the two double beds. With the attack still fresh in her mind, even the knowledge that Heidi was in custody failed to ease her frayed nerves. Hopefully, a few solid hours of sleep would help.

Leaving her suitcase on the floor because she didn't have the strength to lift it onto the bed, she unzipped it and opened the lid. An image of Heidi Lorrimer looming over her flashed into her mind, and Sterling saw herself sprawled across the suitcase as the lid came down on her again and again.

She blinked and the image receded. Hurrying, she rummaged through her things, dragging out her wet pack and the pale-green tracksuit she slept in before zipping up the suitcase again.

Though her rational mind knew Heidi was locked in a cell at the Queanbeyan police station where tomorrow she would be charged with multiple criminal offences, Sterling felt her menacing presence everywhere. It was there when she touched her body: in the soreness of her shoulder, in the tenderness of her scalp when she shampooed her hair and in the dull ache in her spine when she twisted around.

And when she looked in the bathroom mirror after spending twenty minutes soaking in the bath, it was Heidi's face staring back at her, holding the syringe that would plunge Sterling into one final sleep.

Her heart beating too fast, she hurried out into the bedroom to look at her body in the full-length mirror. There was an angry bruise in the middle of her back and multiple purple streaks on her right shoulder. Moving her head from side to side, she lifted her chin, pressing her throat with the pads of her fingers.

Scolding herself as her bottom lip began to tremble, she pulled on the tracksuit, thankful for its comforting softness. She should be grateful she was alive, raiding the mini bar and soaking in a hot bath, not wallowing in self-pity. But no matter what she did, the threat of Heidi Lorrimer stayed with her.

Leaving the light burning in the bathroom, she slipped between the chilly sheets, her tears hot, her body freezing despite the bath. She'd been in such a hurry to escape the bathroom mirror she'd forgotten to blow-dry her hair.

A faint tap at the door made her sit up. It had to be Mitch. Who else would be crazy enough to walk outside at one in the morning when it was zero degrees wearing . . .?

Sterling hurried to the door. 'Yes?'

'It's me. I don't need to come in. I'm just checking that you're okay.'

Sterling reached up to unlock the door, her fingers stiff and sore from fighting for her life. Her life. She still had it. And the guy standing outside was one of the best things in it.

Fumbling with the latch, she managed to get the door open. Flowers was standing there, still in his clothes from today, a stiff breeze lifting his hair.

'I don't think I'm okay,' she said.

He nodded and came into the room, turning to close the door.

'I keep seeing her face, flashing in front of my eyes; she has the syringe in her hand.'

'You should get into bed, Nerida. Don't worry, I'll stay here. I'll sleep in the other bed.'

Sterling did as he said and crawled beneath the covers.

'Now turn the other way,' he said.

She rolled over, smiling at little at his good manners. She'd already seen him naked, but she appreciated the respect he showed her. She heard the closet door opening, heard him hanging up his clothes.

'Mitch,' she said when she heard him sit down on the bed. 'Can I turn over now?'

'Sure.'

He was wearing one of the motel's white bathrobes.

'I'm so cold. I need someone to hold me,' she said, trying to keep the tremor out of her voice. 'No, I need *you* to hold me.'

He stood up and took a slow step towards her.

Sterling pushed back the covers so he could slide into bed beside her.

Forty-seven

Sterling woke up when Flowers left the bed. 'Stay there,' he said, leaning over and speaking in a quiet voice. 'I'm going to jump in the shower. Can I borrow some of your girlie deodorant?'

She smiled. 'You can borrow anything you like.'

'Thanks.'

She struggled up onto her elbow. 'Mitch?'

'Yeah?' He hesitated in the doorway, still wearing the white bathrobe.

'Thank you. That's the best sleep I've had since I moved to Khancoban.'

He smiled a little, his hair flopping over his forehead. 'You're welcome.'

Sterling lay back on the pillows listening to the sounds of him turning on the shower and moving around the bathroom. Nothing physical had happened. She hadn't needed that from him last night, and he knew it. She gingerly turned onto her side. It would happen though, whenever they felt they were ready. More importantly, their emotional connection had grown stronger during this time.

Ten minutes later, he emerged from the bathroom dressed in yesterday's clothes. 'Bathroom's all yours,' he said, glancing at her as she sat up and swung her feet to the floor. 'You have a bad case of bed hair,' he said with a laugh.

Sterling padded over to the mirror and stared at her reflection. 'Oh my God,' she said, pushing back the curls that had sprung up overnight. 'This is what happens when I don't blow-dry my hair.'

'Now I know your weak spot,' he said, moving to the door. 'See you in bit. I'll get back to my room before Sarge wakes up.'

Less than two hours later, Flowers threw open the door to the small room where Elijah Jones sat waiting to be interviewed.

'Good morning,' Flowers said, holding the door open for Sterling to go in ahead of him.

'Hello, Elijah,' he heard her say as he closed the door.

'Oh my God, Ida, I feel like such an idiot,' Elijah said, his cheeks and forehead glowing red with embarrassment. 'I'm so sorry.'

Sterling smiled as they both sat down. 'Don't worry. I didn't take it personally.' She glanced at Flowers. 'It is the first job I've ever been fired from though.'

'There's a first time for everything,' said Flowers, feeling sorry for the publican squirming in his seat. He'd always struck Flowers as a decent kind of guy.

'So, Elijah,' Sterling said, when the formalities had been sorted and they were ready to get underway, 'Can you tell us about the conversation you had with Heidi Lorrimer on the phone yesterday?'

He nodded. 'Sure, what do you need to know?'

'Just run through it,' said Sterling. 'What happened after I left your office?'

'I started thinking about how we were going to be short-staffed without you there, so I rang Heidi and asked if she could come in as soon as possible. It was only ten or fifteen minutes before she was due to start, but you know how busy we can get in that time.'

'I do,' said Sterling. 'Go on.'

'Heidi said "Why, what's up?", and I said, "I've had to put Ida off." Of course, she asked me why. I told her Sergeant Collins had phoned and said he had information that Ida—' Elijah stopped and flushed red again '—Detective Sterling, I mean, had been trying to procure drugs from her while she'd been employed at my hotel.'

'Did Sergeant Collins say who had given him this information?' asked Flowers.

'No, and I didn't ask. I imagine that would have been confidential.' He looked at Sterling then. 'I'm not just saying this because I know that you're a detective now, but my gut feeling had always been that the Ida who worked for me was a person of integrity. I didn't like that I'd been mistaken, so I asked Heidi outright because I wanted to check if it really happened.'

'What did Heidi say?' asked Sterling.

'She said yes, you had done that.'

'Did you get the impression that Heidi was alone in the car when you were talking to her?' Flowers asked.

Elijah shook his head. 'I heard music at the start, but it was turned down pretty quickly. I'm sure she was with someone.'

'Why are you so sure?'

'Because I've called her in for shifts before when she's been in the car with Rodney Garrett. I've heard the same soundtrack.'

Flowers nodded.

'So, how did the conversation finish up?' Sterling asked.

'I think she said something like, "How did she take it?" or "What did she say?", and unfortunately, and I feel terrible about this, I said, "She told me she was an undercover cop working in the mountains trying to bust a drug network." And then I said, "Can you believe that?"' Elijah shook his head. 'That was the end of the conversation and, of course, she didn't show up for work.'

Flowers turned to Sterling. She nodded.

'I think that's all we need, thank you,' Flowers said, standing up and turning off the recording equipment. Elijah's recall of the events yesterday afternoon confirmed what Heidi had told them. Garrett had learned from that conversation that Sterling was a cop. He'd also learned she wasn't at the hotel but at home. He'd known exactly where to find her and exactly how to kill her.

The undercover detective was also a hopeless junkie who'd died of a drug overdose.

Flowers watched as Sterling walked casually to the door, chatting to Elijah. 'If you ever get tired of police work,' he was saying, 'there's a job on offer at the hotel. I'm down two staff members, and you were a gun of a waitress.'

Sterling tipped back her head and laughed, and Flowers thought how lovely she was with her hair up like that, twisted into some kind of loose knot in an effort to control her curly hair. Clearly Elijah thought the same.

'Thanks for the offer,' she said. 'I'll keep it in mind.'

'Well, make sure you drop in for a drink when you're in the area,' he said with a wave. 'My shout.'

Sterling nodded. 'I'll do that.'

At ten o'clock Flowers and Sterling went up to the viewing room. Ryder had just started interviewing Heidi Lorrimer again. Benson was also at the table. Heidi's eye covering was nowhere to be seen, and she looked a little better than the day before.

'So, Garrett prepared the syringe in the car and told you to go into Detective Sterling's place and inject her with the drug?' Ryder asked.

'Yes. He forced me to do it.'

'Did you have a plan?' Ryder asked.

'No, I didn't have any plan. I was just going to say it was me, and that I'd heard she'd been fired, and ask her what the hell happened.'

'But then Detective Sterling let you in?'

'Yes, I knocked, and she opened the door straight away.'

Next to Flowers, Sterling gave a heavy sigh. He turned to look at her. 'Hey, Sarge had just told you Collins would be there any minute. There's no way you could have known Heidi was on the other side of that door.'

When Flowers turned back to the window, Ryder was putting his phone on the table. 'I'd like you to listen to this.'

Flowers tensed at the first sounds of Sterling crying out in pain, followed by the grunts and cries of a violent scuffle. There came a furious roar that didn't sound like Sterling, and then a scream that did. Flowers closed his eyes at what he now knew was Heidi Lorrimer repeatedly slamming Sterling's suitcase down on her shoulder. Then suddenly everything went quiet.

Flowers dragged in an uneven breath. 'That's when we thought it was over,' he murmured, opening his eyes to find Sterling watching him. She moved closer, taking hold of his arm as they waited for her voice.

Don't move. Drop the syringe . . . DROP IT!

'Why did Ryder record the phone call?' Sterling asked quietly.

Flowers shook his head. 'I don't know, I was driving. He must have switched on record when you went to open the door. We all assumed it was Sergeant Collins.'

'Doesn't matter why. I'm just glad he did it,' Sterling said simply.

In the interview room, Ryder had stopped the recording and was turning back to face Heidi.

'Would you agree that what you've just heard was the physical altercation of you attacking Detective Sterling in her residence?'

'Yes.'

Ryder glanced at Benson, who opened the file in front of him and took out some papers.

'Heidi Lorrimer,' Ryder said, 'you'll be charged with assaulting a police officer, the attempted murder of a police officer, as well as the murder of your brother, Arthur Lorrimer Junior at Khancoban. Do you understand that?'

'Yes.'

'Come on, let's go and wait for Sarge to come out,' Flowers said to Sterling. 'Benson's getting out the charge sheets.'

Sterling nodded. 'I've seen enough.'

They didn't have long to wait before Ryder appeared in the corridor downstairs.

'She's been charged, and she's just called Dan,' he said, walking over to them. 'Fortunately, they were in Cooma seeing their lawyer again.'

'What do you want us to do, Sarge?' Flowers asked.

Ryder checked his watch. 'It's going to take them an hour fifteen to get here, and then they'll want to see Heidi.' He raised a hand as Benson came out into the corridor looking for him. 'I've got things to do. Why don't you go and have rest at the motel, or go and grab a cup of coffee? Just make sure you're back here in two hours' time.'

Forty-eight

Ryder and Flowers sat opposite Dan and Ethan Lorrimer in the interview room where a few hours earlier Ryder had charged their younger sister with multiple serious offences.

Dan's eyes were red-rimmed. He looked to have aged ten years in the past two days. By contrast, Ethan wore his stoicism like an armour.

'I can't believe it,' Dan said, his voice breaking. 'I can't believe she killed Art, and then tried to murder your colleague. It's like something out of a horror movie.'

Ethan laid a comforting hand on his brother's shoulder. 'We have to do everything we can to support her,' he said. 'We have no idea what she's been dealing with all these years.'

'If only she'd come to us,' Dan said, pulling a white handkerchief out of his pocket and wiping his eyes. 'We could have tried to do something about it.'

Ethan glanced at Ryder. 'She got in too deep, mate,' he said to his brother. 'They couldn't let her leave because she knew too much.'

Ryder nodded. 'That's the way these groups usually work.'

'She was so desperate she took Art's life to save her own,' Ethan said.

Dan looked at his brother. 'And that's our fault. If we'd explained things to her, about how everything worked, that would have been one less reason for her to do what she did. She didn't even know we were planning to talk Art around because we didn't tell her.'

Ethan shook his head, looking unconvinced. 'Everything's clear in hindsight, Dan. She always gave us the impression she was happy to leave it up to us. We didn't intentionally leave her in the dark.'

Flowers leaned forward. 'I don't know if this helps or not, but she told us she'd always been happy to go along with whatever you wanted to do.'

Dan closed his eyes and nodded. 'Thank you. I'm sorry. I'm just sick in the guts thinking of her working at the hotel to help us keep the property ticking along. And all that time she was a slave to this drug organisation, at first to shield a brother who wasn't even here, and then later to save her own skin, and potentially ours. It's tragic.'

Ryder wasn't often lost for words, but this time he was struggling to find any sentiment that would be of comfort to Heidi's elder brothers. 'I can understand this has come as a great shock to you both,' he said.

Dan took a deep breath and appeared to pull himself together. 'What happens now?'

'Well,' said Ryder, relieved he could finally be of help. 'She'll appear in court tomorrow morning. She won't get bail. And then she'll be taken to the prison. We're assuming at this stage she'll be pleading guilty to all charges.'

'We'll need to engage a good criminal lawyer,' said Ethan, his voice turning husky.

'I'll be in court tomorrow for her first appearance,' Ryder said. 'That's here.'

'We'll make sure we're here, too,' said Dan. 'And please pass on our utmost regret and a speedy recovery to the officer she injured yesterday.'

Ryder inclined his head. 'I will.'

They all stood up and the Lorrimer brothers left, looking as if they had the weight of the world on their shoulders. Ryder watched them go, wondering if they'd sleep tonight knowing their sister would be spending her second night in a police cell.

'That was hard to watch,' Sterling said, coming in from the viewing room. 'They're absolutely devastated.'

Ryder nodded. 'There's a lot of self-blame there, by Dan in particular. That type of guilt can last a lifetime.'

They were sitting in the tearoom when Flowers' phone rang.

'Detective Flowers,' he said, picking up his coffee and carrying it out into the corridor.

'Hello, it's Mhanda Van Engelen here, from Tumbarumba Council.'

'Hello, Mhanda,' Flowers said, pleased to hear a cheerful voice. 'How are you going?'

'I'm well, thanks. I hope I haven't called you at an inconvenient time.'

'No, I'm free.'

'It's just a courtesy call, really, to let you know that the White Winter Station subdivision was approved at a special council meeting last night.'

Flowers frowned. 'How come it was a special meeting?'

'Oh, that's not unusual. We hold them from time to time to clear the backlog. I remember you asking about community opposition, so I wanted to let you know it all went very smoothly.'

'I appreciate you letting me know, Mhanda.'

'No problem, Detective. Have a good day.'

'You too.'

Flowers took a sip of his coffee then returned to the tearoom to tell the others.

'Wow, talk about good news followed by bad,' said Sterling. 'Isn't it preferable to hear the bad news first? What an emotional twenty-four hours for that family.'

Flowers nodded. 'The sale can be settled now, and the Lorrimers will get their money.'

'Not that it will be much use to Heidi in prison,' said Sterling.

'It'll still be there when she gets out,' said Flowers.

They quietened, nodding to a group of uniformed officers who came into the tearoom.

'What about that insurance policy, Sarge?' Flowers said, leaning forward once the officers had passed by. 'Will Heidi get a third share in that too?'

Ryder shook his head. 'She's entitled to the inheritance from her parents, which is her share of the property, but the insurance money will be paid to the company, and she can't share in that. It would be profiting from the proceeds of crime.'

'Right,' said Flowers. 'I imagine Owen Temple's celebrating, and the Buchanans. It looks like their dream is going to come true.'

'Provided Temple keeps his word to Lewis Buchanan,' said Ryder.

Sterling sighed. 'I've never worked on a case like this before, with so much family history involved.'

Flowers caught Sterling's eye. 'This one's been pretty unique.'

'I agree,' said Ryder with a tap on the arm of his chair. 'So, as of now, you're both off duty for the next couple of days.'

Flowers watched as Sterling's face lit up. 'Thanks, Sarge, I could really do with a break.'

'I know.'

'Yeah, thanks, Sarge. We need to pick up Sterling's car and the rest of her gear from Khancoban.' Flowers looked at Sterling. 'Maybe we should do that tomorrow.'

'That sounds like a good plan,' Ryder said. 'And tonight, you're having dinner with us at the Golden Wattle, Sterling, to celebrate the excellent work you've done on this case. It's important for morale that we celebrate our wins.'

'That sounds amazing, Sarge, I'm looking forward to it already,' Sterling said. 'I've been eating pub grub for the last eight weeks.'

Ryder pushed back his chair. 'Okay, I'm off to have a late lunch with Benson. He can't make it tonight—he'll be with his family.'

Finally, Ryder looked at Flowers, his eyes narrowing. 'What about you, Daisy? Are you going to ditch me again?'

Flowers smirked at having been relegated to last. 'Not a chance, Sarge, I'll be there.'

Forty-nine

Flowers' life in this moment could not have been sweeter. Off duty, and with Sterling in the passenger seat, he felt like a teenager entrusted with his father's car on his first date. The future was looking pretty damn good right now, and he was happy to let it all unfold in its own good time.

Time. Flowers looked at the dashboard clock, trying to remember what time the Brumby Cafe and Gallery closed.

'I'm going to call Cate Buchanan,' he said, glancing at Sterling. 'I wouldn't mind stopping in at the shop.'

'Sure, I don't mind.'

Cate answered after the third ring. 'Hello, Brumby Cafe and Gallery.'

'Hi, Cate. Detective Flowers.'

'Hello. I hope you're not traipsing around in the back country again.'

'Unfortunately, I'm not out there today,' he said, gazing at the white-topped mountains in the distance, and a shimmering Lake Jindabyne in the foreground. 'It looks like the perfect day for it though.' He glanced at Sterling and smiled. 'I was wondering what time you close?'

'We have already but we're all still here. Are you after coffee?'

'No, I wanted to pick up a few of those John Gilbert prints, the ones you have in the box. I don't think I'll be able to get in tomorrow.'

'Oh, all right. We'll be here for a while. Just knock on the door and we'll open up.'

'That's lucky,' he said to Sterling after hanging up. 'I was thinking of taking one over tonight and giving it to Sarge—get on his good side again.'

She frowned. 'What did you do?'

'Nothing really. He's invited me over for dinner a few times, but I've been too busy with the game training. I couldn't afford to lose hours over dinner. I think he knew I was making excuses.'

'He's a detective, of course he knew,' Sterling said with a laugh. 'And it's out of character. Your first priority is always your stomach.'

'Aw, c'mon, not always.'

Ten minutes later, Cate was letting them in the door, and Flowers was introducing her to Sterling.

'Come and say hello to Wendy and Lewis,' Cate said. 'They're down the back.'

Wendy and Lewis were sitting at a table in the cafe, an open bottle of champagne chilling in an ice bucket.

'Are these premises licensed to sell alcohol?' Flowers asked in a mock serious voice.

They all laughed.

He introduced Sterling to Wendy and Lewis. 'Nerida is another member of the Homicide Squad.'

'Good heavens, what a terrible thing you've had to deal with,' said Wendy, getting up and coming over to them. 'We've heard a few whisperings about what's happened in the last twenty-four hours— you know how fast news travels around here—but I know you can't talk about that. Suffice to say we've kept our little celebration low-key out of respect for the Lorrimers.'

Flowers nodded and tried not to look at Cate. He had to remind himself that no one knew about her relationship with Ethan. Instead, he turned to Lewis.

'Congratulations on getting the subdivision through council. Mhanda Van Engelen told me the news today.'

'Thanks. It's been a lengthy process, and Mhanda's been fantastic.'

'She was helpful when we visited the council. She seemed to be all over it,' said Flowers.

'Yes, she's done a great job.'

There was a pause in the conversation, and then Wendy said, 'You wanted to have a look through the prints? I remember you being quite taken with them the first day you were here. And you visited John's gallery, didn't you?'

'I did.' Flowers thought back to the conversation with John Gilbert the day he'd learned that White Winter Station was to be subdivided.

Wendy led them over to the box he'd looked through before. 'Do you remember if there was a particular one you liked?' she asked, picking up the box and putting it on a table where they could more easily look through the prints.

'I liked the one of the cemetery.'

'Really?' She raised an eyebrow. 'That's a strange choice, but I admit we do sell a few of them. Oh, here's one of Buchanan Hut,' she said, passing it to him. 'You've been there.'

Flowers looked down at the sketch. 'I like that. I'll take them both.' He turned to Sterling. 'Pick one. My shout.'

'Yeah?' She grinned at him. 'Okay, thanks.'

'Then you can help me choose one for Sarge.'

In the end, they decided on one of Dead Horse Gap for Ryder and Sterling chose one of the homestead.

'Good choice,' Wendy told her. 'I have the original. It's the first one John drew of the old house. My father gave it to me just before he died.'

'It must be a very precious family heirloom,' said Sterling.

'It is now but I wasn't impressed when I was young.' Wendy wrapped the prints individually in tissue paper and slipped them into a paper bag. 'It had a very ornate gold frame that had been broken at one point, and Dad had made a poor job of gluing it back together.' Wendy chuckled. 'I forgot I even had it until I found the exact same frame in Vinnies one day. And it didn't look so ugly then.'

Flowers tapped his card and she handed him the bag.

'I reframed it, and it's been on my wall ever since,' Wendy continued. 'Sounds a little bit loopy, I know, but changing that frame made all the difference in the world.'

'Maybe you were old enough to appreciate it,' Sterling said.

'You're probably right.'

Flowers was eager for them to push on to Thredbo, so they said their goodbyes to the Buchanans and left.

'Thank you for the print,' Sterling said as they walked back to the car. 'I'll think of Heidi Lorrimer in prison when I look at it.'

Flowers swung around. 'Maybe that wasn't such a good idea? It might give you nightmares.'

Sterling laughed. 'You bought one of the cemetery.'

'That's true.'

'I won't hang it anywhere conspicuous, but it will be a subtle reminder of how lucky I am to be here, and to not take anything for granted.'

'That's a positive way of looking at it,' said Flowers. 'Geez, I was a bit on edge in there. A couple of times I nearly said something to Cate about Ethan. It's weird how they don't know.'

'I got a shock as soon as I walked in,' Sterling said when they were in the car.

Flowers turned to look at her. 'A shock? Why?'

'I recognised Lewis Buchanan—he was the man having lunch with Sergeant Collins in the hotel that day.'

Fifty

Flowers and Sterling had gone looking for Ryder when they'd arrived at the Golden Wattle Lodge. The guests were late finishing dinner, so Vanessa had left the three of them alone in the suite to give Poppy a bath. Eva and Jack were trying to coax the stragglers out of the dining room and into the lounge.

'That's interesting,' Ryder said, after hearing that Sterling had recognised Lewis Buchanan as the man having lunch with Sergeant Collins.

'Why don't you call in and ask Collins about it when you're down there collecting your things? It would be good to know. He might not tell you—you know how the country cops feel about us poking our noses into their communities.' Ryder sighed, the familiar emptiness returning to the pit of his stomach. 'It's strange to think that I'll soon be among their ranks.'

Ryder looked at Flowers' and Sterling's crestfallen faces. 'I'm not going to pretend leaving Homicide will be easy, but when I look at you two, I know the future of the squad is in good hands. So . . . here we go.' He handed out the beers Jack had brought in while apologising for the hold up. 'Congratulations. Both of you stepped up and took on more responsibility, and you proved you were up to the job.'

They clinked bottles and Ryder took a long drink of the lager. Once Heidi's court appearance was over, he was looking forward to a few days off himself.

'Thanks, Sarge, for the kind words. I'm always keen to learn, and I appreciate the opportunity.' Flowers held out the paper carry bag he'd brought with him.

'What's this?' asked Ryder.

'We picked up a few prints from the Buchanans' shop this afternoon. There's one here for you,' Flowers said.

'Oh, you shouldn't have done that,' Ryder said, a little embarrassed as he accepted the gift from Flowers. 'That's very nice. And unexpected. I don't really know what to say. Will I open it now?'

'Yes,' said Flowers. 'Sterling chose one of the homestead.'

'It's going to remind me how lucky I am to be alive.' Sterling took a swig of her beer.

'I chose the Buchanan Hut and the cemetery at White Winter Station,' said Flowers.

Ryder frowned. 'The cemetery? You've always been a bit weird, Daisy.'

Sterling sniggered.

Ryder held his print up to the light. 'I like that. It's really nice. Thanks.'

'It's the view from Dead Horse Gap,' said Flowers. 'We thought it was the one with the most meaning. Everything started there with the loss of the snow lease.'

'It did indeed.' Ryder nodded and studied the print before carefully sliding it back into the bag. 'Thank you. I'll get it framed. Vanessa will love it too.'

The door opened and Vanessa stood in the doorway, Poppy by her side in her pink dressing gown.

'Speak of the devil,' Ryder said, and they all laughed.

'I don't know what that's all about,' Vanessa said with a grin, 'but you'd better get organised, it's time to eat.'

Five minutes later, Ryder was sitting at the dining-room table, with Vanessa next to him with Poppy on her knee, and Flowers and Sterling opposite.

'Jack finally got everyone out of here,' Eva whispered, tilting her head towards the lounge room where a few of the guests were still kicking on. 'Now, you three,' she said, looking at Ryder, Flowers and Sterling in turn, 'you just sit there and relax. Jack and I have everything organised, and Vanessa, you've done enough too.' Eva went to stand behind Flowers' chair and put her hands on his shoulders. 'I'm just so excited we finally got you here, Mitch,' she said, giving him a little shake. 'And you too, Nerida. I don't know any details but I'm so happy you're back here safe and sound.'

'Thanks, Eva,' Sterling said.

Ryder thought he saw a shimmer in her eye. Sterling seemed to have survived yesterday's horror, and while issues could still arise from the attack later on, it was with profound relief that he watched her tonight, alive, happy and enjoying herself.

Jack put a bowl of soup down in front of him and someone else put damper on his side plate. Vanessa, he presumed. He missed what type of soup Eva said it was, but it didn't matter. He let the buzz of conversation wrap around him, relieved Flowers had decided to join them. The added responsibility he'd given his partner had seemed to dispel what Ryder had feared was a growing dissatisfaction with the job.

'Can you come to my school?'

Ryder turned towards Vanessa to see Poppy looking at him intently, her arms outstretched towards him.

'Can you?' she asked.

Ryder grasped her around the waist and lifted her onto his lap. 'What about your dad?' he said, catching Jack's eye.

'It has to be a policeman,' Poppy said softly.

'I tell you what, I'll try my best to get there, but if I can't, will Sterling or Flowers do?'

Poppy nodded and, chuffed with her success, climbed off his lap and went to tell her mother the news.

'I find that ointment works really well,' Vanessa was telling Sterling. 'It takes away the inflammation. Remind me to give you a tube before you go home. It'll help bring out the bruising.'

'Yeah, it's a bad one,' Flowers said, picking up his wine glass and taking a sip.

There was a sudden silence around the table, and then Vanessa and Eva burst out laughing.

It didn't matter to Ryder where Sterling's bruise was, and whether Flowers had seen it or not. It mattered to him that he had Heidi Lorrimer in custody, and that Sterling had lived to tell the tale.

'Has Heidi given you any useful information yet?' Jack asked in a low voice. 'I made some discreet enquiries with my army buddies, but I didn't learn anything.' He tipped his head towards the lounge room. 'They've all gone to bed.'

Ryder nodded and kept his voice low. 'She gave me a list of people involved, and she was there when Garrett killed Freidman. She can give us a first-hand account.'

'When did she tell you this, Sarge?' Flowers asked.

Ryder looked up. He must have spoken louder than he thought because all eyes were on him. 'This afternoon. I spoke to her again after I had lunch with Benson.'

'What are the top brass saying?' asked Jack.

'They'll consider giving her protection. We'll be backwards and forwards from prison for a while yet handling this one.' He leaned forward and picked up the bottle of red wine. 'But let's not talk any more about that. Tonight is a celebration and . . . I'm starting to feel better now I've had something to eat.'

'That's the cue for me to get the duck legs,' said Jack.

'Oh my God, I love duck,' said Sterling.

Eva looked up from where she was rocking Poppy to sleep. 'I'm sorry about the late dinner, Pierce—sometimes we'll get a group that want to sit in here all night.'

'Don't apologise, Eva, I've got everything I need right here,' he said, smiling at Vanessa.

Reaching across the table, he topped up Flowers' and Sterling's glasses. He was beginning to enjoy himself, but he knew he wouldn't fully relax until Heidi's court appearance the next day.

Later, when Sterling and Flowers had left and the lodge was silent, Ryder took out the print Flowers had given him. 'Look what Daisy bought us,' he said, handing it to Vanessa as she came out of the bathroom. 'I think it's a farewell gift.'

'That's Dead Horse Gap,' she said, looking down at it. 'It's lovely, and so thoughtful of him. This case seems to have left its mark on all of you.'

Ryder nodded. 'Family trauma. It's the worst.'

Vanessa leaned over and put the print on the bedside table, and Ryder stretched out on the bed.

'It's such a sad situation,' she said, lying down beside him and resting her head on his shoulder. 'The hopelessness Heidi must have felt, and the guilt the brothers are going to have to live with.'

'Yeah. Dan and Ethan Lorrimer always acted in what they thought was the family's best interests. But today, I saw two broken men.' Ryder closed his eyes briefly. 'Not for one second could they have imagined that when they finally sold the property, one of their siblings would be dead, and the other in prison for his murder.'

'No, they would have thought their worries would all be over. It's so horrible,' she said.

Ryder sighed. 'I feel for them, but I'm having trouble dredging up the smallest amount of sympathy for Heidi, because she would have killed Sterling yesterday if she could have.'

Vanessa raised her head and looked down at him. 'I know how worried you've been about her, but she's safe now.'

Ryder tightened his arms around her, inhaling her perfume as she laid her head on his shoulder again. 'Promise me, that if I'm remote, or preoccupied, or crazy busy, or anything that stops you getting through to me, just remind me of this case. What happened to the

Lorrimers was preventable. It's a tragic example of how important communication is.'

'I agree.'

'You know how I often say the courses they make us do at work are generally pretty useless?'

Vanessa chuckled. 'Yes.'

'This case would be the perfect one to study how *not* to communicate. Heidi had a secret no one could help her with, because they didn't know she needed help. Art never called home. When he found out about the sale, he consulted a lawyer and, armed with half the information, flew off with a head of steam, calling Heidi and saying he was coming home to stop the sale. His brothers always imagined they would have another chance to talk to him, but thinking doesn't make things happen. In the end, they never got the chance because Heidi took her brother's life to escape her own nightmare.'

'That's crazy. I've never met the Lorrimers, but from what you've said, it sounds like the two older brothers are measured, but the twins are impulsive.'

'You're right,' Ryder said. Outside, the wind was building in strength, rattling the windowpanes. 'You would have made a good police psychologist.'

She sat up and grinned at him. 'You think so? Okay, let me diagnose you.'

He chuckled. 'We could be here all night.' But he was feeling better already after talking to Vanessa.

'You're tired,' she said, studying his face. 'This case, and the stress of what happened to Sterling yesterday, and the constant worry of her being undercover, it's built up. I know you haven't been sleeping properly.'

'That's your diagnosis?' he said, leaning over and tickling her.

She yelped and scooted off the bed. 'Sleep is my cure for everything.' He watched as she pulled back the covers and slid into bed. 'And if that doesn't work, I go for a ski.'

Fifty-one

At nine-thirty, Ryder climbed from his car in Queanbeyan, his suit little protection against the ferocious wind howling through the carpark. He pulled his overcoat off the back seat, slipped it on and buttoned it up. When he rounded the corner, a huddle of reporters were already gathered outside the courthouse.

Benson immediately came towards him. 'Flowers not here?'

'No, he's driving Sterling to Khancoban to get the rest of her stuff.'

'Ah, fair enough.'

'I want her to have a few days off, and Flowers too. Have you noticed that he's been getting a lot of headaches?'

'No, but then I haven't seen much of him,' said Benson as they jogged up the steps.

Inside, Ryder raked his hair back from his forehead, relieved to be out of the biting wind. The first person he saw was Ethan Lorrimer, a head taller than everyone else. Dan and Kristin were standing close by. Both men wore darks suits, while Kristin was dressed in black pants and a long green shawl. She turned sad eyes towards Ryder, lines etched into her white face.

He nodded, and she lifted her hand. Then he saw her touch Dan's arm to get his attention.

Dan caught up with him as he was about to enter the courtroom.

'Detective, we're still making enquiries about the best lawyer to engage. We haven't had a lot of time to organise it yet.'

'Don't worry,' Ryder said, 'the duty solicitor will look after things today.'

'Thank you. I have no doubt we'll be seeing you again in the future.'

Ryder followed Benson into the courtroom. The police prosecutor was already seated at the long wooden table reserved for the parties' legal representatives. At the opposite end, the duty solicitor was looking through a file. The New South Wales Coat of Arms hung on the back wall behind the magistrate's bench.

Ryder and Benson sat close to the front, on the police prosecutor's side of the courtroom. Behind him, Ryder could hear the familiar sounds of the usual groups that filled a courtroom on any given day. Well-acquainted solicitors and barristers, the press looking for the next headline, and then the families and interested members of the public.

'The Transport Safety Bureau's report finally came through,' Benson said while they waited. 'It contained lots of technical jargon, but the bottom line is the crash was caused by the tractor.'

Ryder snorted. 'We could have told them that.'

'All rise!'

Ryder stood, his shoulder brushing Benson's as the magistrate came in and took his seat at the bench.

'I'll take the adjournments first,' the magistrate said.

One at a time over the next half hour each matter was adjourned, the room gradually thinning out as many of the legal representatives returned to their offices. It wasn't long before Ryder noticed Heidi Lorrimer being brought into the dock while the magistrate was dealing with the last of the adjournments. She was wearing a black pants suit, her pink-tipped hair pinned back from her face. One eye was still slightly swollen where Sterling had eye-gouged her in self-defence.

'Here we go,' said Benson.

'Next, I'll deal with New South Wales Police and Lorrimer.' The magistrate turned to look at the police prosecutor. 'Yes, Mr Prosecutor?'

The police prosecutor stood up. 'Your Honour, Ms Lorrimer has been charged with assaulting a police officer, attempted murder of a police officer, and the murder of Arthur Lorrimer Junior.'

A murmur ran through the courtroom.

'The police are presently preparing their briefs of evidence, Your Honour,' the police prosecutor added.

'How long is it expected to take?'

'The briefs should be able to be completed and served within four weeks, Your Honour.'

The magistrate turned to the duty solicitor. 'Is there any application for bail?'

The duty solicitor stood up. 'We're not seeking bail at this point, Your Honour, but I foreshadow that an application is likely to be made shortly.'

'Very well. I'll formally deny bail, and I'll have these matters relisted for five weeks' time.' The magistrate looked up. 'Next matter.'

'That's us done,' said Ryder, as Heidi Lorrimer, head down and accompanied by a court officer, turned and descended the stairs to the cells.

Ryder and Benson stood, dipped their heads at the magistrate, and then made their way to the back of the courtroom.

In his peripheral vision, Ryder saw Dan, Kristin and Ethan Lorrimer sitting together, stony-faced and staring straight ahead as though they couldn't believe it was over so quickly.

Fifty-two

Sterling gazed at the house through the car window as Flowers pulled into the kerb. It was hard to believe her time here had ended so abruptly. They'd even said their formal goodbyes to Sergeant Collins, and while he'd good-naturedly refused to give up his secret fishing location to Flowers, he'd been happy to tell Sterling about his lunchtime meeting with Lewis Buchanan.

It was during the school holidays, and he'd asked Buchanan to lunch to ask his advice on a right-of-way issue that was causing a problem between two property owners. Over lunch, Collins thought the high school teacher might like to know that his teenage daughter, who'd been staying with a friend while competing in a gymkhana, had attended a large underage party that the sergeant had been forced to shut down.

Collins recalled them briefly discussing the Lorrimers after Heidi had come into the hotel with Rodney Garrett, and Sterling left the station convinced that Collins was a good cop who cared for his community with a light touch, using a firmer hand only when necessary.

'Everything okay?'

She turned to find Flowers watching her, his arm resting on the wheel. 'When are you going to tell Ryder you're leaving?' she asked. 'I thought you might do it last night when you gave him the print.'

'And spoil his evening? No way.' Flowers shook his head slowly, his eyes solemn. 'I'll tell him as soon as we get back to Parramatta. I won't leave him in the lurch, if that's what you're worried about.'

'No . . . I was just wondering.'

'I have time, Nerida,' he said quietly.

'Good,' she said with a smile, deciding to change the subject. 'I'm so grateful you're here with me. I'm not looking forward to going in.'

'C'mon, look on the bright side,' Flowers said. 'You'll be handing back the old Forrester shortly.'

'True,' said Sterling with a laugh. 'It's a bit underpowered for me.'

A few minutes later, she unlocked the door of the rumpus room, flicked on the light, and blinked in surprise. 'It's all been tidied up,' she said. 'I was expecting it to look like a bomb had gone off.'

Flowers followed her into the room. 'I think Ryder organised for Harriet Ono to come up and do the forensics. Honestly, that woman would do anything for him. It looks as though she's tidied it up, though it would be to impress Ryder, not you.'

Sterling laughed. 'I'll have to call and thank her.' She'd been dreading coming back here, worried the mess from the scuffle would conjure up images of Heidi in her mind again. But the place looked as neat and tidy as it had when she'd first inspected it.

'A crime scene,' she said, embarrassed that it hadn't even crossed her mind. 'Honestly, I thought I was a tough cop, but I think something happened to my brain in that fight.'

'You've had a traumatic experience,' he said, walking around and checking the place out. 'Go easy on yourself. It'll take a little while.' He stopped walking and pointed to the old oil heater.

'Yes, that's it,' Sterling said with a laugh. 'That's my hiding place. If you take the fascia off there's a cavity inside, not that I'm going to do it now.'

'I used to try and imagine what this place looked like, when we'd talk on the phone,' he said.

'Those conversations helped me so much,' she said with a rush of affection—*or was it more than that?* 'Thanks, Mitch.'

'You're welcome.'

When he didn't say any more, she went over to look at the pile of things stacked against the wall. Harriet had cleaned out the bathroom and kitchen cupboards and packed everything into green shopping bags.

'I don't care who she did this for, I'm going to buy this woman dinner,' she said.

'Do you want me take those out to the car?' Flowers asked.

'We may as well. No use hanging around here any longer than necessary.'

'I'll get them.' Flowers leaned down and gathered up as many bags as he could carry. 'Have another look around and make sure you haven't left anything behind.'

She did as he suggested, but she soon concluded that Harriet's cleaning and tidying skills were as meticulous as her forensic investigations.

'All good?' Flowers asked, appearing in the doorway.

Sterling nodded. 'Let's get out of here. This is one chapter of my life I'm really keen to close.'

'You're not going to close the entire book?' he said, his eyes turning serious. He shrugged. 'I was wondering about us.'

'Us?' Sterling's heart skipped a beat.

'Yeah. I did try, you know.'

Sterling frowned, not following.

'After you told me we couldn't date, I took an interest in other women, flirted with some, even went out with a few, but then I decided not to do that anymore.' He smiled at her, the way he had when they'd first been introduced at the Homicide office. 'I was happy seeing you every day at work.'

Sterling stepped towards him, a pulse throbbing at the base of her throat. 'I was certain you were going to kiss me when we were walking home last night after dinner, but you didn't.'

'I was this close,' he said, holding up two fingers, the corner of his mouth twitching, 'but we'd both had a bit to drink, and I thought you might regret it, like you did last time.'

'I promise I won't regret a thing,' she said, her heart racing as he moved closer.

'Finally,' he breathed, drawing her into a strong embrace.

Sterling wound her arms around his neck and sighed as his lips brushed her temple, her cheek and, finally, after what seemed like forever, her lips.

On the drive back to Thredbo, Ryder phoned to tell Flowers that a SWAT team had stormed the Garrett compound, but as they'd suspected, he and his dogs were long gone. As of now, Rodney Garrett was the most-hunted criminal in New South Wales.

Flowers glanced in his rear-view mirror at Sterling following along behind in the Forrester. He was grateful she hadn't been in the car to hear what Ryder had said. Flowers had a special dinner organised for tonight, and he didn't want Rodney Garrett occupying her thoughts. It was troubling, though. With Garrett gone, rival drug gangs were certain to move in on the mountain territory, and that meant more targeted murders as they fought for control of the turf.

There was another piece of information he'd learned, though, which was certain to put Sterling's mind at ease. Sergeant Collins had phoned to say the prints lifted from the upstairs break-in hadn't been a match with Garrett's. They belonged to a juvenile Collins had often scooted away from the hotel carpark for trying to coerce members of the public to buy him spirits.

Flowers glanced in his rear-view mirror again. He'd liked Nerida Sterling from the moment she'd turned up in Homicide, a country girl from Taree with invisible braces on her teeth that made it difficult for her to pronounce her 's's. They were friends, work colleagues, and now there was every possibility they could be more.

Making sure there was no one else around them, he raised a hand and waved, and after hesitating for a second or two, he saw her wave back. Flowers grinned, imagining her thinking he was behaving like an immature teenager.

So he turned on his police lights and flashed her three times, just for good measure.

Fifty-three

Two years and seven months later

Only when the orange sunset had slipped below the horizon did the trio leave the car and walk towards the cemetery. The older woman carried a powerful torch, but she didn't turn it on until they were hidden by the tall hedges. Inside, she aimed the beam of light towards her father's grave, illuminating the headstone of the last Buchanan buried in the family plot. If life proceeded in its proper order, she would be the next.

Her father would be turning in his grave if he knew how close she'd come to tossing out the gift he'd given her right before his death. John Gilbert's sketch of the house hadn't been a gift her ten-year-old self could get excited about, not like the horse she'd been asking for forever. Even the frame had been cracked and messily stuck together.

'Never throw this away, Wendy,' her father had whispered. 'You'll realise one day how valuable it is.' Of course, he could never have foreseen them losing the property.

How strange to have discovered an identical frame in Vinnies during one of her visits, and in perfect condition. She'd bought it, tossed it in a drawer with the broken one and left it in the garage.

Then one day, propelled by loss, and the nostalgia that comes with age, she'd decided to reframe the sketch. That's when she'd noticed the cursive writing on the back of the drawing.

'Are you all right, Aunt Wendy?'

She turned at the light touch on her arm. Cate, her face half hidden in shadow, rested the spade she was carrying against her grandfather's headstone.

Wendy nodded. 'I'm fine, sweetheart. I'm worried about *you* and your husband. You still haven't told Ethan about this, have you? That's why we're doing it while he's away.'

'I couldn't tell him while his family owned the property, Aunt Wendy. What was in the ground would have belonged to them.'

'And if we do find it, how are you going to explain your sudden riches?' asked Lewis with a grin.

'If we don't find anything I won't have to worry,' said Cate.

Wendy smiled. For her it was enough to be back on Buchanan soil, to have the keys to the old house jangling in her coat pocket. But the house could wait. This was what her nephew had worked so hard to organise. Were they about to learn if the information passed down through the generations from Buchanan father to eldest child was fact—or fable?

'The coordinates written on the back of the sketch point to somewhere in the graveyard, but I don't know where exactly, it's not precise,' said Lewis, starting the metal detector.

Wendy's smile was indulgent. She hoped for Cate and Lewis' sake that the story of Herbert Buchanan burying gold somewhere on the property he'd established was true. Her father had certainly believed it; he'd told her about the gold repeatedly during his last days, though her mother had always dismissed them as the tormented ramblings of a dying man.

'This is creeping me out,' Cate whispered to her brother, gazing up at the white angel, stark against an inky black sky. 'Hurry up and get on with it.'

Lewis chuckled. 'Don't worry, sis, it won't take long. I doubt there's anything here.'

Cate put her arm around Wendy. 'I really hope we find the gold, for your sake.'

Strange how they didn't know how rich she already was, for having them in her life. She'd never found the right person to share her days with, never had children of her own, but these two had needed her when their parents died.

She watched as Lewis swept the metal detector around the base of the angel and between the smaller headstones. It had been hard to believe that quietly spoken Lewis, dedicated schoolteacher and shire councillor, had seized the initiative and had a quiet word with a friendly developer when he'd heard the Lorrimers were wanting to sell. It wasn't long before Lewis had made his personal interest in the house and cemetery known to the developer.

'It's not going off anywhere around here,' Lewis said, looking down at the machine. 'Where do you think I should try next?'

Cate pointed to the hedge closest to the house. 'Why don't you have a go over there?'

Lewis continued to sweep the metal detector in a wide arc.

Beep beep beep.

Lewis froze.

Cate gasped, then charged towards him while Wendy happily looked on.

These two were more precious than any nuggets they hoped to find. Not that she would spoil their fun, she thought, as she bent down and laid the flowers she'd brought with her on Henry Buchanan's grave.

After all, they'd done this for her.

Acknowledgements

To Annette Barlow and the wider team at Allen & Unwin, including editors Courtney Lick and Lauren Finger, proofreader Tessa Feggans, publicist Laura Benson and cover artist extraordinaire Nada Backovic, thank you.

To my Sydney writing group of four years, aka 'The Dream Team', Vanessa Hardy, Kristine Charles, Nicole Webb and our fearless leader Bernadette Foley of Broadcast Books, thank you. I love having four fabulous women to share this writing journey with.

To pilots Helene Young and Ben Merkenhof, for generously sharing your expert aviation knowledge with me during my work on the prologue, a scene I'd never anticipated writing until this story wormed its way into my mind, thank you.

To Len Klumpp, for your 'on the job' knowledge of a working airport and for sharing that vital piece of tractor information that a city gal like me would never have known, thank you.

To my detective friend in Sydney who prefers to remain nameless, for the hours you spend answering my police procedural questions, thank you. I am forever grateful.

To filmmaker and storyteller Jamie Lewis, for your lively and engaging conversation during several of my live Newcastle appearances, thank you. Your unexpected questions always keep me on my toes. Many thanks also for putting together the video footage for the *Dead Horse Gap* trailer.

To my lifelong friend, Venessa Tripp, who through your animated storytelling over lunch unknowingly sparked an idea in my mind, and so the character of Wendy Buchanan was created, thank you.

To my friend Robyn Proctor, for sharing your stories of growing up in Tumbarumba, thank you. A few snippets of your extensive knowledge of the area have found their way into the story.

To the helpful staff at the Snowy Hydro Information Centre, Khancoban, thank you.

To Claire Rogerson of Snowy Access, for your wonderful four-wheel drive tour to see the historic alpine huts, thank you.

To the many readers who enjoy my books, a very big thank you. Without you, none of this would be possible.

Finally, and most importantly, my precious family. To my husband Damian, for your continuing love and support throughout the writing of this novel and for your decades of legal practise, which I relied on for authenticity during the legal and court scenes, thank you. To my daughter Danielle, for the glasses of wine and endless conversations when we're together and for applying your brief-writing skills to clean up the dreaded synopsis, thank you. You know the story almost as well as I do. To my son Adam, for the regular Facetime calls from the USA, especially during the last two difficult years, and for using your skills as a composer to write the music for the *Dead Horse Gap* trailer, thank you. You three have my heart forever.